FLYING ON THE *WINGS* OF *MERCURY*

by

Mitchell Berg

SYNTHETIC
PROPHETIC

Library of Congress Control Number: 2024918616

SYNTHETIC PROPHETIC ⇌
Kingston, New York, USA
syntheticprophetic.com

ISBN: 979-8-9856091-1-0

Printed in the United States.

For Jenny, who supports everything I attempt to accomplish with enthusiasm, motivation and love. As with everything in my life, I couldn't have done it without you.

"The world, even the smallest parts of it,
is filled with things you don't know."

—Sherman Alexie
*The Absolutely True Diary
of a Part-Time Indian*

Prologue

Have you ever been transfixed by a coin? I mean have you ever *really* looked at a coin and let it ease you into a daydream? It may be a mundane, everyday object, but take a minute to consider how many people have touched it, spent it, and saved it. Can you imagine the places it has been and the events it has witnessed?

Some of these questions can be answered with a quick inspection. We know a coin's birth by the year stamped on it. We can also identify the coin's "hometown" because every one is stamped with a code representing where it was minted. But gathering the story of a coin's journey from its minting to your wallet typically requires a wild imagination.

I am neither an expert in numismatics nor am I even a coin collector. Up until a year ago, I couldn't tell you the difference between today's Roosevelt dime and its predecessor, the Mercury. I knew that some rare coins could be valuable, but my proficiency ended there. I had no clue how to interpret mint marks, and I had never considered how far a circulating coin may have traveled to reach me.

For most of my life, I would have said that any old dime would be worth ten cents to me—nothing more and nothing less. But on August 31, 2018, I found a 1921 Mercury dime, and my life was irrevocably changed. Join me as this adventure unfolds.

Chapter 1

I consider myself a writer by trade and ability, though the reality is that I've always paid my bills through less personally fulfilling means. A literature major in college, I specialized in British Victorian mysteries. There was little doubt in my collegiate mind that my future was to become a recognizable name in the literary world alongside Doyle, Christie and P.D. James. Undoubtedly, the name Zachary (Zach for short) Howard would join those ranks one day.

Reality set in a few years after graduation when my most recent publication attempt was critiqued with similar sentiments to those of my 56 prior rejections. Apparently the consensus was that I lacked "imagination and creativity." Of course not all manuscript readers were so generous with their time to offer me any feedback. However, the publishers and agents I did hear back from all conveyed the same message. Insane! How could people placed in such high-level decision-making capacities all be so wrong?

Some were at least kind enough to offer alternate career paths. Among the suggestions received were: "writing press releases," "proofreading," and if I felt comfortable behind the wheel of a car, "becoming an Uber driver." After several years, I begrudgingly got the message that the literary world was not ready for Zach Howard.

But, I've always prided myself on perseverance, so I'm not one to give up on a dream. I continued to write while I paid my bills as a public relations professional, although I did briefly toy with the Uber driver prospect. My career highlights include announcing the Strawberry Stegosaurus and the Peanut Butter and Jurassic donuts, both on behalf of Dinosaur Donuts. Who said I lacked imagination and creativity?

As my national bestseller had yet to materialize, my fantasized convertibles, yachts and global travels were reluctantly put on hold. The reality was, after paying my rent, utilities and car payments, funding other "luxury" items such as clothing was frequently somewhat of a struggle.

Worrying about relying too heavily on credit cards and the inevitable interest tacked onto balances, I began paying most of my day-to-day bills with my debit card. About a year ago, I decided to become real "old school," periodically forfeiting accumulating points on my debit card to pay with cash when I had it on hand.

I live in a studio apartment in Astoria, which is in Queens, New York. For those lacking knowledge of overpriced city living, I'll elaborate. Beyond semantics, my dining area, living room, and bedroom are all the same. With a few deft moves, the living room sofa transforms into my bed at night only to convert back to my primary piece of furniture after I awake. A scant two inches away from the sofa bed sits a small table holding a ceramic bowl. The bowl, adorned with red, yellow and orange peppers is not for aesthetic pleasure (an overrated and unnecessary attribute), but instead serves a completely functional role. For all I care, the bowl could have painted airplanes or monkeys on the side; it would make no difference to me. Living on a tight budget, I made a remarkable discovery: every penny does count. Whenever I went into a store and used bills to pay for items, I engaged in a subsequent battle of wills. On occasion, the cashier placed the bills in the register, expecting me to walk away and forgo some measly change. Those waiting in line behind me often became annoyed as I would not budge until I received the change owed. Waiting for pennies may have generated a few scowls, eye rolls and curses, but I confidently walked away with my head held high and a pocket full of jangling coins.

You see, I developed the discipline a few months back of depositing any loose pocket change into the pepper-laden ceramic bowl. Initially, the goal was to keep the apartment tidy and, perhaps after three months of savings, convert the change into a dozen eggs and a quart of milk. Little did I know that accumulating spare change would eventually pay for fish and meat in addition to eggs and milk.

Chapter 2

After three months of saving loose change, I emptied the bowl on my table to count and sort my savings. My bounty's mild metallic smell made me think of the upcoming exchange of pennies, nickels, dimes and quarters into usable cash. The bowl had been more than half filled with coins, so that likely would equate to at least an hour or two of sorting while watching Netflix and eating dinner. I pride myself on efficient multitasking.

What could be better than heating up frozen pizza and watching "Stranger Things" while counting money in the comfort of my own home?

I'm friendly enough but have always valued peace and solitude over inane conversation. Being alone provided me with the tranquility that got my creative juices flowing. I knew that at least one brilliant work of fiction was bottled up inside me, just waiting for the opportunity to burst out into the literary world. Interacting with other people would only get in the way.

With a quick glance at the coins, I challenged myself to estimate the total. I made a mental guess of $45.55 and then went to work. The coin sitting on top appeared to be a penny, but I realized it was an old, grimy dime. While unique looking, it was definitely a dime, so I placed it with the other ten-cent pieces. It quickly became apparent that the number of nickels I had saved was considerably fewer than the pennies, dimes, and quarters I had collected. The good news was their quarters made up the bulk of the pile so perhaps my $45.55 estimate was on the light side.

I picked up several free coin wrappers from the bank (it's ridiculous that people pay for them!), and began sorting and rolling. It seemed prudent to turn coin rolls into cash dollars at the bank rather than shopping with bulging pockets laden with coins.

I grabbed the first batch of pennies and dutifully began counting out the 50 that would comprise my first roll. Other than that one grimy dime that had been masquerading as a penny, my sorting had been effective, and rolling my stack of pennies was a quicker process than I had expected. Before long, I had filled five rolls of pennies and three of nickels. $8.50 richer, I turned my attention to the big money: dimes and quarters.

Chapter 3

As luck would have it, the first coin from my dime bundle was the aforementioned misidentified penny. Upon closer inspection, I saw the year 1921 etched onto the face. I had never to my knowledge owned a coin that old and wondered if it could possibly be worth more than all my change added together, or perhaps what I had in my meager savings account.

Squinting, I held the coin under my free-standing lamp, and made out a facial profile on one side. I thought it was a woman's face but was not one hundred percent certain, as it had faded beyond clear distinction. There appeared to be a wing covering the area over her ear. Holding the coin as close to my eye as possible, I discerned the word "Liberty" arcing above the profile.

The back of the coin was in better shape than the front, and at the bottom I read the words "One Dime" and "United States of America" around the middle and top. In the center of the coin's back were branches and leaves surrounding a long cylindrical object. Curious about this design, which I had never seen on a coin before, I looked it up and learned that this coin, a Mercury dime, had on its back an olive branch surrounding a fasces. My initial thought was to question why the U.S. government put an image of an olive branch over an object representing a right-wing political ideology, but then took closer note of the spelling of the words. As it turns out, a fasces is a bound bundle of rods rather than a far-right, authoritarian regime.

My search results also indicated that the coin's condition would be a vital factor in determining worth. eBay had numerous listings for 1921 Mercury dimes ranging in price from $40 to over $500, depending on the state of the coin. I realized that I needed more expertise, so I decided I would track down a coin aficionado.

In the meantime, I set aside my newfound treasure and continued sorting through the remaining dimes. Hoping there was another old one, I soon learned my luck had run out. Four completed dime rolls and $20 later, I turned my attention to the quarters.

To celebrate my evening's good fortune, I thought I would open a bottle of wine, or perhaps have a beer instead. As I entertained infrequently (not once since moving in six years ago) and was not much of a sophisticated drinker, my liquor cabinet consisted of two cans of Coors Lite, a bottle of white wine and a bottle of red wine. My first choice was a beer but as it was somewhere between warm and hot to the touch, I opted for the wine. These wines were grab bag giveaways from last year's office party—a Barefoot Pinot Grigio and a Bogle California red. At the back of a drawer, I located the corkscrew and was able to open the Bogle red.

I drank a toast to myself and my brilliant coin-savings plan. Not a bad outcome: $68.50, including the four rolls of quarters, approximately $5 left over in the bowl as a starting point for my next round, and my real find, a 1921 dime.

I stared at the dime's "tail" side as I contemplated what to do next. I could now more clearly see the olive branch portrayed around the fasces—my new favorite word.

Looking down at the coin again, I saw it was face-side up. Funny, I could have sworn I hadn't turned the coin over. To help prevent this coin from doing any more flips, I decided that two glasses of wine was my hard stop.

Chapter 4

When I woke up the following morning, I had completely forgotten it was the Saturday of Labor Day weekend. Most people had undoubtedly vacated the city, escaping to wherever New Yorkers run to in the hope of salvaging summer's last vestiges. I never was much of a beach person myself, and as there was no one I wanted to spend a long weekend with, I looked forward to the privacy of a half-empty city.

As I mentioned I live in Astoria, Queens, located near something called the Hell Gate train track and the RFK Bridge, which long-term New Yorkers still call the Triboro Bridge. I took my requisite morning coffee and sat by the window gazing at the neighborhood. No matter what time of day it was, my stomach growled from the mouth-watering aromas that emanated from the downstairs Greek restaurant. From my vantage point, I was able to see the Athena Bakery and the Souvlaki King sandwiching Tony's Pizzeria. Leaning forward and peering to my right, I could see the Golden Dragon Chinese Restaurant, Sophie's Empanadas, and Gus's Gyros II. I noted a Blink Fitness among the row of food establishments, which I hadn't really noticed before.

There are also many bars and clubs around this neighborhood—if you are into that sort of thing, which I am decidedly not. I pride myself on being more of the low-key, cerebral type, and much prefer my tranquil apartment nights spent with a good book, an entertaining show to watch, and a hot chocolate.

Astoria has become very popular with millennials due to its proximity to Manhattan. Although technically being a member of that generation, I landed in my neighborhood due to convenience more than design. When E&W Public Relations hired me four years ago, they told me that my predecessor was moving to the West Coast and his studio apartment in Astoria was available. The apartment rent was within my budget, and I signed the lease sight unseen. The previous tenant had no use for the furniture, so I happily bought all the contents (again sight unseen), including the silverware and dishes, for $150. The only household items I needed to bring were my freshman-year pillowcases, sheets, and blanket. All my possessions fit easily in my 2004 Toyota Corolla. At the time I was told parking was manageable, only to discover that what is manageable is open to personal opinion and interpretation.

At some point I probably should have sold my car, but it has been with me since college, and it feels like an old friend—a friend who neither imposes on my privacy nor asks anything of me. So I figured I would continue to keep it. Besides, though I don't particularly like the beach, I do enjoy going to look at the ocean in the late fall and winter when it is pretty much empty. Nothing is more soothing and thought provoking than looking out at the ocean in the wintertime without loud, burdensome crowds.

All the elements were in place that Labor Day weekend for me to have a nice, serene weekend and make some real artistic headway.

I ate a cup and a half of unsweetened original Cheerios with milk and two sliced up bananas for breakfast, then placed the ceramic bowl on the floor beside me in case I was still hungry. I made room for my laptop and the accumulated notes for my novel's plot and started typing. Aside from a bathroom trip I did not leave my work area until I got hungry again at about 2 o'clock.

Hard work always makes me hungry, and while scooping up the remaining peanut butter and strawberry jelly from my plate with the last portion of the white bread crust, I briefly contemplated making a third sandwich. Instead, I glanced around the inside of my fridge, deciding on three carrot spears and a handful of grapes.

Feeling fully satiated and convinced I was ready for more work, the computer screen stared at me as if putting forth a challenge. The white background, letters and, symbols sprinkled with sporadic colors created a hypnotic quality. It was seemingly beckoning me to take a nap as a series of yawns overtook me. Suddenly, I was jolted back into consciousness by the sounds of what must have been an MMA match going on above me. I stared at my ceiling, anticipating a sprinkling of plaster, or perhaps even the entire ceiling falling down upon me. The grunts, screams, and violent furniture moving lasted for several minutes and ended with a high-pitched scream.

I sat in stunned silence for a minute or two until the major disturbance's source came to me: it was the young couple who had recently moved into the apartment above me. I say they were young, but they probably were only a couple of years younger than me, or perhaps even my age. On the two or three occasions I had encountered them on the stairs, they were always fondling each other. Obviously, they did a helluva lot more once they got behind closed doors. I certainly hoped this was not going to be a regular occurrence, disrupting my home life.

I needed something to divorce my mind from my work's intensity and the disturbance of my hormonal neighbors in order to reinvigorate my creativity. Looking around the apartment I came upon the coin wrappers and my 1921 Mercury dime. I was planning on taking the coin rolls to the bank to exchange for bills on Tuesday but figured maybe I could do something with the dime that day. A quick Google search highlighted a coin and collectible shop only a few blocks away. It was open until 5 p.m.

Pulling a short sleeve navy blue polo shirt I've had since college over my head, I hustled down the five flights of stairs with the Mercury dime secure in my denim pants' pocket. As the store was within a reasonable distance and it was a nice day, I figured a good, brisk walk would do me good. The unexpected sunny warmth caught me by surprise, but soon I was taking confident strides down the empty streets.

On my way I was surprised to see my silver Corolla, without another car rammed up against the rear bumper or front fender. The car might have appeared lonely without the usual accompaniment of parked cars, but I was thrilled to be basking in the sun and Astoria isolation during a holiday weekend.

Out of the glare came a strapping looking guy, of a similar age to me, jogging at a fast clip, wearing ear buds. Being in a jovial mood, I gave a brief wave to my fellow athlete as he flew by me without taking notice.

Slowing my pace a bit did wonders to calm my heavy breathing before I arrived in front of Carl Caruso's Classic Collectibles, squeezed between Nick's Famous Pizzeria and the Happy Hellenic Travel Agency. A sign in Carl's window said "We buy and sell collectibles — top dollar paid." Cupping my eyes to see through the dusty window, I was able to tell the store was packed with coins, sports cards, and what looked like 1980s B-movie posters. Scanning further, I was glad to see there was no one in the store other than a heavyset balding man of about 50, reading *The Racing Form* behind the counter.

I walked in somewhat tentatively, and as I did not want to appear overanxious, I feigned interest in a couple of the items on display. I took hold of a box that contained a Slinky toy and turned it over, learning the price was $29.95.

Continuing my cool and casual approach inside the store, I took in a series of signed and framed photographs situated on the walls. Each photo contained younger versions of the man glancing up from *The Racing Form*. Some people clearly do not age well, as was the case with this gentleman.

After a couple minutes, the formerly photogenic man barked, "Can I help you with something?"

Based on the sound of his voice, he was either a long-term cigarette smoker or part terrier. I was going to tell him I was just looking, but instead decided to get right to the purpose of my business. I walked up to the gentleman and stated, "I just inherited this," taking the dime from my pocket and presenting it to him. I decided to say "inherited" rather than "found," as I figured it made the coin sound more valuable.

He furtively glanced at the front and back of the coin, and said, "Not much of an inheritance, is it?" The smell of cigars emanated from his clothing. He proceeded to tell me that the coin, though old, was not valuable unless it was in pristine condition, which this one was not. He concluded his lecture by grinning, exposing teeth matching the color of my khaki pants, and woofing out, "I'll take it off of your hands for twenty dollars."

My response was a congenial, "No thank you," and I turned to walk away.

As I approached the door, I heard, "My final offer—twenty-five dollars." But I kept walking.

When I got home, I took the coin out of my pocket and looked at it before announcing to my empty apartment that I was going to keep it. I proceeded to place the coin next to my computer and resumed writing.

Near midnight, as my yawning bursts increased in frequency, I closed my laptop and placed the dime on top. A good night's sleep would restore my energy and ensure the next day would be equally productive. Little did I know that the next day would be the start of an experience I could never have imagined.

Chapter 5

I'm not a great cook but have always been able to manage some basics. I prepared a hearty breakfast of three scrambled eggs, eight strips of bacon, four slices of toast with butter and jam, and coffee with milk and sugar, I was ready for a full writing day. It was Labor Day Sunday and I was on a mission. When I get motivated there is very little that can stop me from monumental progress.

I removed the dirty dishes from my dining room table and placed them in the sink. As I don't have a dishwasher, hand washing the dishes had to be added to my day's busy schedule. To eliminate as many obstacles as possible from hindering a full day's work, I made the decision to treat myself to a souvlaki platter from the downstairs restaurant for dinner rather than having to shop, cook and clean later.

I've always been a very organized person, and creating and keeping to a schedule is, in my opinion, crucial to all successful people. I decided on a couple of Twix candy bars in lieu of a full lunch, which would not only be more time efficient but would provide a needed energy boost for the busy day ahead. I typically try to exercise at least one or two days a week by walking in the local park, but I realized that such exertions needed to be put on hold as my priority was to write perhaps as many as 5,000 words that Sunday.

With breakfast out of the way and the rest of the day's nutrition already planned, my day was coming together nicely.

Transforming my dining room back to a work area was accomplished by removing the dime from the laptop and then moving the laptop back onto the table. I also placed a pad and pen next to the computer as I sometimes like to jot down ideas the old-fashioned way. I picked up the newest addition to my household, the 1921 Mercury dime, and studied it again. It was either my imagination or perhaps it was due to being seen in a different light, but it appeared to my eye to be less tarnished than I recalled. I placed it on top of my writing pad and opened the laptop.

I had already written a bit over 10,000 words of my novel, *Murder Most Mundane*, and began each writing session by rereading my most recent additions. This allowed me the opportunity to do additional edits, as well as providing an easier transition into the upcoming action. Frankly, I also enjoy reading my writing—though I hope this does not sound too arrogant.

I scrolled up to my starting point from the previous day and read to myself for the next few minutes. I like to read aloud as it is important for me to not only see the words but to also hear them. I've heard that many other great authors follow this same technique.

I came to the very last sentence I had written: "Reginald was found face down in the library with the hilt of a shiny cutlass protruding from his back," when something out of the ordinary caught my attention. Somehow, the writing seemed to continue beyond the last words I remembered typing the night before. Upon closer inspection, I realized the writing was not mine! In what was undoubtedly by any definition, a surreal moment, I began to read words written on my computer by someone else even though no one else could possibly have had access!

I never understood what it meant when someone said "his jaw dropped" until that very moment.

Chapter 6

Charlie LiPari left his small apartment and descended the stone staircase at 345 South Dearborn Street a little after 10 a.m. The thick air greeted him with a sudden blast of heat. He scowled up at the sun as he nearly popped the sleeves on his new wool suit, which had cost him $34.95. "Ooph!" he huffed. He hooked a meaty finger into his shirt collar and pulled it away as sweat puddled off his 225-pound body.

His boss, Johnny Romano, expected everyone who worked for him to dress like businessmen, but this fucking monkey suit was suffocating. The initial novelty for a guy with only a fourth-grade education wearing a suit, when his job description was primarily to break kneecaps and deliver packages, had worn thin. Now it just made him feel murderous.

Charlie knew he was a glorified messenger, delivering envelopes and packages to influential men, but he also knew people gave him more respect than his tasks deserved. Of course, a good deal of that respect could be categorized as fear. Delivering and picking up parcels for Mr. Romano kept Charlie busy most days, and his ham-hock-sized fists were vital tools of his trade.

He walked eight blocks, turned left on State Street, and passed under the swirling red, white and blue ribbons of Vinny's sign. Charlie smiled nostalgically as he entered the haircut joint he had been going to since the days of taking milk money from his kindergarten classmates.

"Hey, Vinny."

Vinny was trimming the bushy hair of Jonas Scupperton's neckline, a lawyer who had enough pockets to hold all of Chicago's south side judges in them.

Vinny just nodded to a window ledge, where a plain manila envelope lay. Then his eyes said scram, so Charlie did so quickly as he picked up the delivery, offering "Beautiful weather," as the door jingled behind him.

Lumbering back down the street, Charlie was hoping to be out of the heat and back indoors by 11:30. Wiping the endless moisture from his forehead, he started licking his oversized lips, imaging an ice-cold beer cascading down his throat.

Charlie was well compensated for work he found easy, and having regular access to booze during prohibition was quite a perk. The fact that he also had his pick of attractive women made his career choice an even better one. He was far removed from being considered good looking. The truth was—and he knew it— he was much more likely to be called homely or scary looking, though never when he was within earshot. Charlie's bulbous nose, which had been broken more times than he could remember, balanced his wing-like ears, plump lips, and a Y-shaped scar across his cheek.

Prior to working for Mr. Romano, women would avoid Charlie as if they knew he had an infectious disease. (To the best of his knowledge he did not have one.) Now, as the influential Mr. Romano's full-time employee, Charlie pretty much had the choice of any of "Mr. Romano's girls" for up to an hour or for however long it took him.

Charlie lumbered along muttering to himself as an approaching man averted his eyes and hastily retreated into the street and right into a pile of steaming horse manure. The man stifled a curse as he readily accepted the lesser of two evils.

A couple of rats seemed to share similar fears as they quickly scampered away from the oncoming behemoth.

On the east end of Cooper Avenue was The Commodore, a large apartment building that Charlie had a lot of memories in— none of them good. As he passed it, a man stepped off the stoop eating a ham sandwich and gave a fleeting glance to Charlie before quickly looking away.

Charlie thought the man seemed vaguely familiar: most likely some out-of-work sucker killing the day hanging around the block.

Unfortunately, like with most jobs there are positives and negatives, as Charlie was about to find out. He felt a searing pain in his back and heard a reverberating boom in his ear before realizing what happened to him. Another blast a second later made certain Charlie would never have the refreshing glass of beer he could almost taste.

Timothy Morris stood over Charlie's unmoving prone body. He plopped what remained of the ham sandwich into his mouth and took a quick look around. He then reached down and took the manila envelope from Charlie's pocket along with a billfold, as his own personal gift. Breaking into a grin, he reached into a back pocket and came away with a brand new shiny dime. Timothy flipped and caught the dime as he contentedly walked away.

Timothy Morris was known to be as cool as a cucumber, but the ten-block walk in 86-degree heat turned his pasty face the color of a ripe tomato. Sweat dripped into his eyes from his previously coiffed hair. He slowed down his pace and saw a kid, about nine years-old, hawking "cold and refreshing lemonade" across the street. Timmy's idea of refreshment was usually something a bit stronger, but he figured a lemonade would hit the spot.

Besides, from a distance, the kid looked a bit like his son Tommy, and wouldn't he want his son to have customers if he was standing in the street on an oppressively hot and humid day hocking lemonade?

Timmy crossed the street and took in the handmade sign that read "Delishus lemonade one cent each." He wondered if his Tommy would be able to print up a sign as neatly as this kid, and whether he would also be able to spell a tricky word like delishus.

"Hey kid, I'll take a cup of lemonade," Tim said, as his tongue innocently massaged his lips.

The boy dutifully ladled out the lemonade to the brim of a cup and handed it to Tim.

"What's your name kid?"

"Billy, sir. Billy Barrow."

"How old are you, Billy?" "I'm eight, sir."

"Eight, huh? I've got a boy just about your age. What do you like to do when you're not selling lemonade?"

"Oh, I love playing baseball. I'm going to be a baseball player when I get older. I'm a catcher."

"You think you could be as good as Bob O'Farrell one day, kid?"

"Actually, sir, I kind of like the rookie catcher the Cubs just brought up, Gabby Hartnett. I think he's going to be a great player one day. Hopefully, I'll be a teammate of his when I'm in the majors."

Timmy smiled. "Oh, yeah? My son wants to play in the majors too. Maybe one day you'se guys will be teammates."

Timmy readily took a refreshing gulf of the lemonade. Its balance of sweet and sour was perfect, and it was well iced. Timmy felt cooler already. "Mmm, that's good! But, unfortunately, kid, while everyone knows that Bob O'Farrell is a top-flight catcher, the chances that an unknown like Gabby Hartnett will even be in the majors in two years is…"

The boy's smile flattened, and the luster of his eyes dimmed instantly. He looked at Tim expectantly.

"Slim to none."

Sucking down the ice cubes, Timmy said, "Son, if you play baseball as well as you make lemonade, I expect to see you in the majors one day." Timmy reached into his pocket and took out the dime, formerly Charlie LiPari's property, and handed it to Billy. Billy began to put together nine cents of change but Tim stopped him and said, "Keep the change."

"Are you sure, sir? That would pay for ten lemonades!"

Timmy patted Billy on the head and confidently walked off, relishing his productive morning.

October 9, 1929

Billy felt like he was going to explode. He couldn't recall the last time he was this excited. He would be taking the train to Philadelphia to see the Cubs play the A's in the World Series Game 3 at Shibe Park in Philadelphia! The first game of the series had been played the day before at Wrigley Field in Chicago, and game two was being played later today. The A's had won yesterday's game 3-1, much to Billy's disappointment. Billy figured the A's would win the series, but in his heart, he held out hope the Cubs might pull it off. The Cubs hadn't won a World Series since 1908, and he figured they were due to be the champs again. His father had been about the same age Billy was now when the Cubs won in '08. His father still exuberantly talked about that series as if it took place yesterday. Billy wanted to share his dad's sense of everlasting joy and wonderment.

The A's were a powerhouse team, managed by "The Tall Tactician" Connie Mack, and with really big stars like Lefty Grove, Eddie Collins, Jimmy Foxx, Al Simmons, and Mickey Cochrane. Cochrane was the best catcher in the American League, and the Cubs had the best catcher in the National League, Gabby Hartnett. Unfortunately, Gabby was hurt for most of the year and wasn't expected to play at all in the series. The Cubs still had other great players like Rogers Hornsby, Riggs Stephenson, Kiki Cuyler, and Hack Wilson, but it would've been exciting to see baseball's two best catchers playing the World Series at the same time, particularly as Billy idolized Gabby Hartnett.

The previous night Billy's dad came home and announced he would be going to an insurance convention in Atlantic City the upcoming weekend. He typically did not like these events, but because his boss was unable to go, he was chosen to attend in his place. Billy had asked, "Does anyone really need to go from your company? After all, it's a long trip."

"That's true, Billy, but then the two tickets I bought for game three of the World Series would be wasted."

Billy's eyes navigated the room. He took in his father's stoic expression, the kind and knowing glint in his mother's eyes, and his younger sister Lucy's expanding smirk.

Reality was slowly setting in, still Billy sheepishly asked, "Who will be using the other ticket, Dad?"

His dad's eyes crinkled up in laughter as he said, "Mom doesn't like the idea of a long train ride, and Lucy doesn't like baseball, so I guess it will have to be you. You better start packing."

Billy had been obsessed with baseball for as long as he could remember. He had dreams of becoming a major-league catcher for most of his childhood but that changed when he broke his third finger on foul tips by the time he was 11 years old. Also, his body type had changed; he was now lean and lanky, built more like a first baseman or an outfielder. His three slightly misshapen digits would always serve as a reminder of his backstop days.

He had become a good student and currently aspired to become a lawyer like his Uncle Matt. He knew he had an excellent chance to make his high school baseball team as a junior next year but realized that was a long way from playing in the majors one day. A career as a lawyer was a much more realistic and practical ambition, albeit less exciting.

He didn't need his father's prompt to take the stairs two at a time and immediately begin packing. He had a small suitcase his parents had given him years earlier when the four of them had taken a trip to St. Louis. Billy quickly got to packing, creating a clothing tornado swirling around the room. Shirts, underpants, socks and pants were all airborne, and several days worth of clothing landed in the suitcase.

He had taken 35 cents out of the canvas pouch under his bed where he kept his change, anticipating a movie outing with friends over the weekend. He realized he now needed more money than that, so he grabbed a few dollars from the little metal bank he kept on his closet's top shelf. Billy's dad would offer to buy him what he wanted on the trip, but now that he was 15 years old, he felt the right thing to do was to pay his own way for incidentals. Besides, he might want to buy his father a present to thank him for this unbelievable surprise.

Billy could already smell and taste the hot dogs, peanuts and Cracker Jack he would devour at the ballpark. He would buy two programs at the game. One he would keep score in as his father had taught him to do when he was a little kid, and one to keep as a souvenir, a keepsake he knew he would treasure forever. He also knew he should buy a third program and give it to his best friend, Stan, who was as big a Cubs fan as Billy. It was definitely going to be an expensive weekend, but, boy, would it be worth it! Good thing that he was thrifty and had saved almost all his newspaper delivery tips.

His parents had always insisted he work so he could have money for extra things he wanted to buy or do. His father had started giving him a small allowance when he was six, but he always had some sort of job to earn extra money: delivering newspapers, mowing lawns, washing cars. He had even sold lemonade when he was about eight years old.

Looking down at the two coins in his hand, Billy recalled when he earned the shiny dime. He had gotten it from a gangster who bought a lemonade from him when he was eight or nine years of age. At the time, he was unaware of the man's criminality. But a few weeks later he saw the man's picture on the front page of the newspaper. *The Chicago Tribune* headline said, "Gangster Killed in Ongoing Turf War." Billy remembered feeling sad and confused at the time because the man had been so kind and generous.

Chapter 7

Whoa, I must have been having a hallucination or an emotional breakdown. The writing on the laptop was absolutely not mine. How the hell had it gotten there? My mind wandered in all directions, none of which I wanted to visit.

Growing up I remembered my mother telling us about an aunt she had—Lydia or Lena? Lena, that was it. She had some sort of mental breakdown and ran away. Every couple of years the phone would ring and my mother would answer it. I would hear mother saying, "Lena, is that you?" Then she would hang up the phone and always look completely shaken afterwards. My siblings and I would ask her about it, and she'd tell us it was her crazy aunt who disappeared a long time ago and periodically would call a relative, say Hi, and then hang up.

Then there's my father's family. He had a much older cousin who never married or had kids, and lived by himself, a recluse. He died a couple of years ago, and when the family went to clean up his house, my father said it was filled with wall-to-wall garbage. He said his uncle was a hoarder who suffered from mental illness. There was obviously a considerable amount of mental illness in both sides of my genetic makeup.

I put down the bag of popcorn I was munching on and closed my eyes. Gritting my teeth, I squeezed my thumb and forefinger as hard as I could into my left forearm while simultaneously digging in my nails. I slowly opened my eyes to see a couple of blood droplets trickling from my raised skin. Satisfied I was not in a bad dream, I realized I needed to get control of myself and begin to think rationally.

I was trained as somewhat of an expert in British mysteries, and the king of all mystery writers, Arthur Conan Doyle, famously wrote in *The Case Book of Sherlock Holmes*: "When you have eliminated all which is impossible, then whatever remains, however improbable, must be the truth."

Somehow, someone must have gotten into my apartment and written on my laptop. I'm a heavy sleeper but couldn't imagine being so far under that someone could've broken in and typed for an hour or so while I was dozing a few feet away. I did only have two glasses of wine.

I took a hammer from my rarely used toolbox, quietly crept across the living room, and threw open my closet to catch the intruder off-guard. No one there. Crawling across the floor, with hammer in hand and flashlight gripped between my teeth, I checked under my sofa, and other than multiple dust balls, again saw nothing. Weapon in hand, on tiptoes, I cautiously moved to the bathroom and swiftly pulled aside the shower curtain. Beyond some traces of emerging black mold, nothing. Nobody there. The momentarily euphoric feelings of safety gave way to the likelihood that I had deep genetic connections to crazy aunts and uncles. I never thought I would have mixed emotions about there not being a deranged lunatic hiding in my apartment.

I needed some fresh air to make sense of things and would have to rearrange my day's schedule. Instead of spending the rest of the day working on my masterpiece, *Murder Most Mundane*, I would contemplate things in the fresh air of the park. I shut down my laptop, placed my lucky dime on it, and with keys and wallet in hand, I rushed out of the apartment and down the stairs.

"This is not possible."

"Laptops don't write themselves."

"Windows and doors were bolted shut."

"Nobody came inside."

"Laptops don't write themselves."

"Laptops don't write themselves."

"LAPTOPS DON'T WRITE THEMSELVES!"

"LAPTOPS DON'T WRITE THEMSELVES! I AM NOT CRAZY!"

Plowing through the front door, I collided with Ricardo, our building's super. He shook his head and asked, "Who are you yelling at, Zach? Is everything okay?"

I nodded, then stuffed my hands in my pockets and charged up Twenty-First Street. My brain boiled with possibilities. Maybe someone, somehow hacked my computer and started to write a story to torment me or to make me believe I was crazy. I've already mentioned that I'm an independent person without a lot of social contacts so such a scenario seemed unlikely. I don't interact much with other employees at work, so I figured it unlikely a coworker would target me with such a bizarre practical joke.

There was certainly the possibility that some social outcast completely unfamiliar to me, who had nothing better to do but sit in front of a computer all day, would try to disrupt the sanctity of someone else by such a dastardly action. But why would I have been chosen?

Another strange thing was that the story I had just read was somewhat innocuous and certainly neither offensive nor threatening. To be honest, I kind of liked the story and was interested to see how it might develop.

The last rational explanation, as much as I hated to admit it, was that I was having some sort of psychotic episode. Maybe I had a split personality and my conscious half was not aware of what the other half was doing. Think Dr. Jekyll and Mr. Hyde.

The more I thought about it, the calmer I became. The two hot dogs with onions and extra mustard I got from the street vendor down my block also helped me relax. Great writers find inspiration and genius in different ways. Perhaps my true creative inspirations were a part of my subconscious and it manifested itself when I was in a trance-like state or even sleepwalking? That must have been it. I had gone to sleep, and once I was in a completely relaxed state, I got out of bed and started writing with an even greater imagination than I possessed when I was fully conscious!

The afternoon tumbled by like puzzle pieces dumped from a box. I walked to the basketball courts, the war memorial, the North Lawn, the soccer pitch, and back more times than I could count. I paced the walkway along the East River, dodging dogs and bicyclists.

I returned to my apartment around 6:15, needless to say, completely exhausted. But I came back with a bit of a sunburned face, a souvlaki platter in hand, and a calmer outlook on things.

I didn't really enjoy my dinner as another wave of nerves hit me with full force. Though my legs were still a bit fatigued from the many miles I clocked during the afternoon, I added to my steps by doing multiple laps around my living room. At every turn I glanced toward my laptop, knowing full well that I could not put off the inevitable forever.

I removed the dime from the laptop, set it aside, opened the lid before quickly closing it again. After ten more trips around the room, I once again opened it, this time powering it up. In a few seconds I would know if a temporary hallucination, or perhaps even, God forbid, a minor stroke had altered my mind.

Not only was the inexplicable writing still there, but there was more of it.

Chapter 8

George and Billy Barrow were set for the adventure of young Billy's lifetime, waiting for the Wednesday 1:07 p.m. train to Philadelphia. They would not arrive at their destination until Thursday night, and his father watched as Billy excitedly paced the platform once the rumbling and whistling of the incoming train was in earshot.

Most of his friends complained about their fathers, but Billy felt fortunate. The only time he recalled his dad losing his temper took place when Billy was about seven. His whole family was walking to the store and came upon three teenage boys poking, prodding and teasing a stray dog with sharpened sticks. His father grabbed the sticks from the boys and came very close to hitting the delinquents in the same manner that they had been torturing the helpless animal. Billy's mom diffused the situation by saying, "George, these boys are animals, you're not."

Billy and Lucy could tell their father was upset whenever his brow began to furrow. They also knew whenever he was about to tell a joke by recognizing a subtle change in his mannerism. No matter how many attempts at humor he made, Billy and Lucy would always preempt the punchline by announcing, "OK, dad, we know a joke is coming."

Billy could barely contain his excitement when the train porter, a Negro named Elijah, brought the Barrows to their private sleeping car. Billy's eyes bulged when he saw the fancy upholstered seats and Elijah's demonstration of how to convert them into beds at night. Billy stood enraptured as he inhaled the aroma of lemon coming off the car's glistening dark walnut wood walls. He couldn't recall a moment in his life when he had felt so simultaneously overwhelmed and joyous.

Elijah smiled. "If the two gentlemen need anything, call me at any time of the day or night."

George Barrow responded, "I believe we have everything we need, and we intend to have our meals in the dining car so no need to bring us any food." He reached into his pocket, pulled out a half-dollar for Elijah and said, "Thank you for your fine service, sir."

Billy was called "a gentleman." This day couldn't possibly have been any better, but the best was yet to come.

The 48-hour train ride from Chicago alone with his dad kept Billy perpetually smiling. Clearly, as "two gentlemen," Billy and his dad's relationship had evolved. Billy recognized he was no longer a child in his father's eyes but was now viewed as a young man. In addition to baseball, they discussed Billy's dreams and aspirations, his career goals and reluctantly, Billy shared his attraction to Dorothy Hamilton. Although Billy and Dorothy had known each other since kindergarten, his feelings toward her were different now: exciting, confusing, and scary. At first he was embarrassed to talk about Dorothy with his dad, but the more Billy divulged, the hungrier his father appeared for more information. Billy felt he had developed a new intimacy with his father and while he thought of his mother and Lucy, he secretly was thrilled to have this time alone with his dad.

Later that evening, his dad proclaimed, "Billy, you are a son any father would be proud of."

Billy tried unsuccessfully to keep his face from turning red as he stammered, "Thank you Dad."

They shared a dinner of shrimp cocktail, roast sirloin of beef with horseradish sauce, green beans with almonds, and the largest baked potato he had ever eaten, which Billy smothered with sour cream. When dinner was over and his father started to smoke his pipe, Billy felt almost unnatural not doing the same. The signal to return to their sleeper car came when his father gave the waiter a silver dollar and said, "Thank you for your fine service, sir."

George and Billy arrived in Philadelphia late on Thursday, October 10th, and took a taxi to The Bellevue-Stratford Hotel. His dad rarely discussed finances at home, but Billy always suspected that compared to some of his friends, his family never really worried about money. When they arrived at the hotel, Billy's eyes opened wide at the grand structure in front of him, and he asked, "Dad, isn't this too expensive?"

George responded, "Billy, I work hard for Kemper Insurance and I do a good job. They show their appreciation by paying me well and making certain I stay at first-class hotels when I travel, as I represent the company. How would it look if Kemper didn't treat their top employees well?"

Walking past two doormen in navy blue suits and white gloves, they continued up the nine stone steps between two looming pillars, and entered the hotel's grand lobby. Billy stopped as if frozen in place as his eyes inhaled the glimmering glass of the overhead chandeliers, while the glistening richness of the gray-and-white marble floor enveloped him.

They were brought up to their room on the eighteenth floor in a lift. Billy could not recall a time he had ever been so far above the ground, even though back in Chicago he had once viewed the city from the top of the Masonic Temple. A porter brought their suitcases up to their room and even offered to unpack them. George dismissed him by again saying, "Thank you for your fine service, sir," and handing him a half-dollar. But even as his eyes scanned the lavish room in front of him, Billy couldn't help thinking that in only twelve hours, he and his father would be seeing the Cubs and the A's in game three of the World Series. Billy knew he was the luckiest 15-year-old in America.

Though sleep should have come easily as his bed felt like a pool of feathers, Billy turned from one side to another trying to coax restful sleep which never arrived. Anticipating the day ahead made Billy's stomach feel as if the 30,000 fans going to the game were using his insides as a walkway to the stadium.

Morning could not come fast enough and for the first time in his father's recent memory, Billy did not eat anything for breakfast. He told his father, "I need to have room for eight hot dogs, plus peanuts, and at least one box of Cracker Jack."

George walked while Billy seemingly floated alongside a herd of other baseball fans toward Shibe Park. As Billy looked up, he could see the stadium's octagonal tower looming over the entrance. The rustling leaves on the many trees surrounding the stadium confirmed the rightness of his decision to wear an extra jacket. Billy scanned the baby blue sky to dispel any concern that rain might dampen, both literally and figuratively, the day ahead. With blue sky outweighing cloud cover, Billy sighed with relief.

George and Billy's seats were behind the first-base dugout, close enough to the field that Billy felt he could touch the trimmed, richest green grass he had ever seen. His excitement somehow grew further when he saw into the Cubs's dugout on the third-base side. There was his hero, Gabby Hartnett, on the bench, in uniform! Hartnett was unlikely to play today due to the injury he had been suffering for several weeks, but just seeing him so close was a thrill.

Billy saw Rogers Hornsby, probably the National League's best player, back-slapping with some of his teammates, and it gave Billy goosebumps. He pinched himself hard enough to hurt, making certain this was not a dream.

The A's had won Game 2 as well, and now that they were on the A's home turf, a four-game sweep was a disheartening probability. The loss in game one was particularly upsetting, as the A's unexpected starting pitcher was a 35-year-old, thought to be washed up, named Howard Ehmke. Not only was Ehmke the winning pitcher in a 3-1 game, he set a World Series record with 13 strikeouts.

"Billy! Billy! Don't you hear me?" George was trying to get Billy's attention, but Billy was so transfixed by his surroundings he had not heard his father.

"Sorry, Dad. What did you say?"

"I said the game will be starting in a few minutes so you should probably get a program so you can keep score."

"Oh right," Billy said, and began to get up when he heard the rumble of cheers and applause spreading around their section.

Billy looked toward the crescendo of noise and saw a man with a round face and a warm smile acknowledging the crowd. Alongside the formally dressed man was a woman wearing a bonnet obstructing her face but allowing wisps of gray hair to creep from beneath the hat's rim. It took a moment for Billy to realize that he was about 100 yards away from the most important person in the country, the President of the United States. President Hoover and his wife were taking their seats at the same event Billy was attending.

The cheers for the President finally subsided, and the President and the First Lady were now comfortably seated. Billy remained standing to take in the moment. After collecting himself, he asked his dad if he wanted a hot dog.

"Sure, I'll take one with mustard. Let me give you some

money."

"No thanks, Dad. My treat." Billy strutted with pride up the aisle to find a hot dog vendor.

Billy purchased three scorecards, then spotted an olive-skinned man with a handlebar mustache carrying a basket and announcing, "Hotta dogs, hotta dogs, get your hotta dogs."

Billy waved to the man. "Four hot dogs please, and a bag of peanuts."

Billy watched as the man deftly opened his basket, allowing aromatic steam to escape. With a long fork the vendor speared four and quickly placed them into warmed buns. With a twinkly smile the man helped Billy organize his mouth-watering haul for the return to his seats. Billy paid for the food, then took the 1921 Mercury dime from his back pocket, handed it over, and said, "Thank you for your fine service, sir."

Chapter 9

Tony Algieri gratefully plopped down on a trolley seat, allowing his weary legs a short reprieve while placing his work basket on the empty seat next to him. Normally, he'd give in to his heavy eyelids and grab a few minutes of sleep, but today, the coins bulging out of his pants pockets kept him alert and attentive. Carefully avoiding eye contact, Tony kept his hands on his pockets to prevent the trolley's movement from creating a coin symphony and attracting unnecessary curiosity.

Once off the trolley and humming the melody of "Vissi D'arte" from his favorite opera, *Tosca*, Tony strolled down Washington Avenue toward the three-story, red brick building on 6th Street where he and his family lived on the ground floor. The lamplighter must recently have completed his task as Tony's front door was illuminated despite the rapidly darkening sky. He lingered a moment or two listening to music he enjoyed even more than opera: the orchestra of his seven children yelling, laughing, and playing. Then he entered his home.

"Papa's home, papa's home," his youngest daughter, Liliane, screamed. Six-year-old Liliane jostled for space with sisters Isabella, 8, and Sofia, 11, as the welcoming committee. Tony picked up Liliane with one arm as he dropped his basket to embrace the other two while four-year-old Christopher wedged his way into the group bear hug.

"Stop it, Chris, he's our papa," Isabella announced.

"He's my papa too," Chris wailed.

"Now, now, bambini, he actually belongs to me," came a voice belonging to a dark-haired woman entering from the kitchen while wiping her hands on an apron. Marie gently nudged her offspring aside as she embraced her husband, though Chris tenaciously retained a hold of his father's ankle.

The family gathering increased a moment later as Tony and Marie's eldest offspring, 16-year-old Tony Jr. entered the fray. "Did the A's win?" Tony Jr. asked.

Tony sheepishly looked at his son and said, "I don't know. I think so. There was a lot of cheering."

"Papa, you work there all day, your customers are all baseball fans, mostly A's fans. You really should learn the game or at least show some interest in it. Baseball is the American game. People will never be interested in *calcio* here."

Following his favorite soccer team, Pro Vercelli, was Tony's passion and he found it frustrating not being able to follow them in the states. Baseball to Tony lacked action, and he had no interest in it despite working at the ballpark. The crowd's cheers and applause were just background noise to him. He only hoped whatever was happening on the field made the fans hungry." What delicious dinner has my bella made for us tonight?"

The response came from the kitchen, partially blocked from Tony's view, "We made risotto." Stella, who was 14 years-old and the spitting image of her mother, came out of the kitchen carrying a large saucepan as proof.

Marie took her husband by the hand and led him to the living room sofa, which was presently occupied by the remaining Algieri clan member, 12-year-old Marco.

Tony ruffled his son's hair as he sat next to him, eliciting, "Stop that. I just combed my hair."

"Watch the way you speak to your father, or you will go without dinner tonight."

"Sorry, Momma. Sorry, Papa."

Marco got up so his mother could sit down next to Tony. The

whole family, even little Chris, knew what was coming next.

"So, was it a good day?" Marie asked.

Tony smiled broadly. "You tell me." He emptied his pockets, change spilling, jingling and rolling off the coffee table onto the floor. The children happily gathered it up.

A few minutes later, Marie exclaimed, "*Dio mio*. Sixteen dollars and eighty cents! How many more World Series games are there?"

"Probably only a couple more," Tony responded.

"We are going to be quite the well-off couple when we visit New York City if you keep having days like today," Marie proclaimed.

Tony and Marie were scheduled for their first visit to New York City the second week of November. Anthony and Stella were being left in charge of the brood so their parents could spend their wedding anniversary in the city they had heard so much about but had never seen.

Chapter 10

Okay, so I had gone insane. Fortunately, I seemed to be an intelligent insane person still in possession of many of his faculties, including being able to view things rationally and with some level of analysis. An insight I could not ignore was that the stories I had just read were about people who had possessed a 1921 Mercury dime, seemingly the 1921 dime currently on my desk.

I was familiar with the stories of Aladdin and the magic lamp, and Jack with his magic bean. I guess somehow I had been transformed into Zachary Howard and the magic dime. But I would have traded my dime for a magic bean or lamp in a second. Frankly, I did not see how a storytelling dime was going to increase my net worth or the quality of my life.

Did I honestly believe that this silver sliver retained memories and then ably wrote them down? Well, the thought crossed my mind that I was fortunate it was U.S. currency and therefore able to transcribe memories into English, or I would have been completely in the dark. Also, it a good thing the coin was so adept at typing. Who knew American currency had such skill?

What other explanation could there be? Perhaps the sulfide on the coin rubbed onto my hands, went through the pores in my skin and traveled miraculously to my subconscious mind? Then, while in a state of deep sleep, I was able to put into writing the messages the sulfide told me. This theory led to an indisputable conclusion: my grasp on reality was slipping.

I figured I should probably pack my bag for what would undoubtedly be a lengthy stay at a local psychiatric hospital, but I decided to first try to seek some answers. Quickly Googling the 1929 World Series, I learned that the series was indeed played between the A's and the Cubs, with the

A's winning the series four games to one. Game three was played at Shibe Park on Friday, October 11, and as it turned out, that was the only game the Cubs won. I was glad Billy was there to see it. And, yes, the President and First Lady had attended. All the facts checked out.

Clearly, as I was born in 1986 and was never a big baseball fan, I didn't have this knowledge, consciously or subconsciously.

Next, I tried to find out if the Billy Barrow from the story ever actually existed and what became of him. I guess I can't with one hundred percent certainty say that the William Barrow I uncovered was the same Billy Barrow in the narrative, but it did seem highly likely. A William Barrow had graduated from Northwestern Law School in 1939, and appeared to have had a very successful legal career.

I discovered a website for Barrow & Barrow P.C., with offices at 353 N. Clark Street, founded by William "Billy" Barrow in 1949, and joined by his son, William Jr., in 1979. The founder passed away in 2003 and his grandson, George, became a member of the firm in 2008.

Apparently, the stories written on my computer were based on real people and events. I could not have knowingly written them, yet their narrative appeared in the body of the saved draft of my novel. The stories had begun appearing after I discovered the 1921 dime, and intriguingly, while my laptop had been shut down. The final clue to the puzzle was that I had placed the dime on top of the closed laptop. Neither Hercule Poirot nor Jane Marple were needed for this case as I, Zach Howard, the great mystery author, was on the job.

I knew I needed to test my theory further. For three consecutive nights after I finished writing, I closed the laptop but did not place the dime on top of it. I did not find a word written by an unknown force on any of the following mornings. To further extrapolate my theory that the dime, and only the dime, was the writing source, I closed my laptop the next two nights, placed a penny on the lid one night and a quarter on it the next night. Nothing happened. I guess pennies and quarters might have other skills, but writing was not among them.

For the time being, I decided to not seek out the help of a mental health counselor, but admittedly my preoccupation with magical writing was taking a toll. I began to fall behind in my work assignments and was also unable to concentrate on my own novel. I knew I needed to test my theory's final portion, so before going to sleep, I shut my laptop and carefully placed the 1921 dime on top.

Chapter 11

There were two more games played at Shibe Park and those games proved to be even more lucrative for Tony. By the end of the series, Tony and Marie had added $54 to their savings. In addition to working at the ballpark, Tony worked construction whenever jobs were available. Hard work and responsible saving was the philosophy Tony and Marie espoused. For the past year, Anthony Jr. had worked as a stock boy at the local grocery, and ever since Stella was old enough to help with the younger siblings, Marie was able to clean other people's homes to earn some extra money.

On Monday, October 14, the little ones were put to bed, and the older kids were outside playing with their neighborhood friends. Marie and Tony went throughout their four-room row house collecting carefully hidden jars. Each jar represented the sweat and toil of the family's hard work since the purchase of their modest home 16 years earlier.

Marie kept insisting to Tony that they should deposit their savings into an interest-bearing account at the bank, but Tony wanted to see and feel the results of their labor whenever he wanted. Every few weeks, they went through the exercise of taking jars filled with money from various hiding spots in their home and placing them on the table in the kitchen. Marie served two demitasse cups of espresso and brought out a pencil and paper. Rather than simply adding the latest savings to the total from a few weeks earlier, Tony insisted they open every jar, take out the coins and bills, and start the tabulation anew. The procedure was tedious but brought so much pleasure to her husband, how could she say no?

This evening they were well into the second hour when their children's return interrupted the counting. Typically the procession of offspring followed the same pattern: the youngest first to the eldest.

When Anthony Jr. and Stella returned together at 10:30, they were immediately beckoned by their father. "Stella, Anthony, sit with your momma and papa and have a drink."

"Marie, bring four glasses to help us celebrate, and I'll get the bottle of grappa."

"Papa, what are we celebrating?" Stella asked.

"First we toast and then we tell you," Tony said. He raised his glass, and Marie poured small amounts of the liquor into the glasses for Anthony and Stella.

"Come now, Marie, you can be more generous than that. They are practically adults. We are celebrating."

Marie followed Tony's direction, filling up Stella's and Anthony's glasses while simultaneously giving looks to her children that left no doubt that most of the liquid better remain untouched.

With his glass now accompanied by three other raised glasses, Tony began his toast. "Momma and I came to this country when we were 19 and 18. We had money given to us saved by your Nonne and Nonni, enough to buy this house. Three months later God blessed us with Anthony's birth and then six times more. We came to this country and to the city of Philadelphia to make a great new life not just for your Momma and Papa, but for all our children and for future Algieri generations."

"Tonight, Momma has finished the calculations, and counted the money we've saved through hard work and sacrifice for the past 16 years. Marie, please tell them."

"Tony, you want me to tell them? Why don't you?"

"Would someone tell us!" Anthony implored.

Marie smiled and said, "We have saved $7,500."

Tony corrected her. "$7,501.45."

"Wow," Stella and Anthony said in unison.

Anthony asked, "What are you going to do with all that money?"

"Momma and I have been discussing it, and we have decided to fulfill a dream we've had since we left Calabria. We want to be our own bosses and start our own business. No more toiling for others and being at their mercy. We want our hard work, sweat and ambition to benefit only our family. When we return from our trip to New York, we are going to the Bankers Trust on the next block to open an account. We will talk to the banker about getting their support to start our business. Momma is right. Leaving our money in jars around the house is not what we should be doing with all of our savings."

"Papa, what type of business are you going to start?"

Marie broadly smiled as she answered her daughter's question: "Momma Algieri's Pizzeria."

Tony smiled and said, "When in New York City we will go to visit Lombardi's in Manhattan. They started selling pizza more than 20 years ago, and I hear they are doing very well. People in South Philadelphia would love a shop that sells pizza like your Nonna used to make, and your Momma makes it even better."

Anthony began pacing around the kitchen to burn off some of his excitement while the more composed Stella asked, "What can we do to help?"

Marie responded, "We'd like to move up our trip to New York. Instead of going in November, we plan to leave on October 27. We'll need you to take care of the house and watch the little ones, okay?"

"Absolutely, and when you get back, we can start planning for Momma Algieri's Pizza Parlor," Anthony said as he completed his fortieth lap.

Monday, October 27

On Monday, Anthony Algieri energetically carried a brand new, black canvas suitcase elegantly trimmed in brown leather in his left hand, and his wife's wooden suitcase in his right, as he and Marie entered the imposing Broad Street Station for their long-anticipated train ride to New York City's Pennsylvania Station.

An anxious Marie had started imploring Tony at 6:30 a.m. to "hurry up or we'll be late." Tony was surprised when they arrived at the station only an hour before the 8:55 a.m. Narragansett train, which fortunately was on time. They would be staying at a Manhattan hotel on Broome and Mulberry Streets in the middle of New York's Little Italy. The neighborhood was not as old as Philadelphia's Ninth Street Italian Market, but after the recent influx of over a million immigrants from southern Italy, New York's Little Italy had more people, more businesses, and more activity than any other Italian community in the country.

The Algieris had diligently spoken English as their primary language since arriving in America, but for the next six days they would speak their native Calabrese dialect once again.

Both Tony and Marie were born in Calabria, in the southern part of the newly unified Italy. Though their roots were Calabrian they now considered themselves true Americans and had not returned since arriving on American soil in 1913. The area they were visiting in lower Manhattan was a melting pot of its own. Immigrants from Sicily, Naples, Abruzzo, and other regions now called America—and more specifically New York City—home.

Tony's hand brushed against the frayed sleeve of the fur on Marie's coat as they exited the train station and got their first glimpse at the wonder that was New York City.

Tony looked around at the endless sea of men in three-piece suits and fashionable hats. The women they observed were mostly wearing cloche hats and overcoats that gave an aura of prosperity.

Walking down the stairs from the lobby of the small hotel Tony grimaced slightly.

"What's the matter, Tony?"

"I remembered when I bought you this coat. We only had Junior and Stella back then, and you thought the coat was more than we could afford. You needed it then, and you need a new one now. It shouldn't be a gift for Christmas; it should be something you like and pick out yourself. We can afford it."

"Nah, this coat has at least three more winters of use."

A short time later Marie and Tony dropped off their luggage in their modest room and immediately went back outside.

Much like a horseman's tug on his animal's reins, the pull on his hand led Tony to a pushcart peddler on the sidewalk barking out his produce in Italian. Though Tony and Marie insisted on only speaking English in their home for their children's benefit, transitioning to their native tongue was as natural as the sun rising in the morning.

"E quell ' arcancia Calabrese?"

"Si, Signora."

Contentedly walking down the street with a bag full of the delicious oranges, Tony was once again a youth strolling a street in Catanzaro, Calabria. This was a mood he frequently felt when in the South Philadelphia Italian Market, but just as frequently there, as here, he quickly jolted back to the moment. The New York and Philadelphia neighborhoods were home to speakers of differing dialects, a far cry from the uniform language heard on Catanzaro streets. Squeezing Marie's hand, Tony inhaled the garlic and basil coming through the open tenement windows along Mulberry Street. They methodically zigzagged the sidewalk, avoiding the knife sharpener and a produce cart piled with cascading mountains of purple eggplant and end-of-season red peppers. As they passed a second cannoli vendor, Tony's eyes pleaded with Marie—but with no luck. The long walk and mouthwatering smells made Marie and Tony hungry, which was pretty much his constant state. The timing was perfect as they were only two blocks away from their destination, Lombardi's Pizzeria on Spring Street. "Marie, can you goddamn believe it, we are going to the first place in America to serve pizza?"

"Tony, you know I don't like it when you curse."

"Sorry, *amore mio.* I'm just so damn excited. Uh, sorry dear," Tony sheepishly tilted his head. He couldn't help himself. Then he boldly boasted, "I can imagine years from now the next generation from Italy going to Philly to visit Momma Algieri's Pizza Parlor. What a great fuckin' country!"

The sigh from Marie could be heard for blocks, but she knew Lombardi's was legendary, and she shared Tony's excitement. Widely recognized as the first restaurant in America to serve pizza, Lombardi's was still thriving over two decades later. Tony thought it best to observe firsthand how a successful business operated. He knew no one made a tastier pizza pie than Marie, but running their own business would take more than just having the best recipe or chef.

Neapolitan-style pizza was typically baked in a hot coal oven with thinly stretched dough topped with tomatoes, mozzarella, and basil. The key to the pizza Marie made was using a tomato sauce rather than just tomatoes. No one's tomato sauce came close to Marie's; its sweet, tangy, and charred sauce placed her pizza in a class of its own.

Couched in secrecy, Marie shared her coveted sauce recipe with no one, not even Tony, though she planned on sharing it with Stella when she turned 18.

A point of pride among most of the neighborhood women back in Philly was the taste of their tomato sauce. Even the haughtiest of her female friends acknowledged Marie made the best version. "Un angulo di paradiso," her best friend Carmela called it. "A slice of heaven." Marie and Tony approached 53 ½ Spring Street, and their pulses quickened as they read in awe, "Pizzeria Napolitano Gennaro Lombardi." Though not as deeply religious as many of their friends, they imagined that this is what it would feel like to stand in front of a venerated religious shrine.

As soon as they entered, they experienced the aromas of charred dough, biting *parmigiano reggiano* and sweet Roma tomatoes, reminding even Marie that hours had passed since their last real meal. The dark, wooden wall panels, dimly lit hanging lights, and the intense heat from the coal oven, further enriched the welcoming experience.

Tony waved eagerly to a lanky young waiter wearing a black vest, who hurriedly came over to Tony's side.

"Buongiorno Signore."

"Due bicchieri di vino per favore cameriere, e una pizza, per favore."

The waiter hustled away as Marie whispered to her husband, "English please, Tony. We are Americans now."

"Marie, everyone here speaks Italian, and we'll always be Calabrian. Besides, Italian is a much nicer language than English.

But I will do as you ask."

The two glasses of wine were delivered a moment later as Tony raised his dark burgundy glass to Marie's, and said, "Saluti. Oops! I mean cheers."

Marie smiled in response and took a sip.

"This is something, isn't it?" Tony asked as he surveyed the establishment.

"Tony, you see they charge 40 cents for a pie. I priced out the ingredients and figured we would charge 30 cents a pie. You think we could charge 35 cents instead?"

Tony just nodded and pensively looked around as he repeatedly tossed and caught, tossed and caught, a dime from his pocket.

Five of the room's eight tables were occupied, include the one at which Tony and Marie were seated. In addition to the man who had brought them their wine, there was a woman dressed in a white blouse, and another man in a black vest taking orders and bringing out food. Both were cleaning as needed. There were two men in long white tomato-stained aprons tending guard next to the oven. They were focused exclusively on making the pies.

One of the men kneaded dough with his fists, sprinkled the marble countertop with semolina flour, then tossed and spun the ball high above his head, letting the centrifugal force spread and thin the dough.

Presented with the perfect base, the other pizzaiolo meticulously placed mozzarella and tomatoes on the flattened dough as Tony watched intently. Marie surreptitiously spied the other chef, now shredding basil, sprinkling it over a pie, and placing it in the coal-fired oven.

A young waiter picked up the pie, freshly removed from the oven, and placed it in front of Marie and Tony with aromatic steam traveling to their noses.

"Buon appetito."

"Grazi," Tony muttered instinctively.

Before a slice met either of their mouths, they devoured it with their other senses. The crust was thin, slightly blackened and revealed a few magical air pockets. Melted mozzarella sat in small pools of bubbling tomatoes. Next Tony devoured the pizza with his nose. Marie laughed to herself as she was convinced that if pizza were eaten through the sinuses, Tony's nose would dwarf W.C. Fields's.

They carefully inspected the charred top crust, the semolina flakes on the bottom crust, and the balance of cheese and sauce. Then they took a deep breath and consumed their first bites. "This is damn good pizza," Tony exclaimed.

Marie simultaneously wiped his chin with a cloth napkin and scolded him, "No foul language." Tony ate ninety percent and with a grin said, "This pie is excellent, but yours is much, much better."

Chapter 12

On Tuesday, Tony and Marie went to explore Macy's, the nation's largest store. It seemingly sold everything, and since Christmas was two months away, this was the ideal place to find presents for the children.

Three steps into the store and Tony's mouth was agape.

Watching Marie smile in wonderment made his own heart flutter with joy. They looked at one another and started giggling. After vowing to limit their purchases to one toy for each of the younger kids, they set off for what for turned out to be a four-hour adventure.

Tony and Marie watched as their fellow customers hurriedly marched through the store while they made their way much more slowly, stopping to gaze at every shelf. Testing the limits of how extensively and rapidly his head could turn, Tony took in the parade of customers hankering over the endless inventory of goods begging to be bought.

Marie scanned row upon row of the latest in women's fashion, until a shimmering satin blue dress caught her eye. Tony wandered towards men's hats. Gently fitting a gray fedora on his head, he strolled over to Marie and asked, "What do you think, am I the next Rudolph Valentino?" Marie's muffled chuckle and an eyeroll answered his question.

Their entertainment continued when, with cautious steps, they maneuvered onto moving wooden steps called an escalator, which magically took them to a higher floor. Two small towheaded boys ducked under Tony and Marie's clasped hands and ran past as a woman's voice called out, "William and Henry, stop that now! And wait for me at the next floor landing."

As the voice got closer, they heard, "Pardon me, I'm so sorry." A blonde woman squeezed past them.

Marie smiled at the woman and steadied herself as she stepped off the escalator onto the safety of the stone mezzanine floor. Turning to Tony, who half stepped, and half jumped behind her, she said, "I'm going to look for some gloves. Maybe I'll even take a peek at winter coats." Pointing to a sign in front of them saying Dried Goods, Marie continued, "I don't want you to get too bored so perhaps we could meet over there in an hour."

"Good idea. It would make me so happy if you bought a new coat. In the meantime, I'm going to look for pipes. I've been thinking I might want to start smoking."

"Oh, I love the smell of tobacco in a pipe. It's much better than cigar smoke. We'll meet back here in an hour."

Marie walked away, doing her best to conceal her furtive smile. She had no intention of buying a coat for herself, or even looking for a new pair of gloves. She needed time away from Tony so she could purchase his Christmas gift: an electric razor.

Tony walked away from Marie with a smile on his face and an air of relief; he hadn't been sure how he was going to get away from her long enough to buy her Christmas gift. Stella had told him before he left that her mom was entranced with the scent of Channel #5, and it would make the perfect, glamorous gift.

Marie and Tony had never indulged in such luxuries before, but both were feeling optimistic about their station in life and what the future might hold.

When they euphorically left Macy's around 4:30 p.m. with a bag of presents including a chemistry set, a musical bear and Lincoln Logs, plus gifts discreetly tucked away in the pocket of their respective coats, Tony and Marie stepped out into the surprisingly quiet streets of New York.

New York City usually had its own distinct sound. It was not easily identifiable like chirping birds in the morning or evening crickets. It was a sound of constant energy–people hustling, laughing, arguing. It was never one noise or volume level but rather a never-ending melody. Yet now it seemed dramatically different than yesterday or even earlier in the day. The cacophony of sounds had ceased, replaced by a suffocating silence and a morose feeling of dread.

"Something is not right, Tony," Marie said. "I can sense it."

Tony nodded his head. "I feel it too.

What do you think has happened?"

Two men wearing expensive looking suits, one charcoal gray and the other navy blue, passed by in silence, wearing glazed, somber expressions.

"Marie, do you think President Hoover died?"

"Oh, I hope not. I pray to God that's not what happened. I also pray that another war hasn't started."

Tony could hear the anxiety in Marie's voice, and his own stomach became queasy with the knowledge that Junior would soon be of drafting age.

He stopped a man briskly walking in his direction. The man, clearly in a stupor, reacted as if punched when Tony called to him, "Excuse me, sir, what is going on? Everyone seems upset."

The man's head swayed woefully, then registered Tony's question. "The stock market is crashing. We're all doomed."

Chapter 13

Marie and Tony decided it would make more sense to return to Philadelphia and their kids the next day, rather than spending an additional day in the gloom of New York City. On the morning of Wednesday, October 30, Marie finished up the packing, carefully wrapping the presents they had purchased to prevent both damage and easy recognition.

They headed uptown to the train amidst numerous faces etched with worry and despair. Boys hawking newspapers were yelling out the bold headlines printed on the papers in their hands. The phrases "Black Tuesday" and "Stock Market Crash" were echoing in the streets like a death knell.

Angst hung in the air like dark storm clouds. Hysterical men in business attire contemplated out loud about whether the banks would follow on the heels of the stock market and possibly also fail.

Marie grabbed Tony's hand two blocks from the train station and asked, "How do you think this will affect our plans to open our business?" Tony's face remained solemn but Marie noted the hint of a smile that he was trying to repress.

"I don't know for certain how we will be affected but why should it be bad? We don't own any stock and we don't keep our money in the banks. Who would have thought the best investment of all would be cash kept in jars?"

They walked in silent contemplation to Pennsylvania Station and passed a man sitting on the stoop of a building with his head buried in his hands, crying. Tony placed his hand on the shaking man's shoulder and asked, "Sir, is there anything I can do for you?"

The man slowly lifted his head to see who had interrupted his melancholy and saw a face filled with genuine concern and compassion. Marie joined Tony at the man's side and said, "It can't be all that bad. What can we do to help?"

The man began rubbing the back of his hand under his red-rimmed eyes and responded, "I have no idea what I'm going to tell them. I've lost all our money."

Realizing their scheduled train was leaving in 25 minutes, Tony silently put his hand into his pocket and took out all the change he had. He handed the grieving man a half-dollar, six quarters, three nickels, four pennies and a 1921 Mercury dime. "May God bless you, young man," Tony said. Then he took Marie's hand, and they walked together to catch their train.

Chapter 14

This dime was astonishing. I wondered whether I would become as universally recognized as Steve Jobs or dangle several notches below? How many people know that Ted Rappaport founded 5G technology, or that Vinton Cerf and Bob Kahn arguably invented the internet (with apologies to Al Gore)? I decided I would aim for Steve Jobs fame, but would happily join the Rappaport, Cerf and Kahn category.

While I did not exactly discover the magical history-telling dime, it did end up in my possession. More importantly, through a well-planned scientific approach, I determined precisely how it operated and under what circumstances it performed. Not only was I not crazy, but once this became public, I imagined the world would consider me an innovator and visionary of great magnitude. I would relish the day when I proved all my doubters embarrassingly wrong.

There had to be a reason I was chosen. My parents were forever bragging about my sister Suzy's "scientific mind and her innate ability to see mathematical equations." They praised my brother Roger's virtue as "a great natural athlete, so good looking and charismatic." The best my parents said about me was that I was "unique and perhaps would one day find myself." Well, Zachary had found himself, all right. It was incontrovertible! I was more than simply unique! Zachary Howard was someone people would be talking about for generations!

Genius comes in many forms and we find our inspiration in many ways. Steve Jobs soaked his feet in the Apple office toilets to relax and help his visionary mind. Nikola Tesla believed that curling his toes one hundred times each night helped inspire him to realize his genius. One of my inspirations and the writer I held in the highest esteem, Dame Agatha Christie, would line up cores of apples she had eaten while writing in the bathtub. My path to greatness was somewhat different, as there was clearly a magical element to it. Nevertheless, I had been entrusted with something special. What needed to be done?

I did not want to be impetuous or shortsighted, so the question was how best to maximize my discovery? Should I tell the world that I identified a magic dime that could type historic stories based on its travels? Would anyone believe me?

Was the real phenomena that a dime produced written work or was it the actual content of the stories themselves? This was a dilemma I needed to muse over and ponder more thoroughly.

The simplest approach would be to build a platform to publicly introduce my creative dime. I could create my own personal website or blog to meticulously chronicle the story of how I discovered the dime, how I systematically uncovered its magical ability and to share the stories it had written. Undoubtedly, this approach would lead to thousands of subscribers willing to pay to read about my magic dime and its historic memory. However, would this popularity endure for future generations? I guess only time would tell, but I have always thought of myself as a writer in a more classical sense, so perhaps a more traditional approach made more sense for a writer of my caliber. Also, by solely focusing on the dime I would be no more than an agent for the star—a promoter, a narrator, an opening act, rather than the actual focus of attention.

The stories the dime had typed so far were interesting but were they as good as writings borne from my imagination? The dime's writing style and storytelling were adequate but fell short of my true ability. I guess for a sliver of silver it was OK, but I was confident that finding this treasure of literary currency was a gift to foster my own writing. I was certain this gift was given to me because I had the ability to turn the proverbial sow's ear into a silk purse.

I needed to take the dime's writings and turn them into work worthy of a true classic. The late 20th and early 21st century belonged to J.K. Rowling. I needed to spin my own magic to make the middle portion of the 21st century the domain of Zachary Howard.

The path became clear; I needed to take the dime's work and improve upon it by fleshing out and embellishing the stories. I would bring the writing to a higher level by using my honed literary skills to ensure artistic and financial success. This path would guarantee my destiny as a great novelist. On the dedication page I would express my gratitude to the 1921 Mercury dime. It would be an esoteric inside reference, and my fans would spend countless hours contemplating the hidden meaning.

Chapter 15

October 8th, 2018

Dear Ms. Schiff:

Please be advised that I will be leaving the employ of E & W Public Relations effective Monday, October 22, 2018, to pursue another opportunity.

I would like to thank you for the mentorship and support you have given me these past four years and wish you all my best.

I have very little in the way of personal belongings in the office so it will not be necessary for me to return to the office to retrieve anything.

I will update you on everything I am presently working on and will provide you with a complete summary before I leave.

Please tell all my coworkers goodbye on my behalf, and that I do not expect or desire any type of farewell party.

With warmest regards,
Zachary Howard

Internal memo from Claudia Schiff to the 18 E&W Public Relations employees:

Dear Colleagues,

———

I want to let you all know that Zachary Howard, an employee for four years at E&W PR will be leaving our employ effective Monday, October 22.

It will not be necessary to replace Zachary, but I would appreciate it if a volunteer would go to Zachary's desk and bag up anything left on his desk. You can get a garbage bag from the storage room.

Thanks!

Snapshot of one of six similar responses received by Ms. Schiff:

Hi Claudia,

Sorry I don't really know who Zachary is or where he sat, but if you direct me to his desk, I'd be pleased to help.

Best,
Kim

Chapter 16

I had to get everything in order before beginning to focus all my attention on this project. As unpleasant as I was certain such a conversation would be, I needed to let my parents know of my exciting career path development. I knew I was obligated to inform them, but it had to be done in a manner that would diffuse hysteria, primarily from my mother.

I studied my phone and realized how much easier it would be to send a group text to my father, mother, sister, and brother announcing my new life-changing focus. However, my mother thought texting was "impersonal and a passing fad," so I needed to update my parents by speaking on the phone, as I had no intention of driving to Fort Lee, New Jersey, for a theatrical face-to-face. Certainly, my mother would find fault in whatever I was going to tell them, and my silent father would express no emotion or offer much of an opinion.

As I reluctantly dialed their landline, praying for the answering machine to pick up, my luck quickly ran out. After only two rings, I heard my mother's nasal voice.

"Hello."

"Hi, mom."

"Zachary, is that you?"

"Yes, mom."

"Edgar, Zachary is on the phone. Pick up the other extension."

The next thing I heard was the subdued voice of my father saying, "Hello."

Before my father was able to utter another syllable, my mother jumped right into a series of questions, answers, and speculation. "Zachary, are you all right? You so rarely call. Are you sick? Is it good news? Are you getting married? Are you moving back home? I knew New

York City was wrong for you. You never listen to me. Edgar, didn't I tell him not to move to New York?"

"Mom, if you give me a chance to speak, I actually have some good news."

But my mother was not ready to relinquish the floor yet. "You are getting married! Where is she from? What does she do? Is she from a good family? There is no alcoholism in her family, is there? Alcoholism is a genetic trait, and I do not want my grandchildren to be alcoholics."

Finally, my father mustered up the courage to break up the drumbeat of my mother's monologue. "Would you be quiet, Beth? Let the boy speak."

I appreciated my father's intervention even though at 35 I was less than thrilled to still receive the "boy" moniker.

"Thanks, Dad. I am not getting married, and I am not moving." I decided to take some artistic liberty and share my upcoming life change in my own way. "I will no longer be working at E&W, as I have been selected to work on a special writing assignment and—"

"You've been fired!" my mother blurted out before I was able to finish. Her voice tends to raise three octaves whenever she is upset, and as being upset is her usual state, ninety percent of her conversations are conducted at an ear-splitting volume. I typically put her on speaker and leave the phone a few feet away when she is talking, but that creates the concern of sharing her opinions with all my neighbors. On this occasion, I simply extended my arm as far as it would go.

"No, mom, I resigned. I was chosen, due to my elegant writing skills, to work on a special assignment."

In response to my mother's follow-up, my stomach became queasy, and my head started to throb. Her words have the unnatural ability to transmit flu-like symptoms across state lines and probably oceans too. For my next writing project, I thought, perhaps I should create a superhero character based on my mother. A diminutive 60-something-year-old woman able to bring bad guys to their knees with just the sound of her voice. I heard an announcer's stentorian voice say, "Able to puncture eardrums with a single remark!"

"Who the hell would hire you for a special assignment?"

I kept my temper in check as I thought about the last laugh I would have and the fame and fortune on my horizon. I imagined future podcast interviews and late-night TV appearances in which I told audiences that I was an orphan.

I concluded with, "I have been commissioned to write a special book, and that is all I am going to say about it now."

My father said, "Congratulations, Zach."

I did not wait for my mother's two cents. "Thanks," I said, and hung up.

Not surprisingly, less than 30 minutes passed before my phone started to vibrate. On the screen was my brother Roger's confident (arrogant) photo. I never have the audible ring on and rarely answer my phone. Famous golfer Fred Couples once said, "I don't answer the phone. I get the feeling whenever I do that there will be someone on the other end." I agreed wholeheartedly.

Roger, my younger brother by two years, is tall, athletically built, and boasts wavy blond hair and a toothy smile that excites oral hygiene advertising executives. At 26, one year after earning his MBA at Wharton, Roger launched his first hedge fund. At 27, his first yacht came aboard to join his fleet of high-priced automobiles. Feeling the need to "settle down" at 30, he broke up with his supermodel girlfriend and got engaged to Priscilla Van Deusen, who, at 30, was two years away from becoming a partner in the New York office of the fourth highest rated global law firm. Priscilla's smile, working in concert with Roger's grin, could light Madison Square Garden, should a power outage occur. The heir to their majestic throne, Roger Jr., was born last year. I assume it's obvious which brother my mother worships.

I was still staring at the missed call when a text arrived from Roger. *Call me bro.*

My stomach was just on the verge of settling down when it started dancing again with the thought of calling back my "bro." It was obvious that as soon as I got off the phone with my parents, my mother had called her two other children with the harrowing news that the middle offspring had somehow further screwed up his life, necessitating a sibling intervention. Either Suzy was unavailable, or Roger drew the short straw.

I thought at the time I would have much preferred speaking with Suzy, and hindsight proved my instincts correct. Suzy, or Dr. Suzanne Howard, as she prefers, a tenured professor in Molecular Biology at MIT, would have focused exclusively on the facts of my new career path. Suzy would have neither commented nor shown concern. She has limited time, and very little interest even when time isn't an issue. In addition to her teaching and research load, Suzy's assets include a Master of the Universe husband, Malcolm, who travels all the time, and three highly gifted children: Stuart, and twin girls Sarah and Samantha. As Suzy lives in Brookline, Massachusetts, seeing me in person was out of the question, which unfortunately was not the case with Roger.

I ate a triple decker peanut butter and jelly sandwich to settle my stomach and then hit the phone number under "favorites" for Roger.

He answered the call almost immediately, but naturally asked me to hold for a minute as he was on a "critically important overseas business call"—his status quo reply. Three minutes later, my brother returned to me. "Sorry about that, Bro. That guy I just rushed off the phone for my big brother is a major client and is easily worth a hundred million. But who is more important, some filthy rich client or you?"

I had to wait for the chunky peanut butter to reverse course and settle back into my stomach region before responding. "Thanks, Roger. What's up? How have you been?"

"Just great, but fucking busy. You really need to come by and see Roger Jr. He's beginning to walk. He's way ahead of all the others in his nanny-baby gymnastics play group. You got to spend time with him before he begins to run and can beat you in a race! More importantly, how are you doing? Mom said she thinks you're out of work and wanted me to check in on you. Do you need a loan? What about another job? My assistant can help with that."

I took a deep breath and said, "Mom is unbelievable. She is the only person I know who can take something positive and exciting and turn it into bad news. I tried to explain to Mom and Dad that I have a great new writing assignment that is going to be career-defining. Things could not be looking more promising."

I visualized Roger rolling his eyes, feigning excitement. "That sounds amazing, and I really want to hear all about it. Tomorrow night at 8:30 I'm meeting a prospective client at a cigar and cognac bar he owns near you. I normally would have invited you to join us but it's business so wouldn't be appropriate. You understand, of course? But why don't we meet for drinks beforehand? What's your favorite bar to hang out? Text me the name and address and I'll meet you there at 6:30. Where do you park your car? I'll need a garage as I'm trying to put some miles on a new Maserati MC20 so I'll need somewhere safe and reliable. Does such a place exist in Queens?"

The peanut butter and jelly sandwich once again defied gravity, reaching my mouth, joined by acidic bile.

"Roger, I'll text you the information on the bar location, but unfortunately I can't help with the car," I said in as calm a voice as I was able to muster.

I hung up and closed my eyes. Breathing deeply, I tried to focus on what tomorrow evening would be like. I knew a couple of drinks with Roger would set into motion the mechanism for disseminating my plans, temporarily satisfying my familial communication obligations. All I needed to do was find a bar I could say is my favorite, text Roger the location, and endure 90 minutes of the Golden Boy's bluster.

I had not been to a bar since moving into the neighborhood so I did a quick Google Map search for bars near me. There were two within five blocks of my address: O'Malley's and Freedom Reigns. O'Malley's sounded like a traditional Irish pub that every New York City neighborhood had, so I opted for Freedom Reigns, which sounded trendy and superficial, therefore ideal for status-minded Roger. I forwarded the address to Roger and added a perfunctory "Excited to see you."

Chapter 17

Standing in front of my sparse closet counting the dust balls on the floor, which vastly outnumbered my footwear, I browsed the few lonely hangers on a precariously hung rusty bar. I didn't think that bar could handle more than my half dozen shirts and three pairs of pants. I had happily found no need to leave the sanctity of my apartment for the last couple of days as the peace, tranquility, and privacy was perfect for serious contemplation. Planning my future, in addition to sorting out the accompanying family saga, was foremost in my mind and solitude was what I required.

Now, what to wear to my brother's interrogation evening?

Thankfully, autumn was my favorite season. It's neither oppressively hot like the summer, nor too chilly. All things considered, I was meeting Roger in the most favorable weather, but I still had no idea what to wear.

My wardrobe, far from extensive, included a couple of pairs of well-worn jeans, and one pair of chinos sadly hanging in my closet. On a top shelf were two pairs of shorts keeping each other company. I knew one of the shorts no longer fit me as I had bought them immediately after a two-week bout with bronchitis a few years earlier. I probably had lost 10 to 15 pounds when I was sick, so naturally once I returned to good health and regained my robust appetite, I quickly added back the lost weight. It wasn't a night for shorts anyway, so I removed the slightly cleaner pair of jeans.

Pants were selected. Next up: what to wear on top. Carefully opening the paper-mâché-like used dresser, I inspected the T-shirt drawer, then the one below it one housing dress shirts. Nothing really jumped out at me as the best choice for the evening.

It was rare to ever see me wearing anything other than a pair of Converse sneakers, though I did own a pair of black loafers. Valuing simplicity, I calculated my wardrobe was sufficient to require laundry once every ten days, so in addition to the few items listed earlier, I had ten boxer shorts and an equal number of socks.

As long as I could remember, Roger had busted my chops about needing to "tone up and lose a few pounds." He, on the other hand, never had a spare ounce of fat on his body. In my opinion, he always looked too fit. I've fantasized about the day he no longer ran ten miles without breaking a sweat, swam two miles without feeling tired or did circuits of weights without feeling sore. That day would come and I was sure he would no longer have a washboard stomach when it occurred. It would serve him right.

I've always had a bit of a paunch. I was certain it's more due to my body type than what I eat or the fact that sports and exercise never really interested me. People are predisposed to certain body types no matter what their diet or workout routine, and I was naturally built on the softer, pudgier side. Why try to change what nature has preordained?

I was meeting Roger an hour later so I placed the jeans on the couch alongside a clean pair of boxers and socks, and figured the sneakers would be fine. The question was, Which shirt to wear?

Appearance was everything to my brother, and I knew he undoubtedly would be dressed in the most stylish and fashionable attire money could buy. It was not so much that I wanted to dress to avoid embarrassing him, but I did not want to endure his pitying glances and condescending comments if my appearance was far below his acceptable standards.

My most comfortable shirt was a 2009 Nickelback concert tour T-shirt. It was the last concert I had attended, and probably was the last concert I ever will attend. I couldn't hear for a full week afterwards, and I had persistent tinnitus that lasted a month. How people truly enjoyed this type of loud and crowded event remained a mystery to me. I never particularly liked Nickelback, but my mother was on my case at that time to try and be more sociable, so when this guy at my first job said he had an extra ticket to the concert, I felt obligated to go. Making matters worse was that the ticket cost me $50. I thought he was inviting me to be his guest, and I never really spoke to the guy much before or after the concert.

I went back to my dresser and pulled out my light blue dress shirt with an only slightly frayed collar, only noticeable if I was wearing a tie. There was no way I was wearing a tie to meet my brother for a drink, no matter how trendy the location, so I felt the blue shirt would be just fine.

I grunted as I began to put on my jeans and figured I must have left them in the dryer far too long the last time I did laundry. I rhythmically breathed in and out with every pull of the jeans. A sense of accomplishment came over me as I tugged and navigated each pants leg over my calves. Finally, I took a rest. Unfortunately, getting them over my thighs took even greater exertion. Finally, I pulled, wiggled, and contorted the pants up to my waist and gave my arms a much-needed therapeutic shake. The clasp resisted closing but finally made it into position on my seventh try.

I held in my stomach and gingerly walked the circumference of my apartment a few times. The exercise seemed to gradually work: after a few laps I regained normal breathing. I left my apartment at 6:15 for my 6:30 appointment with Roger.

It was a slow, mechanical, and slightly painful walk as the jeans still required more movement to soften them up. Google Maps said I would arrive at 6:21 but obviously the app did not consider skintight pants, so I arrived in front of the red brick building with a multi-colored sign announcing "Freedom Reigns" at 6:28.

I doubted Roger would wait for me outside, so I tried to peek through a window to look for him, but the windows were all darkened— such a gloomy contrast to the multiple festive rainbow stickers adorning them. A block of granite about six and a half feet tall and three feet wide positioned at the entrance checked IDs. I couldn't help noticing "TRY ME" tattooed on his right bicep. There was ample room on the same muscle to add "IF YOU DARE." I gave the Incredible Hulk a friendly grin while showing my driver's license, and following a full eye-scan, he grunted, "Okay, go in."

My mother was constantly nagging me about meeting a nice woman and settling down. She has on numerous occasions suggested that I should even go to bars to meet girls. I haven't had the patience to explain to her that no one meets people in clubs or bars anymore. The only way to meet people is through online dating apps. I had been working on my profile for several weeks with only a few edits remaining. Even if I wanted to meet a woman at "Freedom Reigns," it would have been impossible. Once I walked in there did not seem to be a single woman in the bar!

Three bartenders danced down the long bar, attending to bar seats occupied by men ranging in age from their mid-twenties to almost 80. Most of the well-dressed patrons had the "I came straight from work look," which was likely the case. I assumed there was some type of special men-only promotion that night. So many bars seemed to focus exclusively on ladies' nights, so this endorsement of men was quite refreshing.

Leaning against the mahogany bar, a very thin guy with stylish, tortoise shell glasses interrupted his seemingly intense conversation with a much older, silver-haired man, by elbowing him to look in my direction. They were somewhat obviously focused on my too-tight pants and resulting awkward gait. It conjured up self-conscious feelings from seventh grade when my mother sent me to school with a Peanuts lunchbox. I immediately regretted that I had not worn more comfortably fitting jeans.

The two guys appeared to be chuckling at my expense, which repeated itself in a manner like a baseball game "wave." As the two initial guys halted their attention, others took their place, and this exercise repeated itself section by section until my presence seemed to be every bar patron's focal point. It was as if every man in the place took turns smirking and casting a fleeting glance in my direction. Feeling highly agitated, I headed straight towards a table set for two and plopped down in a chair to await Roger's arrival.

A caramel-complexioned waiter with chiseled cheeks, gel-set hair, and a melodic voice came over to ask how he could meet my needs. I told him I was waiting for someone and would order when he arrived.

It seemed a shame that the waiter was intent on restaurant industry service employment rather than capitalizing on his impressive and hospitable persona. I'm no expert, but based on his appearance, stage and screen seemed to be his calling. Avoiding unwelcome stares and snickers, I carefully studied the menu, which included many cleverly crafted cocktail and food options, such as "Sex on Fire Island Beach," "Judy Garland Cosmo," the "Boy Burger," and "Madonna Miso Crusted Ribs."

At 6:38 (on time for Roger), he finally arrived, and I called out his name. Apparently, I was a bit too loud as my announcement triggered dozens of heads looking in Roger's direction with several of them singing in unison, "Hi, Roger."

The usually confident and attention-seeking Roger appeared very uncomfortable. He sent a venomous glare towards me. As he approached, I sensed Roger vacillated between anger and civility. Finally, civility won out as the edges of his mouth peeked upwards though his eyes remained hardened. "Great to see you, Zachary," he said. "Sorry I'm late."

Matching his forced smile I responded, "It's good to see you too. Sit down."

The movie star waiter reappeared, and now completely ignoring me, stared at Roger and asked, "What special treats can I bring you two gentlemen?"

Roger said, "I'll have a Macallan single malt, neat. And you, Zach?"

It had been a few years since I'd ordered a cocktail. I had always been more of a beer man, but succumbing to trends, I confidently ordered a Cosmopolitan. The waiter, never taking his eyes off Roger, gave a smiling, "I'll be back super swiftly. Don't you go anywhere."

As our waiter turned to walk away, a guy at the next table called over to him, "Hey Ty, how did the audition go? When do you think you'll hear?"

Our waiter, Ty, was indeed an aspiring actor. I chuckled to myself, acknowledging my perceptive strengths.

"There were other ways you could have announced your big news, Bro," Roger said, flashing a rare genuine smile. "But I most certainly applaud your creativity! Suzy and I always questioned your sexual orientation, while Mom and Dad remained completely clueless. Suzy assumed you were gay while I just thought you were asexual. I guess Suzy was right. Give me a sec and I'll text her. Or do you want to tell her yourself?"

Roger and I did not have a lot in common, usually struggling to find common interests to discuss, but when we did speak, it was usually in the same language. Not this time, though. I felt as if I had walked into a movie that was half over and had no clue what was going on. Either that, or the movie was in a foreign language, with unavailable subtitles. What the hell was Roger going on about?

"Roger," I said, "I have no idea what you're saying. My big news only concerns my career and the amazing direction it's headed. I know Mom uses creative license to distort information, but I had no idea you shared this awful trait."

The waiter brought our drinks to the table. He dexterously placed mine in front of me without withdrawing his gaze from Roger.

"Chill, Bro. You obviously brought me to this place for a reason, right?"

Keeping my temper in check I said, "I brought you here because it's more upscale and trendier than a typical pub. I know pretense means a great deal to you, so I picked a place I thought you would feel comfortable in and would like."

Smirking, Roger responded, "Why didn't you bring me to a lesbian bar? My understanding is they are also upscale, and I might enjoy that view."

Normally a calm and collected person, I rarely engage in angry outbursts or fits of temper. I looked down at the pink drink in front of me, removed the caramelized, sugared lemon slice adorning the rim, and in one gulp downed the sweet libation. Recognizing that another drink was the only way to survive the next hour, I waved to get Ty's attention. He either did not see my frantic hand or, more likely, he was ignoring me. Fortunately, Roger had more success: with just one raised finger, Ty arrived within seconds, almost knocking over several patrons along the way.

I ordered seconds, and tried to better understand what my brother was saying by calmly inquiring, "Roger, what the fuck are you talking about?"

"Zach, you really don't know, do you? Look around. Tell me what you see."

Tempering my frustration I said, "I see people in a bar. Most of them are drinking alcohol." I hated Roger's condescending behavior, which occurred ninety-five percent of the time.

Ripe with superiority, Roger added, "Very good. Would you be more specific regarding the clientele?"

What I needed at that moment more than anything was more alcohol, and as if by magic, my second Cosmopolitan arrived. Thirty seconds later, my glass emptied, Roger intensified his condescension and criticism.

"Zach, if you keep downing those like tequila shots, I'll need to pick you up off the floor. Take it easy, Bro."

To stop anger getting the better of me, I forced myself to breathe slowly and count to ten. I was so upset by this entire interaction, I began feeling a bit lightheaded, even struggling to get past the number seven. "Roger," I breathlessly blurted,I am a highly functioning adult and I want another drink. No, I *need* another drink. As Ty seems to be under the misconception that we are a table of one, would you do me the honor of ordering me another?"

Roger did not seem pleased but gestured to another Ty-like waiter, employing some sort of secret sign language. A minute later my third cocktail arrived along with a large glass of water. Taking a gulp, I as calmly as possible said, "What I wanted to share with you was that as I was going through some coins I collected, I found a rare 1921 Mercury silver dime."

Somewhat adhering to my brother's concern regarding my sobriety, I took a sip of water. Roger, with a withering look, asked, "Is the dime very valuable?"

I told him it was worth about fifty dollars.

"Zachary, if you need money, I'm sure I could help a bit. I'll write you a check now. My checking account will barely feel it."

"No, no. No, you don't understand. The dime is magic and can write on its own! I'm going to embellish the dime's writing and create my own masterpiece. How exciting is that?"

Roger's lower lip overtook his upper one. "Please lower your voice," he admonished. "Perhaps we should go back to your apartment to discuss this further. I'm supposed to meet this important client for dinner in less than an hour, but I can text him to push it back a bit. I think we may need more time to talk."

I knew Roger was simply trying to prevent me from finishing my drink. First, he had criticized the place I chose, then he had busted my chops for drinking too fast. I was the older brother, but he was treating me as if I was the younger sibling in need of his assistance. Even though he was mightily pissing me off, I realized I needed to regain my role as the more mature older sibling, and it was incumbent upon me to retain my composure. I drew another deep breath and told him, "Roger, don't forget that I am your older brother and I know how to conduct myself. For some strange reason, you have misunderstood everything I've been trying to tell you this evening. I've had the good fortune to discover a unique and precious item—a item that, due to my uncanny writing talents and training, I will undoubtedly be able to use as a platform to earn me great wealth and recognition. Rather than focus on the facts I have presented to you, you have instead, for reasons beyond my comprehension, chosen to question my sexual orientation and sobriety. I'm shocked that someone who is seemingly so successful in his professional life would be so unfocused and distracted."

To his credit, my brother seemed to gather his thoughts. Alas, even with time to gather his thoughts, he responded with absolute gibberish. "Zachary, how did you expect me to react? You suggested meeting in a gay bar, ordered Carrie Bradshaw's favorite drink, which you downed in seconds, causing you to become tipsy and loud. You then told me you found a magic coin which was going to ensure your future success. The obvious conclusion is that you are a gay man, who is finally out of the closet, has an alcohol problem, and is in need of a great deal of therapy."

I sat and stared at my brother in disbelief. Finally, the words came out of my mouth, albeit, in a volume several octaves louder that intended, "I AM NOT FUCKING GAY!"

At that point, I felt I became the central character in a second-rate Broadway musical. Next to me I heard someone in a singsong voice say, "I AM fucking gay." Seconds later other members of the cast began to chime in, "I AM fucking gay," and soon it seemed the entire chorus was singing the same refrain: " I AM fucking gay!" The next thing I knew, the mountainous man from outside appeared, and suddenly I was raised high in the air. The mountain transported me through the bar to the exit door where he sent me airborne into the street. I caromed off a parked car, landed on my backside at the sidewalk's edge. The last thing I remember before everything went dark were the words "I AM fucking gay" emanating from the mountain.

I woke up on my apartment's sofa with ice packs draped across my face and body. Once my vision came into focus, I saw a handwritten letter sitting on my table just a few feet away. As I reached for it, bolts of pain crisscrossed from my elbow to my shoulder and then across my back. Doing my best to suppress agonizing screams, I grasped the letter and read:

Hi Zach,

Quite an entertaining evening. I hope you're okay. I tried to prevent King Kong from treating you like a paper airplane, but he was a few weight classes and species out of my league.

I'll call or stop by to check on you tomorrow.

I can't figure you out but I love you like a brother (haha).

Roger

P.S. I'll just tell Mom and Dad we had a good time and you're doing fine. No need to thank me.

I painfully crawled towards the bathroom with a pit stop at the refrigerator, attempting nourishment. With a Herculean effort I opened the refrigerator door, where I was met by two lonely eggs, a crusty bottle of ketchup, an expired mayonnaise jar and a questionable half gallon of milk. Reaching the milk, which sat way back on the top shelf, and the cereal box, far above me on the counter, proved insurmountable, so I resigned myself to a day of starvation.

Half an hour and a medley of pain-wracked exclamations later, I slithered across for a much-needed bathroom trip, where I swallowed four Motrin and took a rest on the cold tile floor. Then I snaked back to the couch. Knowing productivity would be impossible, I decided to let the coin do all the work for the day. Through labored grunts, and a few tears, I placed the dime on top of the closed laptop and attempted to get some recuperative rest.

Chapter 18

Excruciating discomfort dominated the little sleep I had that night. With every movement, jolts of agony shot through body parts I never knew even existed. I intentionally ignored my laptop because: 1) I didn't want to interrupt the dime's work, and 2) my battered body couldn't possibly crawl to the desk, sit up and position the screen to read it.

The only exertion was periodically checking my phone to see if Roger was on his way over to check in on me, as promised. Yet, as expected—still no word from him. Clearly on my own, I somehow needed to figure out a way to nourish my body and tend to other bodily essentials.

Around 5 p.m. I managed to place a delivery order for Greek avgolemono soup and a gyro platter. I read off my credit card information and asked them to leave the bag outside my apartment, figuring if I started to crawl immediately after hanging up, there would be sufficient time for the food to be prepared and delivered before I reached my front door. Crawling in a style that would be the envy of an eight-month-old, I somehow managed to get to the door, open it, collect my dinner, and slide my tormented body back to my apartment. Exhausted from that workout, I finally plopped down in front of the couch, only to discover the stupid restaurant neglected to send utensils. Seeing no alternative, I devoured it all with my hands, tzatziki sauce emulating shaving cream awaiting the razor's stroke.

A soup spoon would not only have been welcome, but protective. Instead, with considerable effort, I raised the quart container filled with scalding soup. As my swollen, bloody hands hampered my usual dexterity, half the volcanic lava trickled down my cheek, chin, and chest. Third-degree burns were now added to my list of infirmities. I somehow managed to lift my body onto the couch, and there I lay in miserable agony. I was not one to typically indulge in self-pity, but today's situation felt justifiable. Every inch of my body ached, including my head, suffering from a residual hangover. When I was finally falling into a somewhat restorative nap, I heard a knock at the door. Assuming it was Roger finally coming to check up on me, I called out, "I'm coming! Give me a fucking minute!"

Rolling off the couch and once again making the long and painful journey to the door, I screamed, "I'm coming!" At the halfway point, I shimmied and manipulated myself in a sitting position and grasped the door handle. Pulling open the door I said, "Roger, about time!" But my visitor was not Roger at all.

Standing in front of me was a woman about my age with frizzy brown hair and a wholesome, pretty face framed by black, rectangular glasses. Wearing a red blouse adorned with mathematical symbols, she was the slightest bit overweight but certainly nowhere near fat. As I was in a seated position, she was looking down at me with concern.

"Um, hi, I'm Julie. Julie Fields. I live in the apartment across from you. I saw you when you came home last night, and you looked to be in pretty bad shape, so I just wanted to see if you needed anything."

She looked slightly familiar, but we had never actually spoken. Her concerned look gave way to an elongated smile, which quickly eased my misery. For a second I was unable to find my own voice, and with reddening cheeks, I realized how absurd I must have looked in a fetal position on the floor.

Finally regaining my composure, I choked out a response. "I'm better, thanks for asking."

Trying to maintain eye contact, but instead painfully swiveling my head towards my plastic kitchen clock, I watched the second hand make two complete rotations before realizing I didn't want my new acquaintance leaving any time soon. I knew I had better say something else. "I'm Zachary and unfortunately I'm presently incapable of standing up to shake your hand."

For some reason I've always been a bit uncomfortable and, on occasion, tongue-tied around women. This time however, I came out with an impressively witty, "I had a bit of a rough night. A bit too much to drink, and a great deal too much of a 300-pound bouncer."

A smile and giggle in return further emboldened me. Desperately wanting to present a perfect balance between machismo and sensitivity, I continued my clever repartee. "The truth is, I feel like crap. I'm in pain from head to toe, and I just spilled hot soup on myself in a failed attempt to drink it without a spoon. I'm a mess and have never felt so helpless."

Shit, shit, shit, I thought to myself. I put far too much sensitivity and fragility out there. My facial expression must have conveyed my embarrassment. But instead of recoiling, Julie looked on the verge of tears. "You poor thing. Please let me know how I can help. Perhaps I could bring you some things you might need. You don't look to be in any condition to go out."

I knew Roger had already completely forgotten about me, so the realization set in that Julie might be my only salvation and that I really needed to take advantage of her kind offer. But the truth was, I didn't want this conversation to end.

Once I staggered to an upright position, Julie placed my arm around her shoulder, led me to the couch, and gently deposited me. She got us each a glass of water. I was embarrassed I had very little in the way of refreshments, so I offered her a bit of an exaggerated truth. "I'm sorry the refrigerator is empty. Today was my scheduled day to go shopping but because of the accident, I couldn't go. I don't want to impose on you as I'm sure I'll be better in a day or two."

Julie sweetly responded, "It's not an imposition at all. I have a couple of work appointments to do, but if you tell me what you need, I'll be happy to get them for you. I can be back in a couple of hours."

Being a bit old-school and valuing gentlemanly behavior, I responded accordingly. "If it's not too much of an imposition, that would be amazing. But if in any way it would screw up your day, I'm sure I'll be able to manage. What type of work do you do?"

"I'm going to test for my CPA license soon, but right now I'm a test prep tutor, primarily focusing on math SATs. I've always loved math and really like helping others better understand it."

"I can tell by your shirt. The truth is I've always been fascinated by math and have the utmost respect for anyone who can master it. I'm truly in awe of people who can look at complicated equations and formulas and not only understand them but eventually find the hidden solutions to them. To see the different components in math and be able to explain or teach it—that's really a gift."

Julie looked down, and this time it was her cheeks that reddened. Her expression gave me a warm feeling, and she said, "Hah, I forgot I was wearing this shirt. My math skills are really kind of basic.

I do enjoy working with numbers. My job is perfect for me because I'm able to work from home and pretty much make my own hours. I had a job as an auditor with an accounting firm but the daily commute and dealing with the office bureaucracy was such a pain, I just couldn't take it any longer. I like this much better. No worries on the shopping—I need to pick up a couple of things for myself so it would be no trouble to get a few things for you too. I'll be back in a couple of hours to get your list."

"That sounds great," I said as my angel of mercy closed the door behind her.

I closed my eyes and settled my head into the pillow on my couch when I heard muffled voices outside the door. I assumed the female's voice belonged to Julie, and once I heard the cackling laugh I knew it was Roger as well. So, he hadn't forgotten me after all. I was looking forward to a little restorative shuteye before Julie would return, but now I had to force my aching body off the couch again to open the door for my brother. While I struggled to get up, I could hear most of the conversation taking place beyond the door.

"No, Zach is actually older than me. He's always lagging behind our sister and me in things."

I screamed out from across the room, "I can hear you!" as I propelled myself off the couch and landed on the floor. Their conversation continued as I began my now practiced crawl towards the door.

"He seems very sweet and kind."

"Oh, he is. My mother used to call him her little butterfly. He was always kind of delicate. He was never much for sports, but our parents tried to get him involved in activities, so they put him in a recreational soccer league. He must have been seven or so. I remember I was in a younger group and my games were an hour before Zach's. I'd score four or five goals a game and my parents would cheer like crazy as I was in the mix on everything. I'd then watch his game with my parents, and he'd do everything possible to avoid the ball and any sort of physical contact. My father would get pissed at him, but my mother would just say he was our delicate little butterfly. It was kind of funny, I guess, but at the time I was embarrassed that my big brother was such a wuss."

This time I yelled, "I can hear you and I'm coming to open the door!"

Staggering to my feet I threw open the door and was greeted by my perfectly coiffed, grinning brother and Julie.

"Hey, Bro, you seem to be doing much better. I just had the good fortune to meet your lovely and charming neighbor."

Julie turned towards me and seemed to be smiling, the pink cheeks returning. She quickly said, "I really must be going. It was a pleasure meeting you, Roger. Zach, I'll see you in a little bit."

Roger took Julie's hand and said, "Truly, the pleasure was all mine."

Roger followed me into the apartment as I slumped back onto the couch.

"So how are you feeling, Bro? You're lucky to have such a friendly neighbor."

"I'm feeling better. Did you really have to tell her such embarrassing stories about me? "

"I'm sorry. No harm done, and I think she's not the type that would be into the macho jock type anyway. I probably helped your case. What, you've got a hard-on for her?"

"I don't even know her, but I don't think she needed to know that Mom used to refer to me as her 'delicate little butterfly.' Would you like it if I said something like that to your neighbor?"

"Probably not, but then I can't imagine anyone believing I'd ever been referred to that way. Listen, I gotta run. I just wanted to see how you're doing, and it looks like you're in good hands."

Empty-handed, Roger gave me a salacious wink as he abruptly left.

Chapter 19

After Roger left, I began to slowly test my limbs. First, I shook my right leg, then my left, and did the same with each arm. I opened and closed my hands to make certain my fingers were still all functional. Cautiously, I sat up on the couch and moved my head to the left, then to the center, and then to the right. Satisfied nothing was broken or irreparably damaged, I stumbled towards the bathroom with newfound confidence.

I needed a shower, both for hygienic and therapeutic purposes. Leaning on the toilet seat, I started removing the clothing I had worn since the evening before. The socks came off with only moderate effort. I then gradually began pulling up my soup-stained shirt, only encountering difficulty when raising my arms. Anxiety took over as I looked down at my jeans. I recalled last night's ordeal when I wasn't badly injured. The thought of removing them while my body was aching was terrifying.

Recognizing that I had about an hour and fifteen minutes before Julie would return, I needed to focus on the overwhelming task of removing my jeans. I tugged at the left pants leg to see what would happen. Nothing. I attempted the same strategic test with the right leg and experienced the same result. Showering with jeans sounded awful, and I was growing increasingly disheartened until I remembered the pair of scissors in my medicine cabinet.

A thirty-minute ordeal ensued, and I stepped around the tatters of what were previously my jeans, and carefully entered the shower, adjusting the valve so the water temperature was hot but still bearable. I closed my eyes as the water rhythmically pulsated over every inch of my battered body. The hot water's healing effect eased discomfort, and I began to feel invigorated.

My preference was to stay in the shower longer, but I knew Julie would be arriving soon, so I eventually shut off the soothing water and cautiously step onto the tiled bathroom floor. I decided to leave the remnants of my jeans in place for the time being. It was amazing how much better I felt, and brushing my teeth and shaving further invigorated me. I was able to get dressed with minimal discomfort, throwing on a loose-fitting pair of slacks and a T-shirt.

At 4:05 there was a knock on the door, and I quickly got up to answer it. Julie's eyebrows rose when she saw me. "Hello!" she said, with surprise in her voice.

"Hi," I responded as I held the door open for her.

She followed me into the apartment and said, "I cannot believe you're the same person I saw a couple of hours ago. You look one hundred percent better!"

I responded perhaps with a bit too much conceit. "I've always been a quick healer, and I made up my mind I was going to fight through the pain." Realizing I may have sounded a bit too full of myself, I quickly added, "Actually, a hot shower and eight hundred milligrams of Motrin did the trick."

Julie asked, "Would you still like me to do some shopping for you?"

I grinned while working up the courage to suggest, "If you don't mind, I was hoping we could go shopping together."

We returned to my apartment an hour later, having bought a lot more than I initially intended. Julie had brought along a couple of reusable bags and they were both filled to the brim. I concealed from Julie that some of the items I purchased were things I had never bought before. This list included: avocados, whole wheat bread, quinoa, tahini, cashew butter and cauliflower crackers. I honestly never knew there was such a thing as cauliflower crackers, and if I had, I certainly wouldn't have eaten them. Julie had sung oat milk's praises, but I stuck to my guns and left the market with full-fat whole milk.

As I was feeling so much better, I offered to take Julie out to dinner, but she counter-offered to make dinner in my apartment instead. She asked me if I liked avocado toast and I suppressed my instinct to ask "Does anyone?" and instead said, "Of course, that would be great."

Chapter 20

I watched Julie navigate my kitchen area, opening and closing various drawers and compartments. Her jaw twitched on several occasions as if she wanted to say something but thought better of it. Her search of my kitchen netted two plates, two forks, two knives (one of them plastic), a beer mug, a Styrofoam coffee cup, and a frying pan. She took a paper towel off the dispenser and wiped the frying pan. Finally, she said, "I need to get a couple of things from my apartment. I'll be back in two minutes."

She returned carrying another disposable bag, which she placed on the counter next to the sink. She took out two glasses, two bone-white dinner plates, two bone-white smaller plates, a spatula, a frying pan, an assortment of utensils, and two linen napkins.

"I'm sorry, I hope I didn't put you through too much trouble," I said. "I don't entertain too often, but I do have a couple of other plates we could have used."

Julie pursed her lips together. "I figured you were supplying the ingredients so I would provide the dishes and silverware. Where did you find brown plates? I don't believe I've ever eaten off of a brown plate before."

"They were actually left here by the prior tenant. As a matter of fact, just about everything in the kitchen I inherited when I took over the apartment."

Julie smiled and said, "Interesting. I'll get started on dinner."

We ate at the small table that I typically stored folded up in a corner. I think it's called a drink table. Julie had to go back to her apartment to get two wooden chairs for us to sit on.

I had to admit that I really enjoyed the avocado toast. I ate three pieces. Julie topped each with a sunny side up egg and served a quinoa salad to go with it. I'd decided I would definitely eat avocado toast again, but I wasn't so certain about the quinoa. We ate our dinner with a White Claw black cherry seltzer for me and a grapefruit one for Julie.

As I was picking at the quinoa salad with marginal zest, I finally brought up a topic that was weighing heavily on my mind. "What did you think of Roger?" I looked down as I asked the question, but when I felt her penetrating gaze, I felt obligated to return eye contact.

"I know he's your brother and all, so I don't want to say anything rude, but to be honest, I thought he was a bit pompous and obnoxious."

It felt like I got hit with a rush of adrenaline and quickly responded, "He's been like that his whole life. He's always been full of himself and unfortunately was a bully throughout childhood. My parents were always getting calls from Roger's classmates' parents complaining about things Roger and his friends had done. As his big brother I tried to get him to behave better, but he'd just laugh and call me a goody-goody. We've never really been close."

"That must've been hard for you. I'm an only child, which always makes me a bit sad. I never thought about the possibility of having a sibling I didn't get along with. I envied my friends who had another playmate at home. It never occurred to me that having a brother or sister might be a negative."

"I also have a sister, Suzy. She's a couple of years older than me. She is one of those people who approached adulthood as a toddler. She wasn't that much into playing games or running around when we were kids. She'd always have her nose in a book and followed every one of our parents' ground rules. I remember when she was 12, my parents would go out and leave Suzy in charge. She was stricter than my parents. I figured she was my older sister so I did my best to listen to her, but Roger would always do something to get her upset and she would end up calling my parents. Much of the time he'd set me up to take the blame when I hadn't done anything wrong."

"I remember one time he got me into a shitload of trouble for something I didn't do. We had a fish tank with mostly goldfish in it. I used to read a lot too, and I'd just read a book about fish. It said some fish were able to camouflage themselves as a defense mechanism when they felt threatened. I told Roger about it so he said we should set up an experiment to see if our goldfish could camouflage themselves if they felt threatened. I knew they almost certainly couldn't, but Roger suggested that perhaps if we moved our parakeet's cage close to the fish tank overnight, the fish would feel threatened and when we checked the next morning, perhaps the goldfish would've changed their colors. I remember that day like it was yesterday. The next morning, I heard my mother screaming my name, and I rushed out of bed. I found my mother consoling Roger next to the fish tank, which was now completely blue. In between exaggerated sobs, Roger was telling my mother that the goldfish were supposed to change their color to camouflage themselves when they felt they were in danger, and that I placed the parakeet next to the fish tank to scare the fish into changing color. Roger went on to claim that I said it was possible for the parakeet to get out of its cage and eat the fish and warned him that he better not move the parakeet's cage back to the other room. With his remaining tears, he told my mother that I had scared him so much that he was certain the fish would be eaten. So, he decided to help camouflage them by putting blue paint into the water."

Julie looked at me with sorrowful eyes and said, "That's the most horrible thing I think I've ever heard a child do."

"Oh, he did many other horrible things too. The worst of it was I had to take out all the dead fish and then clean out the tank. Of course, I was punished as well."

"What happened to Roger?"

"Absolutely nothing. According to my mother, Roger was the victim.

He suffered enough by knowing his actions caused the death of the goldfish. They believed he was too young to know that pouring paint into the tank would kill the fish, which of course was total bullshit."

I couldn't remember ever having an evening where I've been so comfortable talking with someone. Julie was easygoing and interested in everything I told her about myself. When I shared my lifelong dream of being a critically acclaimed writer, she seemed genuinely enthusiastic. She asked me what I was working on now, and I had to hesitate a bit. The truth was, I desperately wanted to share with her my life-changing news but didn't know the best way to present it. After all, I had just met her and telling her I possessed a magical dime would surely have sent her running.

Nevertheless, I was so overcome with confidence I took her hand, which was surprisingly clammy, and gently led her to the couch. Once we were comfortably seated, I looked into her eyes. She looked up at me expectantly. I took that as a cue, and reached over and took the 1921 Mercury dime from the closed laptop, held it in front of her, and said, "I feel so in sync with you. I'm going to share something I can't imagine sharing with anyone else. I need you to keep what I'm about to tell you between us. The dime I am holding in front of you is magical and will one day earn me fame and fortune."

Julie reacted in a way that I never would have expected. She seemed to shy away from me and her eyes began to crinkle as if she was on the verge of tears. She abruptly stood up and exclaimed, "I'm sorry, but I have to go."

Her sudden mood change caught me off guard, but I quickly recovered and implored, "Please don't go."

My mind flashed back to the disastrous evening with Roger and his reaction to my telling him about the dime's magical power. It occurred to me that perhaps Julie was blindsided by what I had just told her, and realized she perhaps thought me mentally unstable. After all, wasn't my first reaction to learning the power of the dime to question my own sanity? "Wait," I implored. "I know this sounds crazy, but I promise you I'm not insane. Please give me five minutes to explain to you and even show you that I am perfectly rational. Please."

Julie turned towards me with eyes cast down and a face ripe with skepticism. "Okay, I'll give you five minutes to explain."

I told her how I found the dime and how I attempted to determine its value. Then I told her about discovering the writing in my novel document that I knew was not my own. I emphasized that the passages included facts and circumstances that I had no way of knowing. I even expressed my own mental health fears, and how I had run a series of tests to confirm that the dime was authoring pages in my work.

I told her as much as I could as quickly as possible, and concluded by saying, "Earlier today I set up the laptop and dime so the dime would be able to create more of a story. Hopefully the dime has written another excerpt. Please, please stay here and check it out with me."

Chapter 21

Sam Weinstein trudged off the train and began the five-block walk to his home at 529 Saratoga Avenue in Brownsville, Brooklyn. A light rain sprinkled his uncovered head as he mumbled to himself incoherently. Moping along, he looked down at crumpled newspaper headlines blasting the news that the stock market had crashed. He miserably looked around and saw discarded half-eaten chicken bones, the remains of a sandwich, and broken bottles. "Doesn't anyone pick things up around here in this God-forsaken world?" Sam angrily muttered to himself.

A man cursed at him as Sam narrowly missed walking into him, while Sam walked on without discerning the other man's bitterness. As he slowly made progress home, his mumbling became louder and a bit more coherent. "How am I going to tell Ann? How am I going to tell Ann? Danny said it was a sure thing. I've lost *everything*."

He finally picked up his head only to receive the now teeming rain. The ominous sky causing the waterfall stared back at him as if it reflected his soul.

CB Products. CB Products. His friend and coworker Danny Green had guaranteed the stock would triple within three months. Instead, on Tuesday he learned he had lost 90 percent of his $5,000 investment, which represented their entire savings. Danny had said to be patient, and promised it would come back, but today it lost any remaining value it had. All gone.

Sam halted in front of the entrance to his building and took out his handkerchief to wipe away any remaining dampness from his eyes, and then used it to pat his moist hair. He straightened his tie and ran his hand through his wet, dark brown, matted hair. The stairs to his building entrance looked mountainous to him as he took a deep breath, forced himself to smile, and took a massive step.

"Sam, I was getting worried. It's almost sundown," Ann admonished as she simultaneously gave him a hug and a big kiss. "You're soaking wet!"

While helping him take off his jacket and tie, she asked, "Did you have a good day? Where is the challah?"

"Damn, I completely forgot," Sam said, smacking his forehead. "I'll run back out."

"Never mind, they'll be closed now anyway. We can survive one Shabbos without a challah. I have some white bread we can use for the hamotzi. Louise, come out. Daddy's home."

A moment later there was a high-pitched squeal accompanying the sound of slippers running on a wood floor. "Daddy, Daddy, good Shabbos!" Louise jumped into her father's waiting arms as he rained kisses on her soft cheeks.

"Daddy, your mustache is tickling me. I have very, very, very big news. See if you can guess what it is." The space below her upper lip in her radiant smile was a giveaway.

"You've lost another tooth!" Sam exclaimed.

"I've now lost two teeth. Look what I can do," Louise announced as she extended her tongue between her remaining upper teeth. "The Tooth Fairy is going to come tonight!"

"She most certainly will," Sam responded.

Ann called from the kitchen, "Come on, you two, it's Shabbos, and I need Louise to light the candles with me."

Sam put Louise down, and the little girl eagerly ran over to her mother. Ann placed one hand in front of her eyes while holding Louise's hand. Hand in hand they lit two large candles in the brass candlesticks, an heirloom from Anne's grandmother, and chanted in unison, "Baruch atah, Adonai Eloheinu, Melech haolam, asher kid'shany b'mitzvotav v'zivanu l'hadlik ner shel shabbos."

Next, they all sat, Louise in the chair next to the one already occupied by Raggy, her Raggedy Ann Doll. Earlier in the day, Ann and Louise had set the festive shabbos table for four, and seeing Mommy's special fancy dishes Louise felt particularly fond of Shabbos. Every other night, Louise drank from a jelly jar, but on Fridays, her mother gave Louise a grownup wine glass with a stem. Even more special, on Shabbos, Daddy and Mommy let her have a tiny sip of wine from Daddy's wine glass. The truth was she did not really like the taste of wine, but it made her feel very grown up to drink it like her parents. Sam reached over to the decorative bread basket set on the table and took out a slice of white bread. He was about to say the Sabbath prayer over the bread when Louise asked in horror, "Where is the challah?"

"I'm sorry, honey," Sam said. "I forgot to pick one up today."

"Why did you forget, Daddy?"

A cloud of despondence fell over Sam's face, causing Ann to ask, "Are you okay?"

Sam recovered enough to say, "Sure, I just feel terrible that I forgot the challah."

"It's okay, Daddy," Louise said. "We all forget things sometimes. Daddy, are you crying?"

"Of course not. I think Mommy cooked onions tonight. Sometimes they make my eyes water a bit."

Ann brought out a silver platter with Sam's favorite meal: pot roast adorned with pearl onions and potatoes, and a side dish of *tzimmis*. Normally, Sam's mouth drooled at the sight of the carrots, sweet potatoes and plums, and he would eat three platefuls of this meal. Tonight, however, he struggled to finish the single serving given to him. Ann knew there was something troubling her husband but decided Shabbos dinner with her six-year-old daughter present was not the time to delve into it. Fortunately, Louise was too young to sense that this Shabbos dinner was a bit different than other Friday nights.

Chapter 22

Ann and Sam put Louise to bed, securing Louise's lost tooth beneath her pink pillow in anticipation of the Tooth Fairy's arrival.

As they lay in bed, Ann asked, "When are you going to tell me?"

"Tell you what?"

"Tell me what has been making you so distracted and unhappy all evening."

Sam stared at the ceiling's flaking plaster. Ann had always counseled against investing in the stock market. She felt it was gambling, and they were not financially secure enough to afford any sort of speculation. Heartbreakingly, she had been right.

Sam took a deep breath in and exhaled slowly. "Have you heard the news about what has happened to the stock market the past few days?"

"Of course I have. It's impossible not to see the newspaper headlines. Everyone was talking about it at the market today."

At that moment, Ann's face transformed. Sam watched as her eyebrows lowered from quizzical to comprehension. Her lips pursed into "Oh no," but no sound was emitted.

Ann got out of bed and said, "Sam, we will get through this." She went to the bathroom, and all Sam could hear was the trickling of water and muffled crying.

Sam's countenance dropped, seeing Ann return to bed with red-rimmed eyes. One settled in, she said, "Louise should be asleep. We need the Tooth Fairy to make a visit."

Sam got up and went to his closet and felt the back pocket of a pair of pants he had hung up earlier in the week. He manipulated a button on the pants until he felt a handful of change. He recalled the look of both pity and kindness he received when a couple with strong Italian accents had handed him the coins. Sam had never been the recipient of charity before, but at the time he was too mired in despair to protest. The honest, pure warmth emanating from the couple allowed Sam to eagerly welcome their generosity.

He sorted the coins in his hand: a few pennies and nickels, one dime, three quarters and a half-dollar piece. When Louise had lost her first tooth a few days earlier, she received a nickel in exchange. In an act of prayer and hope, in this time of despair, the Tooth Fairy was going to give Louise a dime.

Louise's bedroom door was slightly ajar. She still needed the hint of light from the hallway to help her fall asleep, so her door was never completely closed. Sam tiptoed into her room and watched her pink and white blanket rise and lower slightly with each gentle breath she took. He carefully placed his hand underneath her pillow in search of the folded piece of paper with the tooth inside. Once he felt the paper, he deftly removed it, replacing it with the dime. He resisted the urge to smother his daughter with kisses, and not wanting to wake her, Sam placed a small loving kiss on her cheek, lingering just a bit longer than usual.

Chapter 23

"Mommy, Daddy, I knew it. The Tooth Fairy came last night. I got a whole dime this time!"

Ann and Sam suppressed smirks simultaneously as Ann responded, "That's so exciting. I think you are going to be rich, because you still have so many more teeth that are going to fall out."

Louise responded with a large gap-toothed smile. "What do you think I should buy with it?"

Sam looked at his daughter and asked, "Do you know what I think? I think you should save all the Tooth Fairy money and then when you have a small fortune, you can decide what you want to buy with it. That way, you will know exactly how much money you have and can then decide the best way to spend it. You may want to buy yourself one big toy or perhaps you'll want to buy several smaller ones. You may also decide to save some of your money for another day."

Louise responded with the indisputable logic of a six-year-old, "That's a funny idea, Daddy. Why would I want to save my money for another day? I think I will buy myself a bunch of small toys today or tomorrow."

Louise hurried to her room with Raggy in tow and dropped the dime in the slot of her pink-and-gold horse-shaped piggy bank. A smile spread across her face as she heard the clink of the dime meeting her nickel. Arm in arm, Louise and Raggy skipped to the dining room for breakfast.

Chapter 24

"So you're saying the dime wrote that?" questioned Julie.

"Yup, that is exactly what I'm saying. I'm sure it could have written more, but I think we cut it off early. In the past, I set it up for writing at night and held back all urges to check, not wanting to interrupt it until the following morning."

Julie's eyebrows arched and she seemingly chose her words carefully when saying, "You do understand how unbelievable this is, right? There could be many explanations for how this was written, the easiest being you simply wrote it on another device. I want to believe you, I really do, but logic says a dime sitting on a laptop chronicling history is low on the list of possibilities."

I saw the frustration and fear in her eyes so I said, "Look, you can take my laptop and the dime back to your apartment. Close the laptop, place the dime on it, and go to sleep. Then bring it back tomorrow morning, and we can check it out together. You can also hold onto my phone. I don't have any other electronics so if you have my phone and my laptop I have no way of adding to the story overnight. Please, you've got to show me a little bit of trust. Believe me, I'm not going to sneak out and use another computer. You can also search my apartment before you leave to make certain I don't have another laptop stashed somewhere."

Julie's expression changed as I explained everything. First she wore a look of pensiveness, then skepticism, then contemplation. At last she spoke. "I do think you're an honest person, and I really want to believe everything you've told me. It would be so cool if somehow a dime was able to do what you're saying, but you do know how insane this sounds, right?" I nodded my head as she continued. "There is another way we could set things up to prove your claim." At that point her voice became much softer and I was barely able to hear what she uttered so I asked her to repeat it.

"I could spend the night in your apartment and then together we would be able to check in the morning."

The realization of Julie's suggestion slowly sank in. Of course, that was the easiest and best way to prove my claim, and it wouldn't require me to relinquish my phone for the night. Why I hadn't thought of that? I felt myself smiling from ear to ear.

"Of course, that's the perfect solution! You're brilliant for thinking of it. Why don't you go to your apartment and get what you need?"

Julie's glowing face spread into a broad smile as she danced to the door.

"Wait," I called out. "I hope you have a sleeping bag or an air mattress. I don't have either, and I really need to sleep in my own bed tonight because I'm still recovering from my injuries."

She looked back at me before opening the door and visibly rolling her now moist eyes. I figured perhaps she was embarrassed she had forgotten about my injuries.

Chapter 25

Louise began to stir. At 6:45 a.m she finally forced herself to sit up. A flash of realization came over her. She reached under her pillow, feeling around until locating her prize. The last of her baby teeth had finally fallen out the evening before, and her parents, a.k.a Tooth Fairies, had made the final delivery overnight. Louise was relieved that the last remnant of her babyhood had fallen out. Her parents had even discussed helping her pull this one as a grown up tooth was already pushing it out of the way.

She looked at the nickel in her hand, and recalled sensing her mother had come into her room in the middle of the night. Louise had feigned deep sleep, even exaggerating snoring while her mother placed the nickel under her pillow and gently kissed her on the forehead. A small wave passed over Louise as she recognized it as a pang of yearning for the innocence and gullibility of being six years old again. She vowed never to tell her parents that she knew they were the Tooth Fairy.

Louise looked at her dresser where her piggy bank sat next to her alarm clock. She always loved the clock, with the figure of a ballet dancer displaying the hour and minute with a hand and a leg. Her mother had taught her how to tell time with the clock. She giggled as she recalled the time in kindergarten when the teacher asked, "How can you tell when it is 3 o'clock?" and Louise answered, "When the ballerina's leg with the slipper is on the number 3 and her hand with the glove is on the 12."

She hesitated before putting the nickel into her piggy bank. Instead, she removed the rubber stopper from the bottom of the bank and shook the bank, watching all the coins exit. She added the nickel to the pile of coins, counting out 19 nickels and one dime for a total of 20 coins in all. She had forgotten that on one occasion when losing a tooth, her parents had given her a dime rather than a nickel. She reached for the solitary dime to study it more closely, and strangely felt her fingers suddenly grow warmer. Louise wondered why her parents chose to give her a 1921 dime that time, when she only received nickels in the past. Perhaps, she thought, it was simply that they didn't have a nickel with them that night.

Louise put the dime in her dress pocket in the unlikely event she might find something she would want to buy later in the day. She contemplated a bit longer, and wondered if they had intended to start giving her dimes for all her lost teeth but then they became poor and could no longer afford the additional five cents on each occasion.

She smiled and recalled the times when her dad would come home from work every night around dinner time and they had meals with chicken, beef tongue, or brisket. Louise recognized that for the past several years, her family stopped having meat other than chicken, and then it was only on Shabbos.

She reflected the change in her father, particularly when he lost his job. He always used to be so happy and cheerful, and then suddenly he seemed sad all the time.

Louise glanced at the well-worn Raggedy Ann doll propped on a miniature chair by her bedroom window. She longingly yearned for the times she went to work with her dad, walking into his office snugly holding hands, his face beaming with pride when he presented her to coworkers. Louise recalled the receptionist, Mrs. Walker, her silver hair with shiny bluish streaks, pinching her cheeks, handing her a gumdrop, and proclaiming, "What a beauty."

In his private office, her father took off his jacket and elegantly hung it up. The office wasn't very large but at home he often told Louise private offices such as his were reserved exclusively for the most important people. Her dad ceremoniously moved a second chair next to his so they could work side by side at his expansive wooden desk with its endless array of drawers. Her dad always found work for Louise to do, counting out rubber bands, organizing papers into distinct piles, or asking Mrs. Walker to help her sharpen her father's pencils.

Louise missed those days spent alone with her father, but more than anything, she missed how safe and secure she felt with him.

For several years after losing his job due to what her parents called The Depression, her dad worked washing dishes at Hoffman's Cafeteria. She recalled asking him if he enjoyed working there only to be told, "Not really, but work is hard to get now, and I'm very lucky to have any sort of job."

Louise put on her socks, pulling them above her knees while her mind wandered back to when her mother began working a few years ago. Her mom wanted a full-time job at the time but was only able to get part-time work, and was very excited to get it. She went into Manhattan two or three days a week to do secretarial work. She said a lot of other women were jealous when she got the job. She got it because she was able to type eighty words a minute, which made her more qualified than all the other applicants.

Her dad got a new job about a year ago, working six days a week at Dolly Martin, a women's clothing store. Since then he'd seemed a lot happier. Her mom also seemed to be more content since he began working at Dolly Martin. Louise packed her completed homework assignments and headed to the kitchen.

At breakfast Louise announced that the Tooth Fairy had made her farewell appearance as she no longer had any baby teeth remaining. Each member of the Weinstein family had played along with the charade of the Tooth Fairy's existence, even though it had been understood for some time that Louise knew the true identities of her midnight visitors.

Her mother handed Louise her school lunch bag, receiving a kiss in return. Louise kissed her father goodbye and skipped outside to meet her friend Sarah Roth for the five-block walk to P.S.156, where they were both in the same fifth-grade class. Louise and Sarah had been best friends since first grade, and they knew nearly everything about one another.

On today's walk, Sarah and Louise discussed Sarah's crush on their classmate Freddy Stein, with Louise offering Sarah the best possible advice an 11-year-old-girl who had never had a boyfriend could possibly provide. Sarah listened intently as Louise said, "You know Rhoda Goldman and David Guttman? They are in the grade ahead of us."

"Sort of."

"Well, the boys were playing baseball and a ball was thrown and hit Rhoda in the head! She fell down and started crying. David ran over to her to see how she was and to console her. They have been walking home from school together holding hands ever since."

"So you want me to get hit in the head with a baseball?"

"No, of course not. During recess today why don't you start running, fall in front of Freddy, and scrape your knee? You could start crying and he would console you, and then let nature take its course!"

Sarah thought about it for a minute. "Isn't there a way to do this without me getting hurt? And what if Freddy doesn't come over to me and instead that disgusting Irwin Baum comes over to see how I am? He always has a finger in his nose."

Seeing Freddy bounding up the stairs into school with his friends, the girls quickly agreed to continue the discussion during lunch.

They recited the "Pledge of Allegiance" in the auditorium with the other students and listened to some remarks from the school principal, Mr. Blank. Then Louise headed to her classroom for the first lesson of the day, math.

Louise, a strong and engaged student, seemed to pick up numbers faster than her other classmates. Her ability in math sometimes resulted in poorly disguised resentment from some of the boys. Everyone believed that boys were better in math, and that girls' minds were not made to understand arithmetic computations. Louise was an obvious exception, and her mathematical aptitude resulted in jibes like, "Ask Louise Einstein." She realized the boys who were good students were not the ones who gave her a hard time. Most of the teasing came from the ones who were unable to count the fingers of their own hands.

Louise enjoyed reading and would devour every book she took out from the library. She loved the Nancy Drew series and had read all six books. She checked with the librarian so frequently to see when a new one in the series would come out that the librarian promised she would put it aside for her the day it came in. Louise also recently finished a book, *Little House in the Big Woods*, which she enjoyed immensely. She hoped the author, Laura Ingalls, would write many more.

The funny thing was that as much as Louise enjoyed reading, she equally disliked writing. As a matter of fact, aside from being teased by the boys in her class for her math prowess, the only thing she truly disliked about school was having to write compositions. Whenever her teacher, Mrs. Cohen, assigned homework to write a story, Louise would sit and stare at her composition book for hours in a trance. Mrs. Cohen took the time to speak with Louise to better understand the difficulty. The teacher told her that she was a smart and imaginative girl and just needed to allow her thoughts to flow. Despite the encouragement, Louise continued to freeze whenever she had a pencil or pen in hand.

After school that day, Sarah went clothing shopping with her mother, so Louise walked home by herself. On her way to her apartment building, she approached the Midnight Rose Candy Store. She had the dime from her piggy bank in her pocket, and felt the urge for some licorice. There was also a sign advertising cigars, which she always thought was ironic and even a bit funny. The smell of chocolates was so delicious and inviting while the odor of cigars made Louise feel like throwing up. Why advertise these contrasting scents together?

Her father had always instructed her to never go into the candy store without him, but never explained why. He only said that it was not a good place for kids to go into, and he would explain the reason when she was older.

She already had a pretty good idea of the reason her father did not want her visiting the store. Her classmate, Hy Rabinowitz, had told her that the store was used as a meeting place for gang members of "Murder Inc." Everyone in the neighborhood knew about Murder Inc. They oversaw the neighborhood, and if someone upset them, a bullet-riddled body was likely to be their fate.

As she got closer to the store, Louise noticed a long black car parked in front. There were two large and menacing men engaged in conversation a few feet from the store's entrance. Louise thought about what her father had told her, and sped up her pace as she walked away. Licorice always made her teeth black anyway, so she figured she would instead snack on a banana when she got home.

Chapter 26

Louise smelled the familiar aroma of her mother's liver and onions as she walked past the kitchen. Not in the mood for conversation, Louise quickly said hello to her mother then headed straight to her bedroom, determined to complete most of her homework before dinner. The math assignment was simple, and she knew she would finish it in less than five minutes. However, before she even unpacked her schoolbooks, Louise's mother entered her room.

"Is that it, just a hello? No hug or kiss or 'Mom, how was your day? Mine was good.' "

"I'm sorry, Mom," Louise said as she planted a kiss on her mother's cheek. "School was good. How was your day?" "As if you care," her mother answered with a smile. "We are having liver and onions for dinner."

Louise finished her math homework in two minutes, a new record. Then she guiltily thought about how Sarah sometimes spent over an hour on the same assignment. Louise decided the next time Sarah came over, she would help her with the math homework and give her some pointers on tackling future assignments.

Louise diligently completed her science and history work, both of which consisted primarily of reading. Once these were done, she deeply sighed as she knew it was time for her English assignment, having left the most unpleasant for last. The instructions, plainly written in her own hand, made her anxious: "In one page, write an essay telling the reader what your favorite season is and why." She got up and nervously paced around her room, fixing her eyes on the ballerina clock sitting on her dresser.

Louise went over and picked up the clock, realizing her desk was the preferable location for it. Funny, why was the clock always on the dresser? She would remedy that immediately, and situated the timekeeper on her desk next to her pencil sharpener. She liked the color contrast of the clock: white hands and legs, dark pink numbers, light pink background and an aquamarine trim. The clock showed 5:50, giving her about 20 minutes until her father's expected arrival home. Maybe she should wait in the living room and greet him when he arrives; the essay would just have to wait.

Louise hurried out of her room announcing, "Mom, I finished most of my homework and I want to surprise Daddy when he comes home by waiting for him. Do you need any help with dinner?"

"You can set the table. We'll need sharp knives for the liver and onions."

"Okay, Mom. Mom, what was your favorite subject when you were in school?"

Ann thought. "I would say history. I enjoyed learning about all the things that happened in the past. I also liked reading, and history mostly required reading stories about what had happened centuries before I was born. The events were all so spectacular. They read like fables. I know what my least favorite subject was— math! I don't know where you got your math ability from but it certainly wasn't from me."

"Did you enjoy writing?" Louise asked. "I don't think I particularly liked it or disliked it. I guess you could call it a skill of necessity."

At that moment, they heard the front door's lock opened and Louise ran to her father shouting, "Daddy, Daddy!"

"Wow, this is some reception," Sam exclaimed.

"I finished almost all of my homework and I set the table. We are having liver and onions for dinner."

Sam, with a shining grin and holding out a bag, exuberantly cried out, "That all sounds terrific, and with it we will be having this bottle of wine. Well, two of us will be anyway."

"Oh, Daddy, couldn't I have one sip?"

He walked over to Ann, gave her a big kiss and elongated hug, while excitedly beckoning Louise over to join them.

Ann laughed and told Sam, "You are in a very good mood."

"I certainly am," Sam chortled. "My two ladies will be dining tonight with the new assistant manager of Dolly Martin!"

Chapter 27

Louise loved tonight's unusual behavior—seeing her dad giving her mom spontaneous kisses, and her mom gazing at him as if he was Clark Gable. They became a bit giddy due to the bottle of wine they drank over the course of the night. She was too young to distinctly remember, but she had always thought her parents had seemed happier many years ago. Louise hoped that tonight would be the beginning of a new and better chapter for her parents.

It was a little after 8:00. Louise went to her room for another attempt to work at her writing homework. Since her school-night bedtime was not until 9:30, Louise had plenty of time to write the dreaded assignment. Yet, Mrs. Cohen said the paper was not due until Wednesday so there really was no need to do her homework that night. Besides, her parents were in such good moods it made much more sense to join them while they listened to Al Pearce and His Gang on the radio. Louise vowed to complete the writing assignment tomorrow. She closed her composition book and placed a pencil on top, along with the dime, reminding herself to put it away later. Pleased with her plan, she announced out loud, "Tomorrow I'll write why spring is my favorite season."

Louise joyfully took off her dress and changed into her pajamas. Then she hurried to join her parents in the living room. .

Chapter 28

On Tuesday, Sarah joined Louise for the walk home, the clang of the final bell still resounding in their ears. Louise always enjoyed Sarah's upbeat company and marveled at how Sarah's face lit up as they slowly walked past the Saratoga Avenue dress shops.

Sarah lived to window-shop. The pair briefly paused outside of Louise's father's workplace but decided it best not to disturb him.

Sarah talked nonstop about several subjects simultaneously in a rapid-fire manner. Sarah's petite, pert nose, soft curly auburn hair, freckled cheeks, and glowing hazel eyes perfectly matched her breezy personality. Louise, with her thick, dark, wavy, and unmanageable hair looked longingly at Sarah's delicate curls. It would sometimes take Louise forty minutes to thoroughly brush her hair, battling the persistent knots, which mysteriously reappeared the following day. While Sarah monologued about how annoying Freddy Stein had become, Louise was lost in thought, wondering how long it would take to fight tonight's knots.

As Sarah finally came up for air, Louise asked, "Would you like to come over to my house to do homework and then stay for dinner?"

"That would be great, but first let's stop by my house to make sure it's okay with my mom. Will it be okay with your mother?"

"My mom won't be home till around 5," Louise said, "but she will be fine with it. My mother loves when you're around."

When Louise heard the front door open and close a few minutes after 5 she, with Sarah in tow, ran to the entryway. "Mom, Sarah's here. Can she stay for dinner?"

"I can see that, and of course we would love to have Sarah stay for dinner. Hi, Sarah. How was school today, girls?"

"Hi, Mrs. Weinstein," Sarah said.

"School was fine," answered Louise. "Mrs. Cohen sent Michael Rosen to the first-grade class and made him stand in the back of the classroom because he was misbehaving, as usual." Louise rolled her eyes and sighed. "Mrs. Cohen said that if Michael acts like a six-year-old, he should be in first grade. We are finishing our math homework now. I'm showing Sarah a few math tricks, and then Sarah is going to give me some ideas about the writing assignment."

"That's nice. Why don't you girls finish up your homework and come out in about half an hour? I could use some help setting the table."

Louise and Sarah headed back to Louise's room as she replied, "Sure mom."

The girls sat on Louise's bed and took out their math assignments. Louise figured this was the perfect opportunity to give Sarah some math pointers. Fifteen minutes later, Sarah hugged her friend with more strength than Louise knew she had in her, as she exclaimed, "Thanks so much. You're a better teacher than Mrs. Cohen. You're a better teacher than any real teacher I've ever had. You should be a teacher when you grow up. Definitely a math teacher, maybe in a high school or even at a college!"

Louise felt her face turn red. She was thrilled she was able to help her friend and responded, "I really enjoyed it and it was nothing at all. You're so smart it's easy to give you suggestions. I'm just glad it helped. Now, it's your turn. If you show me how to write essays, I'll squeeze you harder than you squeezed me."

Sarah laughed and said, "Writing is easy. You love to read and you're brilliant. All you need to do is relax and put your thoughts down on paper."

Louise went over to her desk and sat down. She slid the dime from her composition book and placed it on the desk. With a pencil in hand, she opened the notebook. "Wait, what is this?"

Sarah, detecting Louise's shock, came over and asked, "What's what?"

Louise's eyebrows arched in disbelief. Her eyes were glued to her composition book, and she struggled to find words. "This is bizarre," she finally moaned. "My mother wrote my homework assignment for me. Why in the world would she do such a thing? I don't know if I should be angry or if she thought she was being helpful, but this doesn't seem like something she should have done."

Sarah could see how upset her friend was and offered, "Just ask her why she did it."

Louise's face relaxed as she said in an exasperated voice, "I think it will be a long conversation so I'll speak with her later tonight. Since we finished up our homework, let's play checkers."

They played two games, and the girls went downstairs to set the table for dinner. As Ann had worked all day in Manhattan, she didn't have time to cook so she reheated the leftover chicken soup from Sunday for dinner.

A few minutes later Sam walked in singing, which Louise found *so* embarrassing, but seeing two containers of ice cream under her father's arms quickly reversed her embarrassment.

The girls ate little during dinner, as they too busy laughing at Louise's dad's endless silly jokes. Ann cleared away the soup dishes and brought out bowls for the ice cream along with a scoop so the girls could serve themselves. Louise and Sarah devoured their chocolate ice cream while Sam and Ann feasted on rum raisin.

At 8:00 o'clock Sam left with Sarah to walk her home. As soon as the door closed, Louise nervously asked her mom, "Why did you do it?"

A quizzical expression passed over Ann's face and she asked, "Do what, Dear?"

"Mom, you know exactly what I'm talking about."

"Louise, please help me wash the dishes and explain to me what you're asking, because I have absolutely no idea what you're talking about."

Louise's eyes rolled as she stood up and began carrying dishes into the sink. She dropped the plates into the sink with an uncommonly careless clatter, and said, "I'm sure you were trying to be helpful but you shouldn't have done my homework for me."

Ann dried off her hands and put down the dishtowel. She stared at her daughter. "Honey, believe me, I have no idea what you're talking about. I didn't do your homework. Why would I?"

"Mom, are you telling me the truth?"

"Of course I am. Why do you believe I would do your homework?"

"Do you think Dad would do my homework for me?"

"Louise, that is very unlikely. Would you please tell me why you think your father or I would have done your homework?"

Louise grabbed her mother's hand, pulling her upstairs towards her room. Her mother said, "Can't we finish the dishes first?"

"Please, Mom, this is driving me crazy, and I need to show you this now." As soon as they entered Louise's room, Louise opened her composition book, pointed and said, "See, I didn't write that. Either you or Dad must have written it."

Ann picked up the book and looked at the neatly written essay and read:

Why Spring Is My Favorite Season
by Louise Weinstein

Each season has its own special things but spring is my favorite. Summer is fun because the weather is perfect for outdoor activities and going to Coney Island. The fall means school starts again and I get to see my friends every day. The winter brings snow and sledding, but the spring is my favorite season of all.

Just when I get tired of all the freezing temperatures and too much snow and ice, spring arrives with warmer weather. The warmer weather means green grass and flowers will soon arrive.

Reminding me of the arrival of new growth is the holiday of Passover, which is my favorite holiday. I get to see all my cousins at the two seders and we get to eat great food, even though I do miss eating bread a bit.

Spring also means the start of baseball season, which makes my father so happy. He loves the Brooklyn Dodgers and always takes me and my mom to at least one game each year.

Last of all but most importantly, my birthday is in the spring, on April 24th!

After she finished, Ann said, "I think the piece is very good and sounds a lot like you. Are you certain you didn't write it? This isn't my handwriting, and it certainly isn't your father's. But it does look a little bit like yours."

Louise's voice rose three octaves. "It most certainly is *not* my handwriting, Mom! If you or Dad didn't write it, then who did?"

"Honey, I'm sure there is a logical explanation. Perhaps Sarah wrote it for you when you were out of your room. Maybe Dad did write it and tried to change his handwriting to look like yours, thinking it was a cute idea. But I have to tell you it doesn't really sound like something your father would do."

"Mom, I know Sarah didn't write it but hopefully Daddy will be home soon. I'll ask him the second he walks in the door."

A few minutes later, Ann and Louise ran to the front door and before Sam unbuttoned his coat, Louise charged at him, asking, "Daddy, did you write my homework essay?"

"Of course, I'll help you with your essay."

"No, Daddy. Did you *write* my homework essay? I didn't write it, and Mom said she didn't write it, and I know Sarah didn't write it, so you must have written it because someone wrote it."

Sam smiled and said, "Sorry to disappoint you, Sweetheart, but I was at work all day and could not have written it."

"Are you sure? It was probably written last night while I slept. Somebody is playing a joke on me and I don't think it's funny." Louise's lower lip began to quiver so Sam bent down and placed his hands on his daughter's shoulders.

"Why don't you show me what you're talking about, and I am sure we can figure it out."

The three headed to Louise's room, and Louise thrust her composition book towards her parents and asked her dad to read the spring essay. He read the page aloud, and said, "I think it's very good, Louise. I don't understand what the problem is."

Tears started welling up in Louise's eyes as she began sobbing, "I'm trying to explain to you. I didn't write it. Mom says she didn't write it, and you said you didn't write it. I know Sarah didn't write it. So who wrote it?"

Sam held his daughter tightly and said, "There must be a logical explanation. Probably someone at school wrote it when you left your book out today. Perhaps during lunch or when you went to the bathroom one of your friends thought they were being helpful and did your homework assignment for you."

Louise was taking deep breaths in and out, seemingly on the verge of hysterics, as she uttered, "I didn't bring my composition book to school today. I left it right here." She pointed to her desk. "The page was blank last night before I went to bed, and this afternoon when I came home there was a full essay there. So someone here must have written it and it was not me!"

Louise began sobbing uncontrollably. Ann and Sam stared at each other with a combination of confusion and concern.

Once Ann and Sam calmed Louise a bit, the three of them decided it would be a good idea for Louise to call Sarah to make certain that somehow Sarah had not mischievously written the essay. Louise presented the evidence of her friend's innocence like a lawyer in a courtroom, concluding, "So who wrote it?"

Usually, Ann and Sam alternated Louise's bedtime routine. That night however, recognizing her distress, they teamed up to help settle her for the night. Louise became even more upset when she realized she that she had not actually done her writing homework and so had nothing to turn into to Mrs. Cohen. After much discussion, Louise agreed she would turn in the writing she had found in the notebook. She ripped out the original writing and transcribed it word for word on the next page in her book.

For thirty minutes, Ann and Sam took turns rubbing her back, continually reassuring Louise that as a family, the three of them would figure out the mystery the next evening. Louise's breaths gradually slowed down and eventually transitioned into gentle snoring.

Chapter 29

Julie and I had a wonderful evening getting to know each other. I must confess, we even shared a good night kiss. As Julie settled into her sleeping bag (apparently she didn't have an air mattress), I stared at the pitch black ceiling. I was excited at the prospect of someone else sharing my dime's irrefutable magic. Sleep, however, was difficult, as my mind continually raced, anxious about what the morning would reveal. Would the dime continue its narrative or would a blank screen fully humiliate me? I knew Julie was also thinking about the morning's prospects as I heard loud, restless sighs, saw her clenching and unclenching her fists and moving around on the floor.

Sleep finally came to both of us. It was kind of cute listening to Julie's routine. She emitted a large sigh, followed seconds later by heavy breathing and then light snoring. Realizing my guest was asleep, I completely relaxed in my comfy bed and entered my own tranquil world.

When I awoke the following morning I felt almost one hundred percent recovered, though my right elbow kind of resembled a purple eggplant. I looked over and saw Julie quietly reading the book *Americanah*. We made eye contact and said, "Good morning" simultaneously.

"Are you ready for the big moment?" I asked.

Julie mumbled something in response that kind of sounded like, "I was last night," so I reminded her that the coin needed the overnight period to do its thing. Perhaps she hadn't been paying close enough attention to me last night.

While Julie progressed through her morning routine, I removed the coin from the laptop and set things up for the big unveiling.

We put breakfast on hold as Julie and I sat on the couch while I refreshed the laptop. My fingers navigated the keyboard nervously while Julie sat transfixed awaiting the result. A moment later my anxiety washed away as February 19, 1934, appeared before my eyes. Julie let out an audible gasp. "It's true," she said. "I can't believe it."

We read the new prose in silence while I periodically adjusted the text to accommodate our respective reading speeds. When finished, stunned, we sat in silence, both of us trying to absorb what this all meant. Finally, with serious trepidation, I asked, "Well, what do you think?"

Following an elongated pause, Julie replied. "I think this is the strangest thing I've ever seen. Honestly, I don't know if I should laugh or cry or pinch myself. What are we going to do?"

The word that jumped out at me was "we." I had run the full emotional spectrum from confusion to exhilaration, from concern to confidence, from anxiety to enthusiasm, but always alone. Now I had a partner in the unbelievable journey the dime was taking me—no *us*—on.

Julie went back to her apartment with the promise of preparing and returning with breakfast. I used the time to reread my coin's recent literary musings. When I heard thumping on my apartment door, I rose to open it, finding Julie blowing air upward as she attempted to get the hair out of her eyes, while awkwardly balancing two bowls. Julie set the bowls down on the kitchen counter, produced a pair of spoons from her pockets, and placed one in each bowl. The contents were a bit hard to describe. I recognized bananas and what looked like strawberries, but with a weird purple hue. Seeds strewn on top of the whole ensemble created a psychedelic artist's rendition of a fruit salad. Julie asked, "Have you ever had an acai agave bowl?"

"Not that I recall." I also had never walked on hot coals in my bare feet, but I figured I was better off not including that in my response. We sat on the couch balancing breakfast on our laps while Julie's eyes moved back and forth between my face and my bowl. Cautiously, I dipped my spoon into my bowl and haltingly brought it to my mouth. It took a few spoonfuls to realize that the acai agave bowl was delicious.

"This is shockingly good," I exclaimed. "It's kinda sweet and tart at the same time. Really tasty!"

Julie's smile broadened. "I'm so happy you like it."

I finished off three bowls of my newly discovered go-to breakfast. Then Julie and I reread Louise's homework experience. The realization that someone who was born sixty years before me also had a magical relationship with this dime gave me goosebumps. I felt as if in some way I was Louise Weinstein's descendant, and we alone understood each other's experience. I wanted—no, needed—to get more acquainted with Louise and find out if she had discovered how the writing appeared. Did she keep the dime for her lifetime? Did she give it away? Did she lose it? Was it possible Louise Weinstein was still alive in 2018? My mind raced with these questions.

Julie had scheduled back-to-back SAT prep teaching sessions in the afternoon, and then had plans to meet a friend for dinner. We decided to meet the next morning at 9 in my apartment. She promised to show me how to make an acai agave bowl, and then we would read what we both hoped would be a substantial amount of new writing courtesy of my dime.

My expectation was that the next segment of the dime's writing would provide me with some clarity as to my future. I had already quit my job, perhaps too hastily, and needed to determine my next income source. If I was unable to start earning money from my own writing soon, I would need to start driving for Uber or borrow money from Roger or my parents. The Uber option was far and away the more attractive path.

Chapter 30

Louise, sitting in her customary dinner chair, spread the cloth napkin in her lap as she looked up at her father, seated to her right. He met her look with a smile so warm, she was unable to stop giggling. Since her father's promotion, her parents' constant jovial mood was contagious. The arrival of pot roast brimming with red potatoes and bright orange carrots accompanied her mother humming the "Lady of Spain." The white, yellow, and pink lily floral arrangement her father had brought home sat across on the buffet table. All the colors made Louise giggle again.

"What are you laughing at?" Sam questioned his daughter.

"Mom's lipstick on your cheek is the same color as the pink lily behind you!"

Sam took his napkin and wiped his cheek, causing his daughter to laugh again.

"It's the other cheek, Daddy!"

Sam eagerly bit into an onion roll and wiped his other cheek. "We really should do something to spruce up the dining area and the kitchen. Perhaps a new table and a fresh linoleum kitchen floor?"

Ann smiled and responded, "It's a nice idea, but perhaps we should wait until we can afford to buy a place of our own. When we own our home, we'll make everything exactly the way we want it to be."

Louise had no idea her parents were thinking of moving and buying a house.

"Where will we move to? Are you buying a new house soon?"

Ann answered her daughter with a smile. "No, dear. We are just thinking about the future. Now that Dad has gotten a promotion and I only need to work a day a week in Manhattan, we are just thinking about ways we may want to improve our lives."

Looking at her mother and father and how content they appeared, Louise offered, "I'm very happy here. I would be even happier if I knew who had written my homework yesterday."

Sam and Ann shared a glance, and Sam spoke. "Sometimes things happen that can't be explained. There is likely a logical explanation for the writing, but right now the answer isn't clear. We must accept that for the time being. Perhaps in a day we'll find out what happened, or maybe even in a week, or maybe we'll never find out. Think of it this way: if we never learn the truth, it will be a very interesting story that we can tell again and again, and one that you can share with your own children someday."

Louise had the feeling that her parents thought she had written the story but somehow had just forgotten she did. Not wanting to ruin the mood, she simply said, "Okay, Daddy."

After dinner, Louise helped Ann clear the table and then joined her parents for her favorite game, Gin Rummy.

Sitting at the table, examining her dealt cards, Louise decided she would follow her father's advice and do her best to ignore the mysterious writing. She was a good Gin Rummy player, and she won more often than she lost.

The enjoyable evening ended when her dad said he had a stomachache. He got up and said, "I'm not sure if my stomach hurts so much because I've eaten too much or because I keep losing at Gin Rummy to my 11-year-old daughter!"

February turned into March and Louise began to get excited about the weather becoming a bit warmer. The snow of early winter was fun to play in, but three months of snow, ice, and the constant need to wear mittens and boots became tiresome. Everyone around her seemed to be battling colds and illnesses during the freezing temperatures. She hoped the warming temperatures would get rid of the constant sniffling, coughing, and sore throats.

The past month of the winter was particularly hard for her dad, as his stomachache still had not gotten better. He would go to work every day, but he always seemed to be in discomfort and tired when he came home. Instead of spending time after dinner with Ann and Louise, he would go to his bedroom to rest or sleep.

One night Louise asked Ann, "Why does Dad's stomach hurt all the time, and why is he always so tired?"

"Your father probably works too hard and has never had the time to fully recuperate. The new job came with increased responsibilities, and increased responsibilities can cause aggravation. When a person has aggravation, it sometimes creates physical ailments such as stomachaches. Dad is going to see Dr. Underberg right after work before Shabbos this Friday. Dr Underberg will likely give him medicine that will make Dad get better."

Louise had overheard her mother tell her father several times that he should see the doctor. She was happy he had finally listened to her.

On Friday, while they were in the kitchen preparing the Shabbos meal, Louise noticed her mother's distraction and low spirits. Instead of singing while preparing the meal, Ann appeared glassy-eyed, and she made a few miscues in the kitchen, something she rarely did. Half of the sliced carrots ended up on the floor, and Ann nicked her finger while cutting the parsnips.

Louise looked at her mom and asked, "Is there anything I can do besides setting the table?"

"I'm sorry, Louise—what did you say?"

"I asked if there is anything I can do to help prepare for

Shabbos."

"Yes, dear. Please set the table."

"Mom, I already set the table. Is there anything else I can do?"

Ann bit her lip as Louise waited for a response.

"Mom, is there anything else I can do?"

Ann's eyes eventually focused on Louise. "So sorry, dear. I've been daydreaming. Would you please go to the bakery and pick up a challah? Perhaps also get a few pastries as a special treat. Make certain at least one is a prune danish. Dad loves them and it will also help his stomach." Ann handed Louise fifty cents and said, "Please bring me back the change."

Louise took the change, held her mother's hand, and asked, "Dad will be okay, won't he?"

"Of course he will, dear."

Louise would have been happier with her mom's answer if she still did not have such a vacant gaze in her eyes.

When Sam got home that evening, the kitchen smelled wonderful. The chicken was roasting, and Ann was making latkes too. The smell of the frying onions and potatoes wafting in the air made Louise's mouth water and her stomach grumble.

Ann and Louise hugged and kissed Sam with their "Good Shabbos" greetings. Ann appeared to be rather tentative but Louise blurted out, "Daddy, what did the doctor say?"

Sam smiled and said, "Everything is fine. Let's sit down and eat this delicious dinner your mom made."

Ann and Louise lit the Shabbos candles and said the prayer while Sam eased himself into his chair while grunting audibly. He reached for the challah and hastily sang, "Baruch Atah Adonai Eloheinu Melech ha'olam ha'motzi lechem min ha'aretz."

Ann poured two glasses of wine and a glass of grape juice, and Sam recited, "Baruch Atah Adonai Boray Pre Ha Goffen."

Louise took a sip of her drink and asked her father, "Could you tell us now what Dr. Underberg said?"

"He wants me to take Pepto Bismol each morning. Ann, Dr. Underberg scheduled another appointment for me to see him next Friday at 4:30 and would like you to come with me. By then he should have the results of the tests, and he wants to discuss with you changes to my diet. It sounds like he is convinced that I'm having a problem with some of the food I eat. He knows you're in charge of the meals so he asked if you could join us."

"Of course, Sam. I hope roast chicken and latkes won't be banned!"

While Sam discussed with Louise her day at school and weekend plans, Ann played with her food. Louise caught her mom staring into the living room on a few occasions as if watching a show only she could see.

><

Sam was a little more energetic over the weekend. Ann insisted that they all go to shul Saturday morning for services. They always went to synagogue on the high holidays, and Sam would go about once a month on the Sabbath, but it was a bit unusual for them all to go together for regular Shabbat services. Louise was certain her mom wanted to go so she could pray for a cure to her husband's ailment.

Louise sat upstairs in the synagogue with her mom and the other women while her dad sat with the men downstairs. Louise never fully understood why the men and women sat separately, but rationalized to herself that by being upstairs the females were the ones closer to God.

Louise was usually a bit fidgety during the lengthy Shabbos

services, but she was not on this day. She sang along with most of the prayers. Her mother had her eyes closed for most of the service, quietly chanting prayers. Louise, having attended Shabbos services nearly every Saturday when she was younger, read Hebrew well, and knew all the prayers in the correct order. She wasn't certain why, but a couple of years ago, she and her parents had decided to attend services less frequently.

Louise could tell that her mom really needed to be in synagogue today, to ease her worries about Sam's health. Louise was herself growing concerned that her dad's pains were due to more than just pressure at work. She wasn't a young child anymore, and she knew that a regular stomachache should not take weeks to disappear.

Louise closed her eyes and chanted the prayers quietly alongside her mother.

When Louise got home from school the following Friday, the apartment was empty. It was the day of the appointment with Dr. Underberg. Her parents would not be home before sundown.

Louise went to her room and took five nickels from her piggy bank. She decided it would be a nice surprise for her mom if everything was set for a festive night. She left the apartment and walked down the street. In addition to picking up a challah for the hamotzi, she bought a prune Danish for her father. She knew a pickle seller who set up his barrel every Friday afternoon on Saratoga Avenue. Her father loved sour pickles, and she was hopeful that after his doctor's appointment he would be able to enjoy one. She smelled the garlicky brine of the pickle seller's barrel before she even saw him. Louise bought two, planning to share the second one with her mom. Then she hurried home to prepare for her parents' arrival.

Ann and Sam opened the door just as Louise was placing two candles in candlestick holders. Her parents' facial expressions contrasted: her father was smiling and appeared happy, while her mom's face had the same glazed look from the past few weeks.

"How is my perfect daughter?" Sam asked.

"I'm great. More importantly, what did Dr. Underberg say?"

"As I had thought, the doctor said the problem was the food I've been eating. I guess I can't digest certain foods. He spoke with mom for a while, and they conspired to change my diet. On the subject of eating, it looks like you've taken care of everything for our Shabbos dinner."

Louise smiled and said, "That's great news, isn't it, Mom? We are having the chicken soup Mom made yesterday, but I bought the challah and got sour pickles from the pickle seller. Are you able to eat pickles?"

Sam turned to Ann and said, "I'm pretty sure I can but I guess I need to check with my lovely warden."

Ann responded with a smile. "Of course you can have the pickle Louise bought for you. It's some of the fried foods we will need to cut back on a bit."

At the dinner table, Sam carefully studied the pickle as if he was inspecting a newly discovered treasure. He brought it slowly towards his eyes as if to understand indecipherable writing. He then turned it over and over until seemingly evaluating each side. He finally brought it close to his nose and began to sniff. Nodding at Louise, he then took the largest and loudest bite of a pickle she had ever witnessed.

"Far and away the best pickle I've ever tasted. Undoubtedly because it was purchased by the best daughter in the whole world."

Louise smiled broadly attempting to hide her own concern, which she saw reflected on the face of her mother, who was unsuccessfully attempting to smile.

Chapter 31

By the beginning of April, Louise knew that her father's health was worsening. He began missing work, and he spent a lot of time in the bathroom. Louise frequently heard her father throwing up and trying to stifle moans.

Her formerly robust father now appeared frail, with shriveled and yellowing skin. Worst of all, her dad seldom left the bedroom. Louise came to understand that her father was very, very sick and unlikely to ever improve.

On April 4th, Louise approached her mother in the kitchen while her father slept. She knew her mother was trying to protect her, but this could no longer be hidden. Perhaps because Ann saw the look in her daughter's eyes, she spoke before Louise did.

"Louise, let's go sit on the couch." As they sat, Ann took Louise's hands in her own and said, "I'm sorry. We should've had this discussion sooner. It's obvious your father is very ill, and unlikely he will get better." The tears from Ann's eyes mirrored her daughter's and in a halting voice she continued, "When Dr. Underberg spoke with me privately, he told me that Daddy has large tumors in his stomach. They are cancerous, and unfortunately too large to remove."

Ann pulled her daughter close to her as Louise asked, "Did daddy know he had cancer the night he came home from the doctor with you?"

"No, he didn't. Dr. Underberg and I thought it was best to let him know the truth slowly. However, the symptoms progressed faster than Dr. Underberg had hoped. Your father and I spoke with Dr. Underberg last week, and he learned how bad his condition really was. On Monday, Daddy told his Dolly Martin boss that he wouldn't be returning to work."

"Does the doctor think Daddy might live for a few more years?"

Ann stared at her daughter with a love that pained her own stomach and said, "No, sweetheart. Daddy is so sick right now that the doctor thinks he probably won't live more than a few days or weeks. However, God does sometimes make miracles happen so we can pray that He will make one for your father. The thing is, we really don't want Daddy to continue to suffer, do we? If he goes to Heaven, all his pain will disappear."

Louise's chest was heaving, and she was crying uncontrollably as she blurted out, "But baseball season starts in a few days, and we were supposed to go to Ebbets Field to see the Dodgers!"

Chapter 32

I walked to the door promptly at 9:00 a.m. to let Julie in. I had a feeling she would be punctual, and she didn't disappoint. I had just completed making breakfast for the two of us. She had been nice enough to make breakfast for the previous morning so I figured I should reciprocate.

The afternoon before I had done a bit of shopping for some food items, a few additional dishes, and some cutlery from the Dollar Store to fill out my kitchen supplies. I'd gotten the impression that Julie thought my kitchen was not as well stocked as it should have been, so I took prompt action to remedy the situation.

I had the table set and had two glasses of orange juice poured.

I was brewing coffee and included a milk container on the table in case Julie wanted milk with her coffee, as is my preference. Actually, I much prefer milk to coffee so my cup of coffee typically includes at least fifty percent milk. While some like their coffee with milk, I guess I prefer my milk with a hint of coffee.

I asked Julie to sit so I could serve my breakfast specialty, which I took off the stove and served using a newly purchased spatula. I placed breakfast in front of Julie and watched to see if she could figure out what it was. As her face contorted with confusion, she poked at it a bit with her fork. But still recognition did not seem set in.

"Give up?"

She nodded.

"It's a Spam and cheese omelet! Would you like some mustard with it?"

"No, thanks, I think I'm good without mustard."

I served myself, and as I was rather hungry, I ate my omelet in five big bites. Julie, on the other hand, pecked at her omelet like a bird, though I knew she liked it by her persistent, almost forceful, smile.

I asked her, "Have you ever had a Spam and cheese omelet?"

It's funny, I could have sworn I first heard her mumble. "No, and I've also never walked on hot coals in my bare feet." More clearly, she said, "No, but it is very unique and has quite an interesting taste."

Encouraged, I suggested, "We could alternate making breakfast for one another."

Julie gave me a strange smile.

After breakfast, I cleared away the dishes and set my laptop on the table. A feeling of anxiety permeated the air as we waited for the screen to come to life. A few taps of the keyboard and the screen was ready to show us if the plight of Louise had continued.

"There," Julie blurted out as a description of a dinner scene with Louise's family emerged, and we leaned forward to read the newly written prose.

Next to me, Julie began sniffling and wiping tears from her eyes. "This is too sad," she said in a choking voice.

"Yeah, it is, but there wasn't a word written about additional magical writing, which is what I really wanted to read." I sensed that Julie was not thrilled with my comment, so I quickly followed up with, "I really hope that Sam somehow miraculously recovered."

There was a moment of silence between us. "Do you need your laptop today?" Julie asked. "If you can, maybe you should set it up so there could be a full day of writing when we check again tomorrow."

I thought about it for a while before responding. I really needed to work on my own novel, but I was at a crossroads because the lines between my words and the dime's writing continually blurred. Waiting until the dime produced more work became my new strategy. Also, Julie was obviously into the story and wanted to come by the next day to read more. Since I was weirdly enjoying her company, I finally said, "I'll set it up now."

Julie smiled and said, "Great, I'll bring muffins. You can make the coffee."

Chapter 33

Louise didn't think she had any more tears left. The previous day, Monday, May 7, had been the final day of sitting Shiva. Her father had died more than a week earlier, and the agony kept coming at her in waves. She angrily threw a wet handkerchief in the direction of two others already on the floor of her room, when she heard a gentle knocking on her door, and her mother's voice.

"Louise, Sarah is here to see you. Can she come in?"

"Yes, Mom."

The door opened, and Sarah sat next to Louise on her bed. The cover on her bed had red roses on it. Her father had picked it out years earlier, saying it was a perfect blanket for a girl with all the beauty of a rose.

Sarah had made two visits during the shiva period, but Ann and Sarah's mom thought it would be comforting for Louise to also spend some time alone with her best friend.

Sarah saw her friend's puffy red eyes and tear-lined face and sat next to her. She gently placed her arm around Louise's shoulder, and Louise nestled her face on Sarah's bony shoulder while sobbing quietly. In time, Louise sniffled, picked up her head, and asked, "Do you think I will ever be happy again?"

"Of course you will, Louise. Your father would want you to be happy forever and ever. You have your mother, who loves you, and me as your best friend. We will make certain you are happy again."

"I probably won't even remember much about my father in a few years. He was supposed to be a part of my life for a very long time."

Sarah wasn't sure what to say. Hesitantly, she suggested, "You have photographs of your dad, and you'll always have those. Maybe you could write about what he was like. That way, you will have your memories of him saved, and you could read about him while looking at his photos whenever you want."

Louise spent the day with Sarah, who did a great job keeping Louise occupied and as upbeat as possible. Louise recognized how fortunate she was to have Sarah for a best friend. Her mom came into her room after Sarah had left, just before bedtime.

Together, mother and daughter held each other tight, talked, cried, and even laughed a bit, remembering some of her father's jokes and antics.

"Mom, Sarah suggested I write about Daddy so I can remember him my whole life."

"That is a great idea. Sarah is so smart to suggest that."

Her mom kissed her goodnight and asked, "Would you like me to shut off the lights?"

"No, thanks. I have a couple of things I want to do before going to sleep."

Louise reached for the stuffed rabbit on her bed, seated next to her Raggedy Ann. Her father had bought her the rabbit when she was a very little girl, because he called her his "little bunny." The frayed and discolored fabric, with one chipped plastic eye, was—Louise knew—a treasure for the rest of her life. Holding the rabbit, Louise reached for some writing paper, which she laid out on her desk alongside a pen.

The weather had warmed, so Louise opened her window to let in some fresh air. She sat at her desk as the breeze from outside relaxed her and rustled the writing paper. She gazed absentmindedly at a framed photograph of her and her father and moved it on top of the paper along with the lucky 1921 dime she always left on her desk.

Ann had told Louise that she didn't need to return to school until Thursday, so Louise was able to sleep in Wednesday morning. It was already past 8:00 a.m. and Ann was cracking eggs in the kitchen when she heard Louise shriek, "Mommy, Mommy, Mommy, come quick!"

Ann rushed to her daughter's room and flung open the door to find her daughter shaking and holding a paper in her hand. Ann's heart sank as her daughter crumbled to the floor crying. Ann knelt beside Louise and held her tight while soothingly saying, "It's all right, I'm here. We will get through this, I promise."

"No, Mom, it's not just Daddy. Look at this." She thrust the wrinkled writing paper at her mom.

"It's happened again. Daddy died, and I'm going crazy."

Ann kept one arm secured around Louise's waist while holding the paper so she could read it.

"What is this?"

"When I woke up this morning and went to my desk, I saw someone had written about Daddy. I know it doesn't look like your handwriting, but did you write it? You must have written it, because there was no one else in the apartment last night, and I didn't write it."

Ann did not respond right away as she looked pensively at the words written in front of her. She curled her upper lip, fighting back tears, and finally said, "Louise, this is beautiful. I wish I wrote it, but I did not. If you didn't write it, it must be a miracle. God works in mysterious ways and all we can do is accept it as a blessing from God."

My Father, Sam Weinstein

———

My father was Sam Weinstein and he went to heaven when I was 11 years old, and he was 40.

He had brown eyes and wavy brown hair and was an average size for a man but he seemed very large to me. He would dance with me when I was little, and sing songs to me, though his voice wasn't really good. He would tell me jokes, some of them funny, and some of them not. I would always laugh, even if they weren't funny because he would laugh so hard once he finished telling the joke he made me laugh.

He would play games with me and my mom, and especially loved playing cards. He would make me believe he was angry whenever I won, but I knew he was really happy for me.

He would take me to Brooklyn Dodger games and he was the biggest Brooklyn Dodger fan in the world even though they were never very good.

He was always very kind, and I know he loved me and my mom more than anything. Even when things weren't going well he would never get angry.

I know he was sad after he lost his job and we did not have much money, but he never got angry with me.

I would watch him sometimes when he looked upset, but as soon as he saw me his whole face would brighten up and he would hug and kiss me. He would always make me feel so special and loved.

My daddy, Sam Weinstein, is in heaven now. I'm not sure how my mom and I are going to do without him, but I know I will always love him and miss him.

———

Chapter 34

Sarah and Louise walked in silence most of the way home from school. Louise was emotionally exhausted, and Sarah had run out of things to think of to say to support her friend. Sarah knew being back at school was supposed to be a return to normalcy for Louise, but what was normal for Louise anymore? Sarah knew that when she got home, her mother, brother, and sister would greet her, and that her father would be home shortly afterwards. Her friend was going to go home to a new life, a life without her father.

It comforted Louise to have Sarah walk by her side, but it was also nice to be quietly immersed in her own thoughts. Louise contemplated the grass beginning to grow around the concrete sidewalk, and how the leaves had begun to emerge on the isolated trees standing between the sidewalks and streets. She hadn't realized how many cracks there were on the sidewalk, or even how much bubble gum was permanently stuck on the surface beneath her.

As they approached Louise's building, Sarah grabbed Louise's arm and said, "See you tomorrow. It's good to have you back at school." Louise hugged her friend and went inside.

Ann was at the dining room table. Louise came in and gave her mother a kiss.

"How was your first day back at school?"

"It was fine. Everybody was so nice to me. Mrs. Cohen even told me I don't have to do the homework she assigned, but I'm going to do it anyway. Mom, I really want to talk to you about that unexplained writing. I know you probably think I wrote it, and you and Dad thought I wrote that homework assignment last time. The handwriting looks a bit like mine, and the words are things that I could have written, but I honestly didn't write either one."

Ann took Louise's hand into her own and looked into her daughter's eyes. "Louise, the world is full of strange events, things that we may not understand and are unable to explain. If you say you didn't write those pages, of course I believe you. And I know Dad believed you. I'm just wondering if there is a small chance that maybe you wrote it without realizing it."

"Mom, I swear I didn't write it. I didn't write it when I was awake, and I didn't write it when I was asleep. I did not write it."

During a dinner of mushroom and barley, which neither Ann or Louise ate with much vigor, Ann said to her daughter, "Louise, I spoke with the boss of the secretarial pool, and beginning next week I will be going back to work. They have always liked my work, and I'm going to be going into Manhattan five days a week. It's going to be an adjustment for both of us, me being away from early morning till sundown. I'm not accustomed to working five days a week, and you're not used to me not being home when you return from school. We will both need to adjust to the schedule change, but I know we will be fine. We have each other and we will always have each other."

Louise looked at her mother stoically and said, "I understand, Mom." Louise glanced away, quietly asking, "Do you believe in magic? Like, do you believe something could have magical powers?"

"Do you mean like a Ouija board?"

"I guess, sort of. I really mean like an object, like a coin."

"There are so many miracles in the Bible that are hard to explain, but they happened. As I said, there are things we don't understand, and me, a simple housewife, why would I understand them?"

Louise watched her mom's face—a mirror into her own emotion. Tears streamed down her face as their new reality took shape.

Louise and Ann held each other for a while, both softly sobbing. Louise finally stood up and went to her room to begin her homework. She had an intuitive feeling she knew the source of the magical writing but needed to test her theory to make certain.

She always had a special feeling, a feeling she could not explain, about the 1921 dime she received from the Tooth Fairy all those years earlier. When she touched it, she would get a warm sensation, a feeling she never had when she felt any other coin. There was something about the coin she was unable to explain, but something she knew. This sensation was the reason she had never spent the dime even though she always carried it with her.

She recalled that both times the magical writing had taken place, the process had been precisely the same. Prior to each occurrence, she had focused on what she wanted to write, and then she placed writing paper on the desk. She had then put down a pen on top of the paper, and finally set her special dime on the paper. Both times the routine had taken place at night right before she went to bed. The next day the paper had words seemingly from her own imagination written on it. The style of the writing was even typical of Louise, but she knew for a fact that she did NOT write these words.

Louise decided that on this night she was going to recreate the conditions that had resulted in the magical writing. She decided to once again place writing paper on her desk with a pen on top of it. She made up her mind that she was going to concentrate on answering the question, how does grass grow? The only difference this time: her special dime would spend the night on the dresser instead of on the writing paper.

Her plan in place, Louise completed her homework.

Fortunately, a writing project was not part of her homework assignments.

On most school mornings her mother, or father, would knock on her door at 7:00 a.m. with morning greetings to rise and shine. On Friday morning, Louise was restless for most of daybreak and found it impossible to remain in bed past 6:40. As soon as her feet hit the rug she headed to her desk and turned on the lamp. A smile emerged on her face as she saw the writing paper was blank. The first half of her theory proved true. Tonight, like a true scientist, she would attempt to complete the experiment.

Louise sat in the wooden chair with her elbows on her school desk. Why was the second hand of the clock on the classroom wall moving so slowly? Of course, the lethargy of the seconds hand caused the minute hand to take forever to move, and the hour hand didn't seem to ever budge. Mrs. Cohen sensed Louise's distraction and logically attributed it to Louise being in mourning and needing more time before she would once again be an attentive student. When the bell finally rang announcing the end of the school day, Louise quickly gathered her school bag and waited for Sarah on the school steps entrance.

On the walk home Sarah was pleased to find her friend so chatty and animated. On this rare occasion, Sarah was finding it difficult to keep up with Louise—both her walking pace and her dialogue. Sarah's mom had told her that Louise would probably be sad and moody for some time, so she wasn't sure what to expect. All she could do was walk faster and listen. Finally, Louise asked a question.

"Do you believe an object can be magical?"

"Well, my Uncle Mort is great at magic tricks. Sometimes he uses props that seem like they create real magic. My dad told me that most of the time it's just Uncle Mort using some kind of trick to make it seem like real magic but it's actually just a fake."

Louise's eyes crinkled as she said, "I mean real magic. Like something people can't control. I'm doing the second part of an experiment tonight, and if I'm right it will prove that I own something that's truly magical. Can you sleep over tomorrow night? If my experiment works, I'll have proof by then, and I could show it to you this weekend."

The smile on Sarah's face was wide and genuine as she responded, "I'd love to but let me check with my mother first."

Louise offered her a big smile in return as she skipped away.

During dinner Ann watched Louise as her daughter intermittently tapped her fingers on her plate. Louise's eyes kept focusing on the walls and ceiling for things apparently only she could see.

Louise did not seem depressed, just preoccupied.

Ann was in deep mourning herself, but her primary concern was for her daughter, who, after all was still a child. Ann had lost her own mother to cancer when she was just 17, and her father when she was 20. Ann still remembered when her parents told her, at age 15, and her older sister Rachel, who was 21, that their mom had a large tumor in her breast. Watching her mom wither away was at that point the most painful period of Ann's life. It was almost merciful that Sam suffered for only a few months in comparison to the two full years Ann spent watching her mother deteriorate. The feelings of helplessness watching her mother and later her husband die were indescribable. Three years after her mother's death, her father was gone too. The doctors said it was a sudden massive heart attack at the age of 49, but Ann knew that her dad died of living for three years with a broken heart.

Louise had gone upstairs to do her homework, so Ann sat at the dining room table in deep contemplation. She really did not have anyone in her life other than Louise. Both of her parents were dead, and her sister lived in Colorado with her husband and their four sons. She had only met Rachel's husband once and disappointingly, none of her nephews. Why, Ann thought, had she never met her nephews?

She and Rachel never had a falling out, they had just grown apart. The geographical distance was certainly a large contributing factor, but she knew in her heart that if their parents were still alive, there would still be family gatherings and she would have maintained a relationship with Rachel.

When Sam died, she received a call from Rachel asking if she should come, but what good would that have done? The two sisters, separated by six years in age, and now thousands of miles in distance, had not been close for such a long time. For more than a decade she had Sam and Louise, and that was enough for her. Now she only had Louise. In many ways that would be sufficient for Ann, but would that be enough for Louise?

It took Louise considerably longer than usual to finish her homework as her eyes kept wandering between the clock on her bed and the dime situated by her elbow on the desk. Once she finished with her schoolwork, Louise took out some paper. She carefully placed a pen and the coin atop the blank paper. Louise stood over her desk, concentrating on how she would like to write a paper about why grass grows. With the mission completed, she went downstairs.

Louise enjoyed her mother's favorite radio show, "The Major Bowes Amateur Hour," kissed her mother good night, and went to her bedroom. As she entered her room her eyes focused on the desk, where she was hoping and expecting a miraculous event would take place overnight. She stood over the trio of components needed for the experiment, closed her eyes, and once again thought about how much she would like to write a paper about what causes grass to grow. Satisfied all preparations were in place, she took out *Emily of New Moon* from her small bookcase, pulled her bedcover down, fluffed her pillow, and got into bed to take her thoughts elsewhere.

The first glint of sun squinted through the blinds on Louise's bedroom window at 6:25 a.m., and Louise was already wide awake to receive it. She threw off her bedcover, pushed away several strands of hair from her eyes, and swung her legs off the bed and onto the chilly floor. She took a halting breath and hastily took the ten steps to reach her desk. She could feel her heart pounding in her chest as she peered down at the paper in front of her. Her lips quivered and her hands shook as she turned on her lamp. Tentatively sitting as her desk, Louise slowly read the new words on the paper.

Louise started to run into her mother's room but instead, sat back in the chair and reread the writing.

What Makes Grass Grow

Grass grows at different times during the year. There are three primary things that help to make grass grow: the proper temperature, the amount of sunshine it receives, and the amount of moisture or rain it receives.

In New York City, cold temperatures and the snow in the winter will make the grass disappear, and the grass will not start to grow again until spring, when the weather warms up again. Temperature starts to rise into the sixties in April, which is ideal temperature for the grass to grow. Also, in April there is usually a good amount of rain, which is very helpful for the growth of grass. Too much rain is not good for the grass as too much rain can wash away the nutrients that grass requires to grow healthy.

The sunshine is also very important to the growth of grass. Sunshine is very important because it is a part of photosynthesis. In a way, photosynthesis helps create the energy that grass needs to grow.

Too much heat is actually bad for grass and will make the grass stop growing and turn brown instead of green.

In order for grass to grow it requires the perfect formula of warm temperatures, rain, and sun.

For good measure, Louise read the writing a third time, and then took it into the bathroom with her to brush her teeth. She wasn't certain her mother was awake yet as she still hadn't heard movement from her room. Louise paced a bit in the small bathroom and began to sing, "*Frère Jacques, frère Jacques, dormez vous, dormez vous, sonnez les matines, sonnez les matines...*"

She heard slippered footsteps as the bathroom door opened and Ann said to her daughter, "Good morning, young lady. I'm glad you are in such a good mood. What a beautiful way for me to wake up, with a lovely concert. Singing, and in such a loud voice, you must really be ready to start your day."

"I'm sorry, Mom. I didn't mean to wake you. Well, sorry, I did. I have something to show you."

Ann laughed as Louise grabbed her hand, half leading and half pulling her into Louise's room.

"Better yet, Mom, you go to your room, and I'll bring what I have to show you to you."

Louise returned to her mother's room to find her sitting on the edge of her bed brushing her hair while looking into a handheld mirror. Louise sat on the bed next to her mom and gently took the hairbrush from her and began brushing her mother's long brown hair.

"Mom, I know you still think I may have written the magic essays but I now have proof that I didn't do it," Louise said as she handed her mother the composition. "The paper wrote itself overnight. Last night I set up an experiment to figure out this mystery, and I now have the answer. It makes no sense and I completely realize it's impossible to believe, but I'm certain what's responsible for the writing. I'm not going to tell you now; it will be a surprise. I've invited Sarah to sleep over tonight. Oh, I'm sorry, I forgot to ask, is that okay with you?"

"Of course it is, dear."

"Tonight, I'm going to set up the experiment and prove to you and Sarah how the writing is being done."

Ann smiled and said, "That sounds like a great plan. Let's have breakfast, and then we'll go to Synagogue. I would like to say Kaddish."

><

Louise, Ann and Sarah collectively finished cleaning the dinner dishes and returned to their seats for tea and the special dessert Sarah had brought over, rugelach.

Louise positioned a poppy-seed-filled pastry next to an

apricot-jelly-filled pastry on a plate in front of her, then looking intently at her mother and her best friend, announced, "I know you both have had doubts about what I've told you about the magically appearing writing. I know you both trust me but kind of doubt that the writing somehow appears without me writing it. You probably thought that I do it in my sleep. It made no sense to me either. I kept thinking about it and thinking about it, and I've figured out what is causing the writing to occur. I know what I've discovered will seem impossible, but I'm pretty sure I can prove to both of you how it happens."

Ann put her hand on her daughter's hand and said, "It's okay dear, I believe you, and I'm sure Sarah does too."

"That's right, Mrs. Weinstein, I definitely believe Louise."

Louise took a deep breath to calm the mounting feeling of frustration. "I still want to prove to you both what is responsible for the writing. It's really, really important to me that you not only believe me, but see it for yourselves."

Ann squeezed Louise's hand, smiled, and announced, "We would love to see what you have to show us."

Ann and Sarah followed a determined-looking Louise into her room. They stopped at the entrance as Louise announced, "Please look at my room now and I'll explain what I'm going to do. Please don't touch anything. I want everything to be perfect for the experiment."

Ann suppressed a laugh and said with a stoic face, "Tell us what we should do."

"Mom, I'd like you to sleep in my bed tonight and please let Sarah and me sleep in your bed, if that's okay with you."

"Hmm, if it's only for one night, and it's an important part of the experiment, then it's fine with me."

"Thanks, Mom. Now let me show you what I'm going to do."

Louise reached for a couple of pages of writing paper and put them down on her desk. She was not sure how much paper to put down, but she figured if the dime needed a second page to write on, it would be available. As Ann and Sarah both intently watched, Louise took a pen from the side of the desk and placed it on the paper. Finally, she reached into the pocket of her jumper and took out her special dime. She carefully placed the dime next to the pen and exclaimed, "We're all set. Oh, wait—what should the magic writing be about? I need to think about a topic and then concentrate."

They looked at each other. "Well," Sarah proposed, "how about our homework assignment? We're supposed to pick from one of the three explorers we have been discussing in class and write a report on him. Either Columbus, Ponce De León or Magellan."

Louise grinned from ear to ear and said, "Perfect. I'll focus on Ponce De León. Most of the kids will probably pick Christopher Columbus anyway."

"Mrs. Cohen said we have to make certain to include biographical information, and it should be one page long." Sarah laughed and remarked, "Hey, if a report is magically written, maybe this includes a bibliography."

"Absolutely, but now I have to concentrate. I have to stand over the paper and think about the writing topic."

As the three walked out of the room, Ann asked, "Louise, why do you need me to sleep in your room?"

"If Sarah and I sleep in your room, and you sleep in ours, you will know for certain that I didn't write anything unless I snuck back into my room in the middle of the night."

"Dear, I completely and totally trust you. Besides, why do you believe the writing can only take place in your room? Maybe it would work if you set up your experiment in my room or any other room in the apartment?"

Louise's lower lip enveloped her upper one as she thought about what her mother had just said. "You're right, perhaps it would work in any room. I'll set it up in your bedroom, and I'll go into your room before Sarah and I go to sleep to think about the Ponce De León."

Normally an excellent Parcheesi player, Louise lost all seven games played that evening, nor did she seem to even care. Her mind was on a sailing vessel somewhere over the Atlantic Ocean.

At 7:00 a.m. the following morning, two doors simultaneously flew open in the Weinstein apartment. Ann and the girls narrowly averted a collision with some deft pirouettes. The eldest of the three had a piece of paper in her right hand with writing on it: a one-page paper about Ponce de León, to be precise. It included biographical information.

Ponce De León

Juan Ponce de León was an explorer who not only discovered Florida but he also named it. He actually called it La Florida but in English it became just Florida.

Ponce de León was born in Spain in 1474. His family was wealthy when he grew up, and he was a member of the Spanish military as a teenager. He first came to the land we now know as The United States of America in 1493 with Christopher Columbus. Columbus had discovered America in 1492.

Ponce de León was so good at his job in the military that in 1508 he was sent to Puerto Rico where he became its first Governor in 1509. He was so valuable to King Ferdinand of Spain that it was decided he would be most valuable in exploring other parts of the world for Spain.

So in 1513, Ponce de León was put in charge of his own exploration ship and he went out searching for the Fountain of Youth. People at that time thought there was a magical stream called the Fountain of Youth, and that anyone who drank from it became young again. Ponce de León did not find the Fountain of Youth but he did find Florida!

When Ponce de León went back to Spain he was so famous and popular that the King knighted him!

In 1521 Ponce de León went back to La Florida to try and help the local people, but they did want any help so a big fight took place. Ponce de León was very seriously hurt in the fight and he ended up dying in 1521 when he was 46 years old.

Chapter 35

Julie reached over with a paper napkin to wipe my cheek, coming away with a sizable chocolate stain. She had brought over absolutely delicious chocolate-banana muffins. I devoured three, washing them down with a large glass of milk, then brought our dishes to the kitchen sink. We then settled back on the couch, Julie with a coffee mug in hand, and both of us prepared for what the laptop screen had to tell us. However, my nerves got the better of me and I hurriedly headed to the bathroom to unload my bladder.

Julie blurted, "There's more writing! Zach, come here right away. I don't want to start without you," abruptly aborting my bathroom diversion. Julie practically sat on top of me. "This is so cool! Let's get to reading."

We read the latest installment in Louise's life twice before discussing the content. For me, the biggest revelation was that there were three people in 1934 aware of the dime's magical ability, but before I could say anything, Julie offered her thoughts. "For an 11-year-old, Louise's plan to understand how the coin operated was mature and methodical. You must give her a lot of credit. It's strange how the dime works differently for you and for Louise. For you it's more historical and biographical, while for Louise the writing seems to transcribe her own thoughts and style."

"Yup, there's a lot we don't understand about how or why it works."

A preoccupation of mine was the three people aware of the magic coin's powers. What did they do with that knowledge? What happened to them? There clearly was never any disclosure or publicity about it. But the biggest question was, What should we be doing now?

We both sat in quiet contemplation a while. Finally, I said, "The other real-life issue I've got to face is finances. I've got to figure out what

I'm going to do to earn some money. I probably resigned my job before thoroughly thinking things through. My family has always said I'm a bit of a dreamer and wouldn't amount to anything until I rely on hard work and dismiss lofty aspirations. Unfortunately, they may have been right."

Julie moved right next to me again. I really liked her but she clearly had issues respecting other people's space. She took a hold of my hand, looked me straight in the eyes, and said, "We will figure this out together."

Julie's message of support meant a lot to me, though it would have been just as effective delivered from a distance away. She suggested we go for a walk through the park to talk things out, so we decided to meet in front of our building in 15 minutes.

Julie was already waiting for me as she was busily texting away on the sidewalk.

"Work related?" I asked.

"Yup, just trying to rearrange my schedule a bit."

We headed east, and shortly Astoria Park came into view. The feel of the grass under my feet after the concrete was welcoming as I wondered if more trips to the park were in my future. Julie pointed out a sign, partially hidden behind branches of a tree, for a trail that we wordlessly followed to the outset of a path. What I thought was going to be an effortless trek through the woods was about to turn into an endurance event.

Every few minutes I looked over at Julie, who smiled and gave off an aura of freshness and contentment. Though the weather was beginning to cool a bit, the sun was bright in the cloudless sky. Sweat dripped down my face as I periodically pried my flannel shirt away from my body as I wondered why Julie appeared freshly showered without a hair out of place.

I've never spent too much time in Astoria Park, but a lot of people certainly seemed to like it. Couples were still hitting balls on the tennis courts, though the large pool was empty. As we came to an arrow indicating two options to proceed, Julie took my hand as we veered to the right. "This one is my favorite trail. It's where I go to really think about things."

People have said New York City parks can be dangerous, and unfortunately, we were about to experience it firsthand. We were leisurely walking on the path, taking in the fallen leaves of varied green, yellow, orange and brown above us, when out of nowhere a woman put our lives into heart-stopping jeopardy.

I felt a trembling underfoot, quickly looked behind me, and saw a woman doing an auto racer impersonation with a Ferrari disguised as a baby stroller barreling down on us. She never uttered a word of warning or caution, and if it had not been for my keen sixth sense, we might have spent the rest of the afternoon in the emergency room. At the last moment, I pulled Julie with me off the path, and we tumbled onto the grass, Julie heavily landing on top of me.

Concern came over me after a little while as Julie had not gotten off me. She felt as if her whole body had relaxed into a position of comfort—perhaps she was unconscious?

"Are you okay?" I nervously asked.

Breathlessly she responded, "I'm fine."

My pounding heart and labored breathing lasted for several minutes. Then we dusted ourselves off and were able to resume our walk. We continued walking until Julie stopped at the side of the path and stared at a cluster of trees. My eyes followed the trajectory of her gaze, landing on what had caught Julie's attention. "Wow," I exclaimed. A beautiful bird with an orange body and a black head sat perched on a branch about fifteen feet above us.

"You'd never expect to see an oriole in a city park, would you?" she said. Julie seemed to be daydreaming. After another minute or two had passed, she told me in a voice huskier than her usual one, "You know, I was almost engaged to be married a couple of years ago. He was an accountant and a really nice guy, but he had insisted that once married we should live with his widowed mother. I knew I didn't want to start off married life living like that. After all, up to that time, the most instrumental woman in Gary's life was his mother, and I didn't want to compete with her. Plus, she wasn't a particularly nice person, and the idea of seeing her day in and day out was too much for me. She was always critical of everything I did in a passive-aggressive way."

"I'll never forget the first time I made dinner for Gary and his mother. I was so nervous and wanted to make sure everything was perfect to impress her. As Gary and his mom were leaving, she whispered to say the dinner was very nice, but the chicken could have used a bit more salt. I cried myself to sleep that night. It wasn't so much that she was critical of my cooking, but that I knew then that I couldn't spend the rest of my life with a man whose mother was such a bitch and still played such an important role in his life."

I smiled and said, "If I ever get married, the last person I would want to include in my domicile would be my mother."

She smiled even more broadly at my comment and asked, "Have you ever been close to being married?"

"I guess I've always been independent, and to tell you the truth, a bit of a loner. The idea of sharing my life and my personal space with someone has always intimidated me. I've probably rationalized it a bit by thinking that until my career took off, or until my first novel got published, I was not ready for a real relationship. That's the long answer to your question. The short answer is no."

Julie was quiet for a while as she appeared to be deep in thought, which was a good thing because it gave me a chance to catch my breath. I've always found it easier to walk without talking and talk without walking. However, the tranquility didn't last long; Julie began to pepper me with questions.

"If you met the right person, do you think you'd be able to share your life? Don't you feel if you had a partner, you might have the support needed to help you reach your career goals? Privacy is important to everyone, but can't you still be in a relationship while respecting each other's space?"

I laughed a bit at the last question as it came from someone who would be comfortable standing in a phone booth with someone else.

Finally, she asked, "Don't you ever get lonely?"

That one I had to think about.

An hour and a half later I collapsed on my sofa while Julie served us both iced tea from my refrigerator. Observing the energy Julie still possessed after our grueling, almost two-mile walk had me thinking I probably needed to be in better shape. Exhaustion aside, I had enjoyed every part of the adventure, even the intense discussions. They certainly inspired some self-reflection and soul-searching.

Probably the best part of our time together was that Julie was able to get me a remote interview for the next day with her boss to become an SAT English tutor. She said that with my experience writing and editing, the company would likely be able to charge $500 an hour for my time. Of course, I would only get a portion of the fee, but if I was able to tutor for even 10 hours a week, I'd be able to pay my bills while continuing to work on my book. As a further bonus, I'd have the necessary time to investigate Louise Weinstein. Best of all, I wouldn't need to ask Roger for a loan.

Julie had some work of her own to do but promised to return that evening with dinner. She said she had a great bottle of wine at her house that she was dying to try and she had a recipe it would go with perfectly. She noticed how achy I was from the long trek we had, and even offered to give me a massage after dinner, but I told her a hot shower would do the trick. She certainly was considerate.

I was getting used to Julie's company, and I had to admit I was developing some amorous thoughts about her. The problem was I had no idea if she had similar feelings about me. I always found women so difficult to read.

><

We had an unbelievable meal that night. Julie made a stir-fried steak with sautéed vegetables that was amazing. I don't think I've ever eaten a steak without a baked potato and sour cream before. This meal certainly expanded my epicurean horizon.

I'm not much of a wine drinker, but I knew that if Julie needed someone to share an excellent bottle of wine with her, I could give it a shot. That night was a night of firsts for me.

Admittedly I'm not a wine connoisseur. One type of wine is the same as another to me. I find it hard to differentiate between wines, unless of course it's a red wine compared to a white one, which is more of a visual thing for me. This wine was a Bordeaux, a 2019 Château Laroque, to be precise. Julie was so excited about the bottle I even played along with the whole pretension thing. I watched as she removed the cork with a corkscrew. Then she set it on the table to allow it to—in her words—"breathe." After about five minutes, she poured a couple of drops into each of our wine glasses. She had to go home to get two more glasses as apparently my everyday glasses were not suitable for a quality wine.

I watched as she gave her glass a little shake, so I did the same with mine. My only apparent error was downing the one ounce of wine in my glass while Julie took a small sip and then looked as if she was gargling the liquid. Julie didn't say anything, but the look in her eyes was the same one my mother used to give me when she thought I had done something wrong, so I was quite accustomed to those looks.

To top everything off, Julie had baked delicious oatmeal cookies with cranberries, which we ate while she gave me some tips on what to say and what not to say during the interview with her boss.

"I just want to warn you that Justin Cowley, who is the owner of the company, will be the one interviewing you. He's a good guy, but he does have a rather healthy ego. It's important that you support his opinion that he is an expert in all areas of knowledge and tutoring. Even if you think he is wrong about something, or you think you know more than him, don't give him that impression."

"Of course," I said, thoughtfully. "However, we both know that unless Justin has a decade's worth of experience writing and editing, I'm fairly certain I know more than him about crafting an essay. But I'll keep it to myself. I'll portray enough of my ability to get the job but keep a lot of my expertise in check so as not to intimidate him."

Julie appeared to grimace slightly. "Right," she said.

After dinner and the job-preparation discussion, we focused on what was undoubtedly the most important thing in our lives at that time—and potentially for a very long time. I suggested we move to the couch as I wanted us both to be as relaxed and comfortable as possible in preparation for what we would be doing for the next couple of hours.

Julie had orchestrated a magnificent meal, but the next segment of our night was my domain, and I wanted to take charge right away. It was funny—Julie sat on the couch and had this look on her face that seemed to anticipate what she wanted me to do. Hopefully I was up to the task and didn't disappoint.

First, I asked if she was comfortable, and she responded with a sheepish smile. I then reached behind her neck to a side table that had a pad and pen on it while she closed her eyes. When her eyes were open, I could tell I had surprised her. The laptop was open to Louise's last event, and a pen and pad were at the ready for note taking and planning!

We planned and plotted until 10 p.m., at which point I told Julie I was tired and needed to get a good night's sleep in preparation for my interview the next day. Julie looked disappointed—but I understood: we both wanted to spend more time strategizing our approach to the mystery of Louise Weinstein. I suggested we meet up the next evening to finalize our approach and discuss how my interview went—I'd take care of dinner. Julie arched her eyebrows and gave me a look of confusion. Her lips moved as she was about to say something but then stopped. She repeated the process, then said, "Sorry, but I have to wash my hair tomorrow night."

I watched as she abruptly left a minute later without saying good night. What strange creatures women are. How long does it take to wash your hair?

><

Try as I might, I could not think of what I did to upset Julie. Right after my interview the next day, I sent her a text telling her that I thought it had gone well and that Justin was going to let me know within a couple of days. I thanked her for setting it up, asked if she was still washing her hair that evening, and then I suggested the following night if she still couldn't make it that evening. She responded, "My pleasure. I hope you get the job. Pretty busy, perhaps another time."

Justin called and hired me the next day, asking for my availability and saying he would schedule tutoring sessions for me. Next came an email with a link to a two-hour video outlining "the Justin Cowley tutoring approach" for SAT verbal prep. Outrageously, he required me to watch the video and answer a subsequent quiz before final approval to tutor my first student.

Wanting paid employment as soon as possible, I watched the video and passed the quiz easily. Honestly, I had about thirty suggestions to improve the Justin Cowley approach, which I would share them with him once I got to know him better.

Pleased I had my employment plans in order, I was able to turn my attention to my magic dime and what was going on with Julie. I realized I needed and wanted Julie's help with the dime, and the fact was, I enjoyed her company. I figured I needed to first focus on making things right with her. The mystery was, why was she upset with me?

As my knowledge of women was on par with my knowledge of nuclear physics, I knew I needed some help to figure out what to do about Julie. As much as I didn't want to, I knew the one person who was an expert when it came to the female mind was Roger.

I texted Roger, explaining in detail my latest interactions with Julie. I mentioned we shared a special interest, without specifying the magic dime. I told him how she arranged a perfect job for me, which allowed me freedom to continue working on my special project. I even shared with him about how easy it was being with her. I received this response from my brother:

"Thanks for reaching out. Sounds like you found someone good for you, and this is an easy fix. Gifts are the answer. You should have already given her two presents. Probably flowers for the first time you banged her, and maybe a bottle of good wine when you got the job. You said she likes wine. Keep me posted." Aside from my brother's presumptuous attitude and his crass language, Roger's advice made sense. Julie was the one who got me the job—of course I needed to thank her. I couldn't believe I had been that thoughtless and insensitive. As far as Roger's other assertion, how was I to know if Julie even thought of me that way? Sure, we kissed a couple of times, but the last thing I wanted to do was to scare her away. I decided I would take things one step at a time and begin with thanking her for the job referral.

As I was finishing up my fourth slice of sausage pizza, my phone pinged and alerted me to a text message from Julie. In my haste in reaching for the phone, I dripped red-tinged oil down my shirt. Dabbing at my shirt with an already oily napkin, I opened my messaging app, expecting an effusive thank you for the flower arrangement I had left outside Julie's door a couple of hours earlier. I had checked in vain for a local flower shop, but the only place I could find that sold flowers was the Korean market where I usually bought my beer. The flowers looked good and even came with a packet of vitamins to put in the vase water. Who knew that flowers needed vitamins?

Julie's message did nothing to put my mind at ease, and instead led to my greater confusion.

"Thanks very much for the flowers. It was totally unnecessary as it's a pleasure to help someone you care for. I've attached a link you might find interesting."

Curious what Julie sent me, I clicked the link, "Mates for Life," and immediately saw two seahorses bobbing around on the screen with one nuzzling the other. Assuming their purpose was as a cute introduction to the video, I raised the volume so as not to miss anything. The narrator stated that sea horses typically had one mate for life. Next up was a video of wolves, penguins, beavers, barn owls, and gibbons frolicking and playing in their habitats.

I was about to send back a response to Julie with a series of question marks when I realized I had misread her in the past and didn't want any further misunderstanding. Perhaps she was trying to share her interest in natural science or zoology? Maybe this was her way of suggesting that our friendship was intact we should plan a trip to the Bronx Zoo?

Not sure what to do, I sent a message to Roger.

"Roger, thanks again for the advice. I bought Julie flowers and left them by her door with a thank you card for helping me get the job. I got this text back a few minutes ago. What the hell is she talking about? How should I respond?"

I received the following response within two minutes: "I can't believe we have the same parents. The woman likes you. There is no mystery here. She wants you to commit."

Was it possible that Roger was right? Did this smart, attractive woman really like me romantically? I wanted to think about my next step and not rush into anything, so I worked on my novel a bit before calling it a night. The last thing I did prior to going to sleep was place the life-altering dime on the closed laptop.

When I woke up the next morning, I contemplated whether the right move was to check for any new writing myself or invite Julie to join me. I'm glad curiosity got the better of me as this is what was I read.

Hi Julie—

I've been such an idiot. The time we have spent together has been unbelievable, and I don't want to jeopardize anything. I should have made it clear how I feel about you, but I just didn't understand how someone as smart, pretty and talented as you would feel similarly about me.

How about we drive to The Bronx Zoo this weekend? I'd love to see pairs of owls, gibbons, and wolves with my own perfect pairing?

Zach

Wide-eyed, I sat and stared at the screen trying to get my thoughts together. I was stunned that the coin understood and had written on my behalf words that I couldn't express on my own. The coin revealed my inner thoughts and what I should have said to Julie all along.

I copied the message verbatim and sent it to Julie. Then I deleted the writing from my laptop. Strange, I was beginning to think differently and contemplate things more strategically.

Julie's response, short and simple:

I'd love that

Things were coming together. I had the ideal job, which allowed me sufficient time to work on my novel while investigating the historical facts presented by my magical dime. Most importantly, I now had someone I really liked to spend time with—remarkably, someone who seemed to genuinely like me. I guess I didn't want to admit it, but I did get lonely at times. It's true, I had always preferred being by myself, but that was probably because most people didn't really want to spend too much time with me. Finding someone I enjoyed being with, and who enjoyed my company, made me feel something new: true happiness.

Julie and I went out to restaurants, museums, and especially to the Bronx Zoo. We even went dancing at a club one night. It took quite a lot of pleading for Julie to get me onto the dance floor, but once I got loosened up I think I wasn't too bad. Of course, the girl dancing next to me whose foot I inadvertently stepped on wasn't particularly thrilled, and neither was her hulking boyfriend, but once I bought them drinks to apologize, everything was okay. However, of all the things we were doing, our biggest adventure was still on the horizon.

Chapter 36

We sat in a local Indian restaurant that Julie said she had been dying to try for a while. Indian food was not my first choice, but I read somewhere that one of the keys to a successful relationship is leaving your comfort zone and sharing the interests and choices of your significant other.

I sat in contentment in a plush red chair as I gazed at the rich fabrics of orange and yellow hanging around us. Lights, seemingly encased in paper-mâché, were dangling down from the ceiling. In contrast to my mellow mood, Julie seemed quite animated. As she studied the menu, she exclaimed, "There are so many things I want to try. I'm not sure what to have. What would you like?"

Trying to be as supportive as possible, I offered, "Honestly, whatever you would like. But at least one dish with beef, chicken, or pork. Otherwise, I'm good." I smiled. I was pleased with my new cooperative self. I had become a more balanced person—someone able to put aside his own preferences for someone he cared about.

Julie's eyebrows rose a bit and a somewhat bemused look overtook her. She haltingly replied, "Beef isn't really a part of the Indian diet."

"No problem. Either chicken or pork would be great," I cooperatively offered.

"Zach, I'm fairly certain I told you this was a vegetarian restaurant. There's no meat or poultry on the menu."

"You were being serious? I thought you were just joking."

I noticed a slight cracking in her voice as she said, "If you prefer, we could go somewhere else."

There are times in a man's life when he must make a choice, a choice that can greatly impact his future. The old Zach would have told this lovely woman that yes, he preferred that they get up and leave the vegetarian restaurant and instead go to the most welcoming looking burger place next door. However, sitting in that restaurant on that autumn evening, I fought my natural instincts and instead said, "Definitely not. You pick whatever you think we should eat, and I'm sure I'll love it."

I watched as Julie placed the menu on her plate, stood up from her chair, and walked around the table to hover over me. Before I could react to her once again invading my personal space, she leaned down and gave me the most intense and passionate kiss on the mouth! As her lips locked onto mine, I heard applause from the diners at the tables to the left and right of us. I guess I was learning to say the right thing.

Over chana masala, vegetable biryani, basmati rice, dal chawal, rajma, and hara bhara kebab (whoever heard of a kebab without meat?), we discussed our impending search for what became of Louise Weinstein and the journey of the otherworldly dime. The meal was somewhat tasty but would have been much improved if it had included portions of poultry, cow, pig, or lamb. The three glasses of mango lassi hit the spot, at least satisfying my sweet tooth. I also successfully secured a commitment from Julie that the following week we would be going to one of my favorite restaurants, "Meet Meat."

We started our planning by reviewing what we knew about Louise Weinstein's life. Her parents were Ann and Sam Weinstein, and she had lived in Brooklyn. We knew Louise's birth date was April 24, 1923, and were fairly certain she was born in New York City. With these facts in our possession, and a few hours spent in the library reviewing census records, we would be able to fill in the blanks. With sites like 23andMe and Ancestry.com available, there were additional resources to help us with our quest. While Julie looked somewhat mesmerized watching me eat a plateful of gulab jamun, she asked crucial questions. "What are we trying to accomplish? What do we expect to achieve?"

The last of my sweet fried balls of dough in honey slid down my throat like a softball through a garden hose. "I think we need to prioritize figuring out what impact the coin had on Louise's life. How did she use it, if she used it at all?"

"What's your Monday schedule like? I'm teaching in the morning, and afterwards, if it's good for you, we can start our search on a Brooklyn genealogy site."

"I'm pretty busy until 4, but afterwards I'm good."

As we walked home, there was a chill in the air. Julie placed her hands into her pockets, but I plucked one out and held it in mine. We continued home that way, stopping only briefly for me to remove a scarf from my pocket, which I gently placed around Julie's neck. We decided we would spend the night in her apartment. The need for a sleeping bag that night never came up.

While Julie was preparing breakfast Sunday morning, I went to my apartment to set up for what was hopefully a final coin update prior to our scheduled Monday afternoon research center visit. I set my closed laptop on the table and placed the dime on top of it. Because of my recent successful experience with the apology letter penned to Julie, I thought long and hard about my wish to learn as much as possible about the weeks and months after Louise, Ann and Sarah learned the truth about the writing.

My stomach began to rumble as soon as I opened my apartment door for the short walk to Julie's. The smell of sausage made my mouth water as I increased my pace down the hall. Julie let me in wearing an oversized shirt that said, "I'm a Nerd and Proud of It" over a π symbol. In the kitchen she resumed flipping pancakes with a spatula. She gave me a big smile and asked, "Would you mind pouring two glasses of orange juice?"

I opened the door to the fridge, took out the carton and began pouring. "The coin is in position. By tomorrow we should have a substantial amount of additional information to read regarding what has taken place with Louise."

I sat down at the table, and Julie placed a plate of fluffy pancakes and grilled sausage patties in front of me. I inhaled the aromatic feast, then attacked it with my fork. Not wanting to appear ungrateful, I gently asked, "Do you happen to have any syrup?"

She brought organic Vermont maple syrup.

"Wow." I took the small glass jar and poured a good amount over my breakfast. It came out faster than expected, much waterier than normal syrup. The color was too light, not sweet enough, and frankly, inferior to my syrup. I briefly contemplated getting the Log Cabin from my apartment and educating Julie, but a little voice in my head counseled me otherwise.

The pancakes were great, and the sausage was as good as I have ever had. I had to once again compliment Julie on her culinary skill. "This breakfast is amazing. What type of pancakes are these?"

"Oh, thanks. They're oat and banana pancakes. It's a recipe I've used for a while. Do you like the sausage too?"

"I love the sausage. I've got to tell you, this is the best breakfast sausage I've ever had. Where did you get it?"

Julie giggled. "It's actually Impossible Sausage."

I guess she could see the lack of comprehension on my face so she quickly followed up, "It's not made of meat. It's plant-based, made from soy products."

"You're kidding me, that's not possible. It tastes much too good to not be meatless."

The giggle turned into a laugh as she said, "That's why it is called Impossible Sausage. Not only does it taste like real sausage, it's actually not bad for you."

After breakfast, we headed to the subway to catch the 7 train to Grand Central Station with the New York Public Library as our destination. We figured we would start our research at an in-person resource and make a day of it.

New York has many libraries throughout the five boroughs, but the one truly known as The New York City Library is located on Fifth Avenue from 40th to 42nd street.

We navigated our way to the massive structure around clusters of people sitting indiscriminately on the stairs. Many of them were eating lunch, and one couple was sharing what looked like a warm salted pretzel with mustard. My stomach growled in response.

I had never been to the New York Public Library, and my first impression blew me away. The breathtaking marble facade with massive pillars and imposing stone lions adorning the entrance, was both intimidating and inviting.

"So sorry," I mumbled to an elderly man as I collided into him, distracted and mesmerized by my surroundings. I vaguely heard Julie calling my name as I meandered, staring at the library's central lobby ceiling. Julie, doing her best to ground me, grabbed my hand, led me to an information desk, where she asked the woman, "Would you please direct us to the genealogy section?"

The woman looked up to reply, "I'm so sorry, we close the genealogy room on Sundays. However, it's open every other day. I recommend making an appointment before you come. You can do so online."

The word "closed" caught my attention, and I somewhat ineffectually asked, "Are you sure we can't go in today?"

"Quite sure," was the curt response.

Julie grabbed my hand and said, "Look, you haven't been here before, and it's really a great place to explore. For someone who loves books and writing so much, you won't find a better place. Let's look around."

———

Once again, Julie was right. Though we didn't make any headway into our Louise research, we had an amazing day visiting the most magnificent library I ever stepped foot in. We saw ancient maps from around the world and myriad volumes of books. The library's architecture was intense, and the aura within the study rooms was ideal for a writer of my caliber.

Walking back to the subway, Julie told me that *Breakfast at Tiffany's* filmed several scenes in the NYPL, but that information seemed useless. She also told me that the library appeared in *Sex in the City* episodes, which interested me even less. A minute later Julie added, "Did you know that they filmed parts of *Ghostbusters* there too?"

"Really! Why didn't you tell me when we were there? Do you know what part, which scenes were in the movie?"

"I'm not certain but the lions in front were definitely part of the film. They're kind of iconic."

We picked up dinner from the Greek place in our building and brought it up to my apartment. A large souvlaki platter and two pieces of baklava for me, and a medium Greek salad for Julie. We agreed to use restraint and not check on the dime writing's progress until after dinner. When we cleared the table, Julie pointed out a large tzatziki stain, so I changed my shirt. We settled in, opened the laptop, and read the next part of Louise's story.

"I can't believe how nervous and excited I am," Julie said. "It's like when waited for the next Harry Potter book to come out."

"Yeah, I heard of people who lined up at bookstores hours in advance waiting for them to open up so they could be certain of getting a copy before it sold out, and they were forced to wait longer for it to be restocked. We are clueless about what to expect, or even if there will be another chapter. We also don't know for certain what the formula is for the writing. Like, if I were to leave the dime on the closed laptop for, say, three days, would there be three times as much writing as if I left it in place for one day?"

"That's a good point. Wait—the screen's up."

We sat in silence as we stared at the screen, and then at one another. The screen was blank.

"Maybe it needed the overnight period," I offered.

Julie countered with, "You said it before—we really do not understand the process at all. Did you do anything differently this time?"

I scoured my mind. "Come to think of it, I may have tried to give the dime a mental message about what I wanted to read about. Perhaps I shouldn't have done that."

"That could be it, but who knows? We are clueless about what is going on. Tonight, before we go to bed, maybe you just place it on top without giving it any subliminal messages?"

I nodded in affirmation while also taking note of her use of the plural pronoun when referring to the bedtime arrangements. As much fun as it would have been to utilize the hands-on resources of the New York Public Library, much of the genealogy information was available online through various websites. Most of the information stored by the New York Public Library was also accessible online, which certainly made things a lot easier. We decided that Monday evening we would begin our search for Louise in earnest. Hopefully by then there would be additional particulars chronicled by the magic dime.

As difficult as it was to wait, I did not open my laptop until Julie arrived back at my apartment Monday at 4:45. We made small talk, asking about each other's tutoring sessions but it was clear we both were anxious to see what, if anything, the coin had transcribed.

What if the dime wouldn't or couldn't write anymore? Nothing about this made sense so it was certainly possible that the stars aligned for a brief period facilitating the writing to take place, and now they weren't. Something somewhere might have changed, like a weather condition or some other paranormal element, and we would never see the magical writing again. I could not believe how nervous I was. Butterflies were running rampant in my stomach as I rubbed my sweating palms on my pants. I could wait no longer, so I said, "Okay, let's check. You turn it on. I don't think I can look."

Julie solemnly reached and pressed the power button on. I looked at the screen and then towards Julie before looking away again to stare at the refrigerator. After a little Julie said, in a voice much calmer than I would have been able to muster, "There is writing."

Chapter 37

Louise carefully removed her old jewelry box from the closet. She fought a losing battle against the long-dried glue, trying to reattach the tiny faux jewels to its top. The box had traveled with her to many homes during the different periods of her life and held countless memories. Through the years, she had frequently looked at and felt the now fraying purple velvet that lined the inside of the container protecting these precious remembrances. She reach inside and took out what was likely the least expensive—but in many ways the most valuable—piece of jewelry she had ever owned. She gently sniffed at the small plastic ring in her hand, trying to sense if any hint of popcorn or caramel from the Cracker Jack box she had gotten it in from all those years ago remained. Her mom would tell her she had gone to five Brooklyn Dodger games with her father, but Louise had always been certain it was six.

Louise had another jewelry box in which she kept her bracelets, earrings, brooches and rings, but this was where she kept a large part of her heart. She had not taken out the most curious and fascinating relic the box contained for almost 50 years. As many times as she had opened the vessel, there was one keepsake she had always left inside. She did a quick calculation and realized it had been 47 years since she put the dime away, not to see the light of day for almost half of a century.

She picked up the little round piece of silver. Her fingers began to tingle with an unnatural surge of energy that caused an indescribable wave of emotion. The strangeness of the feeling it inspired made her want to laugh out loud and sob with grief.

She reached into the box and gently lifted out a yellowed

folded piece of paper. The letter was a lifelong reminder of the most important man in her life for her first 11 years. Her father had been gone now for forty-seven years. He had not seen her graduate college, receive a Masters degree, teach math for thirty years, get married to a wonderful man, have two great children and three grandchildren. The oldest of her grandkids, five-year-old Sam, was named in memory of the father she had lost all those years ago.

Love is an emotion that can be seen and felt in many ways. Reading the letter for what was likely the thousandth time in her life filled her with a warmth that could only be described as intense adoration. The writing contained the perspective of a heartbroken young girl on the saddest day of her life about a man she would never see again. She knew the letter was written from her heart, but she also realized that a bit of magic was instrumental in creating the treasure she now meticulously folded and placed back in the box.

The dime still looked relatively new, in part due to a pact that had been made many years ago—a pact she honored, though so many times through the years, she had been tempted to take out the dime and once again experience its remarkable power.

She thought vividly about the day when she, her mom, her best friend Sarah experienced confirmation that the dime was truly magical. Inexplicably, the coin, somehow, someway, had the ability to put into written words Louise's thoughts and emotions.

Once its true power was acknowledged, her mom had said they needed to speak with Rabbi Alter for guidance. Sarah had joined Louise and her mom in the rabbi's cramped office. The rabbi did not typically meet with women but as Louise's dad had recently passed away, he consented to make a compassionate exception. He appeared to be less than comfortable during the entire meeting, scowling frequently, and he was decidedly condescending. In hindsight, Louise realized it was not just that there were three females in his quarters, but also two of them were children. Perhaps the biggest issue was the purpose of the meeting had to do with the absurd concept of a coin possessing magical powers. All these years later, Louise realized that Rabbi Alter had thought Louise and her mom were two fragile females who, due to their great loss, were suffering from female hysteria.

Louise recalled that the rabbi talked about things that were impossible to understand and how God worked in mysterious ways. He cited miracles that took place in the Bible, including Moses parting the Red Sea and plagues that God had brought down upon oppressors of the Jewish people. Louise recalled Rabbi Alter's dark eyes boring into her own as he said, "There are things we are not expected to ever understand. We must simply accept them as truths beyond our comprehension. There are things that occur that can neither be dismissed nor logically figured out. Dismiss them at your own risk. Under no circumstance should a gift that God blesses you with be used for personal fame or fortune. It would be a terrible insult to *Adonai* to use his gift for something like homework. Never forget what I am telling you now. The magic of a gift from God can bring a great deal of happiness and charity, but it may also bring heartache and problems. For now, you should put the dime away. There may be a time when God will let you know the use He intends for it. However, even then, you would need to be very, very careful." The rabbi then turned to Mrs. Weinstein and said, "Please see to it that Louise puts the gift away and avoids the temptation to take it out."

Sarah, Louise, and her mom walked home feeling a bit intimidated and slightly scared. They each understood that the rabbi's advice had to be observed, and almost unfathomably the three of them never discussed the dime together again.

Louise and Sarah had remained best friends through eighth grade, when Sarah's father received a job opportunity in Los Angeles. The two girls corresponded regularly for a year or two, until the communications became infrequent. Finally, at some point, the two girls who were once inseparable and shared an incomprehensible secret, lost touch with one another. Every so often, Louise wondered if Sarah had a family of her own and if she had spoken of their mystical bond.

As she held the mysterious treasure in her hand again for the first time in years, Louise wondered if she would ever again utilize the special ability of the dime. Of course, she had no idea if the dime was still able to write on her behalf, or frankly if it had ever really created the writings in the first place. It had been such a long time ago, and was such a traumatic and emotional time, it was likely there was a more logical explanation for how the writing appeared. Even if the dime never wrote another word for her, she felt good holding it again, feeling it, and seeing with her own more aged eyes the solemn profile of Mercury in his winged helmet.

Louise was 58 years old and now sadly alone. The love of her life, David Graber, had been killed in a tragic car accident a little over a year earlier. He had been walking back from Synagogue on a rainy Friday night when a driver skidded off the road and onto the walking path into the man Louise Graber expected to grow old with. The driver, a man in his eighties, should not have been driving at night in those conditions.

A heartbreaking irony was that David had been killed observing God's word. He was returning from Sabbath prayers on foot, as driving to and from Synagogue on the Sabbath was forbidden. David had done everything right—why was he taken from her at such a young age? He was a warm and loving husband, a great father and grandfather, and an accomplished and caring dentist. For patients that were unable to pay for his service, he would reduce his fee dramatically, and in many cases not charge them at all. He went to shul every Sabbath, and volunteered his dental service at a group home for wayward youths.

Louise closed her eyes as she visualized her time with David. They had made a wonderful life together. Home for the past twenty years was in Great Neck, Long Island. Their son Philip was now thirty-two years old, a doctor living in Mamaroneck with his wife, Donna, and their two children, five-year-old Sam and three-year-old Rachel. Philip's sister Esther had just turned twenty-nine and lived with her husband, Donald, in Englewood, New Jersey, along with their two-year-old daughter, Molly. Esther had followed in her mom's footsteps, becoming a teacher, teaching fourth grade in the local elementary school, and loving every second of it. Each child and grandchild was a blessing, but Louise was supposed to share it all with the love of her life. All of their dreams for the next chapter of their journey together had been cruelly taken away that horrific Friday night.

After David's death, Philip and Esther had spent a great deal of time with Louise. Esther even suggested Louise move in with her and Donald, saying that she would be the best caregiver Molly could possibly have when they were at work. But Louise felt that a young family, no matter how good the relationship with a parent might be, needed the space to grow on their own. No, she would remain in Great Neck, where she had a beautiful home, friends, and wonderful memories.

Louise recognized she was still a relatively young woman with what should be many more years of life adventures ahead of her. Louise and David had so many plans for when David joined

Louise in retirement. They had discussed traveling extensively abroad, going on a safari, visiting all of the European countries, and experiencing Israel. They were going to take classes together, go to the theater, and dote on their grandchildren endlessly. Most of her friends were married, and though she knew she would be invited to many social events, Louise realized she would far too frequently be a third wheel.

Most unsettling, she knew at some point her friends would attempt to set her up with eligible single men, men who were widowed or divorced. Undoubtedly her friends would mean well, but she knew in her heart that David would always be her one true love. She was certain she wanted to remain without another partner for the rest of her life.

Louise realized she needed to do something meaningful and fulfilling with the rest of her life in David's absence. He would have wanted it that way, and she knew she needed the direction and fulfillment that would come with set goals and achievements. She had discussed various possibilities with Esther and Philip, and the most obvious choice was to be involved doing some sort of charitable work. Fortunately, she was financially comfortable, so earning money was not a necessity. She wanted to devote her time to helping others but also wanted a challenge and intellectual stimulation.

She had spent her professional life helping to develop and nurture young minds, but she also appreciated the wealth of knowledge and experience senior citizens possessed. She decided she wanted to devote quality time to residents of a senior citizen home in order to make a difference in the lives of people approaching the end of their time on this earth.

Louise felt the trickle of warm tears creep down her face as she recalled the last year of her mother's life. Ann Weinstein had been such a good, vibrant and loving woman. Nearing the end of her life her body had begun to fail, but her mind remained as sharp as it had been fifty years earlier. Arthritis and heart disease kept her bedridden during the final months, and Louise treasured the hours she spent simply talking and holding her mother's hand. The remaining time they had together was as much of a treasure for Louise as she was certain it was to her mother. Those days together, laughing, crying, and reminiscing would never be replicated but they would always be a part of her. It broke Louise's heart that her grandchildren, Ann's great-grandchildren, would not remember or ever really know their great-grandmother. Of course, they would never know Louise's father either, who died in the 1930s, but at least a token of remembrance existed describing him, through the loving eyes of his then 11-year-old daughter.

The eldest members of society have so much to share and teach, not only to the younger generations but also to those who follow. Louise felt she also possessed a unique gift that could assist her in chronicling the story of many people: mothers, fathers, grandparents, and great-grandparents who were facing the end of their lives but were still very relevant. She could help them produce everlasting written legacies.

Chapter 38

Louise started working at The North Shore Home in November 1981. Her title was simply Volunteer, and her primary role was to serve as a companion to residents. She would read to the senior citizens, play cards, or watch television with them, but mostly she would talk with them. She would sit in their rooms discussing politics, music trends, recipes, or anything else they might care to discuss. More than anything else, they wanted to reminisce about their pasts, their days of youth and vitality.

Louise volunteered at the home four afternoons a week. The director of the home, an imposingly large man named Ralph Young, met with her on her first day to discuss both Louise's expectations and the goals set for her by the home's administration.

Louise sat in Mr. Young's office and smiled at the irony of a director named Young in an facility that catered exclusively to the old. Mr. Young—and everyone called him Mr. Young—must have been close to six feet, five inches tall and at least 300 pounds. She glanced from the comfort of a cushioned chair at the gold-framed photographs sitting on the rich walnut-colored desk across from her. The first photograph was undoubtedly of Mr. Young's wife, a woman with dark blonde hair, a wholesome face and warm smile who couldn't have been more than half the size of her husband. Positioned in the next framed photo was a handsome portrait of the entire family. In this photo, a slightly hunched Mr. Young, stood behind his wife, with hands on her shoulders, alongside two blond teenage sons. The Youngs, all formally dressed, posed with their dog, were the picture-perfect family.

Mr. Young was on the phone. He mouthed, "I'm sorry—two

minutes" and offered an apologetic raised two fingers.

Louise smiled in response and took in another photo, this one on the wall behind Mr. Young's desk. A caption on the bottom identified the subjects as the 1951 Army football team. Louise figured that Ralph Young had probably been about twenty years old at the time, so he would now be about fifty, which made sense, as his hair and bushy eyebrows had sprinklings of gray. It certainly was not a surprise that he had played football or that he had a military background.

"I'm so sorry, Mrs. Graber, I really had to take that call. It was the daughter of one of our residents, and she is understandably upset that her mother's senility is getting worse."

"Of course, Mr. Young, I completely understand. You have a lovely family."

"Thank you, Mrs. Graber. I'm truly blessed, and I'm so pleased you're here." He stood and filed a folder in a cabinet, then walked around the desk to envelope Louise's hand in a warm handshake.

"I'm very excited to be here. I'm looking forward to getting to know many of your residents."

"That's wonderful to hear. I'd like to discuss what my thoughts are regarding your day-to-day involvement and see if they are acceptable to you."

Louise nodded in response, and Mr. Young returned to his desk chair. "There are a lot of nursing homes, and many have reputations that are less than stellar. The North Shore Home is different for one primary reason: I insist that staff treat our residents with consideration and compassion. I don't tolerate anything bordering on disrespect or indifference towards our residents from our employees, and I expect the same from our volunteers. I believe we have the absolute best staff in this industry, and certainly in the region. That being said, our employees can only do so much. What makes North Shore truly special are the generous volunteers such as you, Mrs. Graber. Our staff members feed, bathe and support our guests as needed, but what most of our residents need more than anything is companionship. That is a gift you can provide."

"Many of the residents here have served in our armed forces defending this country. Others were doctors, nurses, lawyers, and engineers. These people were vital contributors to their communities and to our society. They accomplished great things and in their younger days helped mold and influence others. They used both physical skills and trained minds to make life better for not only themselves and their peers, but also for generations to come. Many of our residents feel forgotten and experience limited daily joy. We do the best we can to provide everyone staying here with activities and social events so they are once again able to feel a part of something. However, my experience tells me what they want more than anything else is to converse with people who are genuinely interested in what they have to say."

Louise remained silent as she absorbed the emotional introduction from Mr. Young. Knowing she made the right decision, Louise asked, "What do you envision me doing on a day-to- day basis?"

Mr. Young sat heavily back in his chair. "Most of our residents have family or friends who actively visit and support them here. Unfortunately, we also have several people here who are alone in the world, with no friends or family to visit them. It would mean so much to those without family in their lives to be able to receive the benefit of companionship. It would be something for them to look forward to and add so much to their time here during their twilight years."

Louise felt the warm flush of satisfaction as she contemplated what Mr. Young was outlining, and responded accordingly, "What you're proposing is exactly what I was hoping for. Selfishly, I couldn't ask for anything that would be more fulfilling. Getting to know the likes, dislikes and achievements of your guests would be a shared experience that I hope would benefit them, and if I could be frank, would benefit me as well."

"I appreciate your enthusiasm, Mrs. Graber. I've already given it some thought, and I've prepared a list of five residents I would appreciate you initially working with and getting to know. I've included their room numbers, ages, and a little bit about each one."

Louise took the paper from Mr. Young to study it. She saw there were the names of three women on it and two men. Mr. Young interrupted her concentration, saying, "My chief administrator, Mrs. Crawford, is looking forward to meeting with you. She's been with us for ten years, and frankly both this place and I would fall apart without her. She'll take you on a tour of our facility and will undoubtedly be an invaluable resource for you. Of course, please feel free to stop by to see me whenever you would like. My door is always open to you."

Louise got up and followed Mr. Young out of his office to another office door about ten yards away with a wooden sign on it that said, "Diane Crawford—Administration Head." Mr. Young knocked on the door twice before opening it, announcing, "Mrs. Crawford, please meet Mrs. Graber, who I believe you spoke with on the phone last week."

A thin middle-aged woman with short, neatly coiffed black hair and glasses came from behind a desk, extended her hand to Louise, and said, "It's a pleasure to meet you in person, Mrs. Graber. I am so pleased you will be joining us."

Louise accepted Mrs. Crawford's hand as she responded, "I'm

really very excited to be here. Mr. Young has made this sound like the perfect place for me."

Mr. Young's smile was a foot wide. "I'll take my leave. I'd only be in the way. Mrs. Graber, you are in great hands with Mrs. Crawford."

Once the door closed behind Mr. Young, Louise turned to Mrs. Crawford and said, "Mr. Young seems like such a caring man."

"Oh, he really is a great person to work for. But please call me Diane. I was never in the military, and I appreciate Mr. Young's formality, but when we aren't in his presence, I'd prefer Diane. Is it okay if I call you Louise?"

"Absolutely. I'd much prefer it."

"Why don't I give you a tour of the facility, and when we're done, I can go over some of the specifics regarding the list of assigned residents I see you holding."

Ninety minutes later Louise and Diane chatted in Diane's office. A mug of black coffee sat in front of Diane while Louise sipped on a glass of Tab with a wedge of lemon.

The past year had been a very difficult one for Louise, but she had the feeling that volunteering at North Shore would go a long way toward advancing the healing process. Diane could not have been more welcoming or kind, and Louise had taken an instant liking to her.

"Now let's take a look at the list Mr. Young gave you," Diane said as she came around the desk with her chair and sat. Louise placed the paper on the desk for both of us to see.

1) Mrs. Arlene Schwartz
Room 202
Age 86

Widowed former elementary school teacher
No children
Prefers to be in her room by herself watching television

2) Mr. Walter Morrison
Room 306
Age 90
Never Married
No children
Owned a dance school
Still has his cognitive skills but daydreams all day and appears melancholy

3) Miss Linda Carmichael
Room 214
Age 79
Worked as a bookkeeper
Never married
No children
Can be argumentative and does not interact well with other residents

4) Mr. Robert Kramer
Room 315
Age 71
Wife left him
Two daughters, both estranged
Worked as a salesman for a hardware supplier
Can be abrasive and threatening to other residents

5) Mrs. Dolores Rotkowski

Room 232
Age 83
Secretary
Recently widowed and lost her son in Vietnam
Cries a great deal and prefers to be left alone

Once both Louise and Diane had reread the list, Diane said, "Mr. Young put a lot of thought into this, and he clearly has a great deal of confidence in you. Ms. Carmichael and Mr. Kramer will certainly be challenging and frankly may be a bit resistant to your involvement at all. However, I definitely believe you'll enjoy spending time with the other three, and I'm certain they will be thrilled to get to know you."

"I'll do my best for all five. Hopefully Miss Carmichael and Mr. Kramer will at least give me a chance. Thanks, Diane, for the tour and giving me so much of your time. I'm excited to start on Monday."

"You'll do great, Louise," Diane said as she stood and walked Louise to the door. "And let's definitely have lunch one day next week. See you Monday."

Chapter 39

Louise was nervous when she woke up on Monday, November 16, 1981, for her first official day at the North Shore Home. She typically rose around 8 a.m. but this morning she found herself awake before 7. She hurried downstairs, started the coffee pot, and dropped two slices of bread into the toaster. Then she dashed back up the stairs to wash up.

Her kids had called the night before to wish her luck with the new endeavor. She wasn't certain why she was so anxious—after all, she was just a volunteer. But she figured nerves could sometimes be a good thing.

She changed her outfit three times, finally settling on a dark blouse with a floral print. In the kitchen, she spread some butter and marmalade on toast and poured herself a cup of hot coffee. A soft thump and sliding sound told her that *The New York Times* had just been lobbed onto her driveway by the delivery boy. The weather forecast was for temperatures in the upper forties with cloudy skies.

Louise absentmindedly stared at an article while taking small bites of a piece of toast. Though her eyes fixed on the print, she realized she had not digested a word. She rinsed a few dishes and left the house.

Louise pulled her silver Honda Accord into the North Shore parking lot and strode towards the entrance. A husky, middle aged man with a crew cut directed Louise to an office where she would receive her official ID card. Ripe with satisfaction, and a healthy dose of nerves, Louise headed to Diane's office for the day's instructions. Diane's slightly ajar office door afforded Louise a glimpse of Diane sitting at her desk writing on a pad.

Louise gently knocked and said, "Good morning."

"Good morning, Louise. You're here bright and early. Couldn't wait to get started?"

Louise smiled and said, "That's the truth. I was too excited to concentrate on anything at home, so I figured the best thing to do was to head right over."

"Well, I'm glad you're here. I see you already have your identification lanyard. If you give me a couple of minutes, I'll introduce you to the residents you've been assigned."

Everywhere Louise looked she sensed the influence of Mr. Young's military background. The eggshell white corridors had an antiseptic smell while the vinyl floors glistened and gleamed.

Walking through the halls with Diane, she got a sense of how difficult it must be to work in such an environment every day. While there were many happy faces eager to greet Diane and engage her in conversation, there were also a lot of vacant stares. In addition to chattering conversations, Louise heard incomprehensible calls and screams. Jarring at first, Louise soon understood that the sounds came from disorientation and not anger or shock.

Diane noted Louise's discomfort and said, "The truth is, you will get used to it. A lot of our residents suffer from senility and varying degrees of dementia. I know it's painful to listen to the yells of anguish and frustration. We do our best to engage them as much as possible and keep them comfortable, but there is only so much we can do. When I first started here, I had years of experience as a nurse, but even that training didn't fully ready me for the intense sadness I've seen here."

Louise clasped her hands and held them thoughtfully to her lips. "I hope I am up to the task."

They reached Room 214, where Miss Carmichael resided.

Diane knocked on the open door and announced, "Miss Carmichael, I would like to introduce you to someone."

A heavyset woman with short silver hair and thick black glasses briefly looked up from the book she was reading as Diane and Louise approached. Louise extended her hand and sweetly said, "Good morning, Miss Carmichael. I'm Louise Graber. It's very nice to meet you."

Louise had heard the term "harumph," but had never actually experienced the response until Miss Carmichael greeted her. That reception followed with, "What, are you a shrink? I don't need a shrink, nor will I speak with one. I'm perfectly sane. I just prefer my own company to that of others. Okay with you?"

"That's perfectly fine with me, and I'm not a shrink. I'm a new volunteer. I was hoping I could get to know you better by spending some time with you. I see you're reading *Sophie's Choice*. I read the book a few weeks ago, and I'd like to come back later to discuss it with you if that's okay."

Miss Carmichael picked up the book to continue reading, which served as her visitor's clue to leave.

In the hallway, a harried young woman with freckles, not much older than twenty, wearing a nurse's uniform approached Diane and breathlessly blurted out, "Mrs. Crawford, I have been looking for you everywhere. Mr. Young would like to see you right away. He sent me to look for you a while ago."

"Ms. O'Brien, you could have used the loudspeaker to page me."

"I'm sorry, I didn't think it would take me so long to find you."

"Okay, I'll be right with you," Diane said before turning to Louise. "I'm so sorry. Would you mind introducing yourself to the other residents? The others will be much more receptive than

Miss Carmichael, I promise. I'll try to catch up with you later on."

"Of course, Di—Mrs. Crawford," Louise said while glancing over at Ms. O'Brien. "You're so busy, and it may even seem a bit less formal if I make my own introduction to the other four. I can report to you later if you would like."

Louise made the remainder of the rounds on her own. Mrs. Rotkowski and Mr. Morrison were both napping, but she was pleased with her initial visits with Mrs. Schwartz and Mr. Kramer. Diane had told her that Mr. Kramer could be difficult, but her first impression was that he was personable, and perhaps a bit flirtatious. She promised Mrs. Schwartz she would be back at 1:30 to spend more time with her, and she told Mr. Kramer she would try to stop by again before she left for the day.

Diane also suggested that when she wasn't with her assigned residents, it would be helpful if Louise would check with the Activities Coordinator, Mrs. Colby, to see if she could assist in the Activities Room. Louise headed down to find Mrs. Colby on the ground floor, where she worked. A man in a wheelchair and his attendant exited the elevator in front of Louise and headed to the Rehabilitation Room, which was next door to the Activities Room. Most of the residents had sessions with physical therapists as part of their weekly schedule, and the elevator was usually congested due to the cumbersome wheelchairs. Louise made note of the stairwell door location as she realized the stairs would likely become her most expeditious way to navigate the home. Louise opened the door to the Activities Room and took a glance around.

Four silver-haired women were playing cards at a table to her far right, while a group of residents, both male and female, sat with vacant stares, watching a black-and-white movie. Five smock-wearing residents sat at a long perpendicular table busying themselves with art supplies. Board games and cards adorned smaller tables throughout the room.

Though she had never met Mrs. Colby, Louise had no difficulty picking her out among the staff members in the room. A raven-haired woman with messy bangs in her eyes was moving rapidly from one station to the next, with a grin etched on her face. She appeared to Louise like a dancer moving gracefully around the room. Louise carefully intercepted Mrs. Colby between a game of Monopoly and a card game to introduce herself.

"So sorry to interrupt you. I'm Louise Graber, a new volunteer here and—"

Before she could finish Mrs. Colby said, "I heard you'd be starting. It's nice to meet you. I'm Nina Colby. If you don't mind following me, it looks like I need to mediate a dispute between Mr. Gross and Mr. Kendrick. Their backgammon games can get testy."

Louise hurriedly followed Mrs. Colby as a red- faced man in a button-down short-sleeved shirt used his cane to propel himself from his chair and yelled at his backgammon opponent. The man in the opposite chair struggled unsuccessfully to rise from his chair and equal the fighting sides.

Mrs. Colby arrived before either combatant could do any harm to the other or to themselves. Replacing her smile with a stern frown, she uttered, "Gentlemen, what is going on here? You two act like children. You claim to be best friends but every day you end up fighting. Mrs. Graber, would you mind sitting here with Mr. Kendrick for a bit while Mr. Gross and I take a walk to the other side of the room?"

"Of course not, Mrs. Colby, it would be my pleasure." Louise assumed the chair vacated by the still huffing and puffing Mr. Gross.

Mr. Kendrick sheepishly looked at Louise and said, "The funny thing is, I was an elementary school principal, and Sidney—that's Mr. Gross—was a psychologist. It's ironic that the staff always reprimand us like a duo of misbehaving boys. I'm sure our old students would love to witness it. By the way, I'm Donald Kendrick."

Louise enjoyed every second of her ensuing conversation with Mr. Kendrick. When Mrs. Colby announced it was time the residents began to get ready for lunch, Louise looked down at her watch to see they had been talking for almost an hour. She was genuinely disappointed her discussion with Mr. Kendrick had to end. He promised he would do his best to stop arguing with Mr. Gross if Louise promised to visit at least once a week, which she quickly did with a warm embrace.

At 5:15 p.m. Louise got into her car with a feeling she had not known since prior to the accident that took David's life. The emptiness that had been growing in her ever since that fateful day had shrunk. Her first day at the North Shore was a healing salve. Meeting new people, many of whom were suffering from similar loss and loneliness, was therapeutic. Enough of this medicine, and her spirit might be fully restored.

Chapter 40

Louise smiled at the elderly man seated on his bed. She suggested they go for a walk, but Mr. Morrison said he was content remaining propped up on the bed.

Mr. Morrison's clear, deep blue eyes mesmerized Louise. Even though his age was 90, his eyes exuded warmth and friendliness. Scanning his 250-square-foot room, Louise took in the requisite hospital bed, nightstand, tray table, and an Ikea-looking metal dresser with four drawers. She then surveyed the countless photographs hanging on the walls, resting on all available spaces, and above the headboard.

Louise's eyes focused on a framed photograph of a young dancer in a white leotard and a light blue top, elevated off the ground with toes pointing down, arms extended skyward. Louise recognized the piercing blue eyes in the photographed man, who exuded graceful exuberance and athleticism.

Mr. Morrison, noticing Louise staring at the photo said, "Yes, that was me. Age can be a terrible thing. Once able to routinely run and jump so naturally, today I can't get from the bed to the bathroom without assistance. Scientists should figure out how to bottle virility for later in life."

"Who are the other people you have on the wall?" Louise continued to scan the photographs.

"Well, I'm in almost all of them." Mr. Morrison turned towards his left and pointed to the one furthest away. "That's me with my staff. I ran a dance school a few miles from here. People would come from all around here to take classes at my school. We had students from Suffolk County, the city, and even a few from Jersey and Connecticut. We had quite a stellar reputation.

Of course, most of it was attributable to my staff. We had a bunch of wonderful and highly accomplished instructors. Many of them were performers at Lincoln Center and other top venues. That photo up there is from 1947. Next to it is a photo of me with my favorite dance partner, Irene Skowron. The two of us performed many times together at The New York City Ballet. We even performed once at the Royal Albert Hall in London, in 1928. Irene passed away about 15 years ago—cancer."

Louise saw a glistening in the old man's eyes. She pointed to the next photo. "And this one?"

Mr. Morrison clear his throat. "That was my best friend, Lionel Rasmussen. He was an amazing dancer, much better than me."

Louise then noticed the gold-framed photograph on the nightstand. The photo was of a man, probably in his late fifties or early sixties. The angular face, though older, was the same as the young male dancer in the previous picture. Mr. Morrison saw the recognition in Louise's eyes as she glanced between the photos, taken decades apart.

"Yes, that is Lionel, my very special friend and roommate for more than 40 years. He died in 1979, and frankly, it's been a struggle ever since. I relied on him for everything. I finally decided a few months ago that it was too hard to live on my own, and that's when I moved here."

As the emotional intensity in the room engulfed Louise, she moved her chair close to the bed and said, "I lost the love of my life recently. My husband, David, died not too long ago, and I'm still trying to adjust. I'm not sure if I ever will. In a way, I too have come here searching for something. I'm looking to give my life a new meaning."

Mr. Morrison then reached out his hand and gave Louise's a

squeeze. Compassion emanated from the bony hand, conveying the intimacy and friendship Louise longed for.

Later that day, Louise spent quality time with both Mrs. Schwartz and Mrs. Rotkowski in addition to checking in again with the cheeky Mr. Kramer. With a wink and a smile, he insisted she promise that she would spend more time with him soon. She decided she would give Miss Carmichael space for the next day or two and attempt to break the ice with her more gradually.

Louise periodically poked at the leftover roast chicken left. She alternated mechanical sips of red wine with bites of the now dry chicken. Her mind kept wandering to the time spent earlier that day with Mr. Morrison, Mrs. Schwartz and Mrs. Rotkowski. They each had experienced so much of life, and now each one had in their own way expressed that their days of productivity were in the past. They all had loved and felt the pain of loss. All three had made a difference in the lives of those around them and now shared similar feelings of loneliness. Louise couldn't imagine how she would be able to survive without her family and friends.

What Mrs. Schwartz had told her that afternoon was a heart-wrenching representation of the feelings of not only Mrs. Rotkowski and Mr. Morrison, but countless people who have reached their senior years: "No one knows that I was once young and truly mattered. I had an impact on hundreds of lives. I would take little children and teach them, care for them, and impart lifelong knowledge to them for eight hours a day, two hundred days a year. Many of my students accomplished great things when they got older, and I'd like to think I was a contributing factor to those successes. They became doctors, lawyers, engineers, and teachers. Hopefully, some of the skills I provided also gave them the platform to become wonderful mothers and fathers later in life.

As a matter of fact, in my career I had the privilege of teaching many children who were the offspring of students I had taught a generation earlier. The parents of these second-generation students came up to me and told me how excited they were that their own children would have a wonderful second-grade year like they experienced. I never had children of my own, but I gave a little of myself to each one of my students. Now it's all in the past, as am I. I'm a distant memory without anyone to care about me or really know who I was or what I contributed."

Mrs. Rotkowski and Mr. Morrison shared similar sentiments. Their productive lives that impacted those around them were long forgotten by the current generation and invisible to future generations.

Louise gulped down the remaining wine in her glass and pushed away the chicken. How she could help preserve the legacies of lonely residents of the North Shore Home? How could she help these warm and wonderful people know that they truly had made an impact?

The realization of what she wanted to do transported her up the stairs and into the room in the house she now considered the den but which was formerly David's office. The leather chair behind the mahogany desk had remained unoccupied since David's passing. She opened the door to the closet, reached for the top shelf, and took down a black composition book. After checking there was no writing in it, she turned off the light and left the room.

"Louise, calm down, just relax." Louise wondered if talking to oneself was a common trait of people living alone. In her bedroom, she sat with the composition book in one hand and the Mercury dime in her other palm, which was now moist with sweat. She stood up and exhaled as she placed the book down gently on her nightstand and placed the dime on top of it. "Louise, you forgot the pen," she admonished herself. She took out a Pilot Precise V7 in blue with rollerball tip and ink-viewing window from her pocketbook and placed it next to the dime. As she was leaving, she said out loud, "Please, just a paragraph or two."

Chapter 41

Louise smiled warmly at Mrs. Schwartz, who returned it with equal sincerity as Louise spoke. "I thought a lot about our conversation yesterday, and it reminded me how great an influence a grade-school teacher has on the young. I'm confident that countless students remember you with great affection. However, you're right, many people just aren't aware of the impact a teacher truly has, not just for a year, but sometimes a lifetime. I'm sure you have quite a story to tell, and I have an idea, a suggestion, if you agree. Why don't we work together on an account, or memoir, of your experiences as an educator? Come to think of it, it doesn't need to be only about your career as a teacher. It can be about any personal experience or thoughts you may want to record."

Mrs. Schwartz took several deep breaths, trying to control her emotions. "That's very generous of you and quite flattering, and something I would love to do. My vision isn't good enough to write anymore. Are you sure you'd be willing to help me with the writing?"

"Of course." The image of the magically written page Louise read a few hours earlier flashed in front of her. It was only two paragraphs long but reading about the importance of helping others, as crafted by the dime, convinced her she was embarking on a path she was destined to follow. "I'll come back to see you later this afternoon, and we can prepare."

Louise made her rounds, spending time with each of her other assigned residents, though her time with Ms. Carmichael didn't go beyond a cursory "Good afternoon." At 4 p.m. Louise returned to Mrs. Schwartz's bedside ready to begin working on their writing. Louise's plan relied on the magical ability of the

1921 Mercury dime. However, if something went wrong with her scheme, she figured she would somehow be able to muddle through on her own.

"I hope you don't mind, Mrs. Schwartz, but I've always been a bit superstitious, and whenever I write, I follow a very specific routine. I've followed this formula since I was in grade school, so I guess old habits are hard to break. I'm going to take notes on a pad, and I would like to place a composition book on your nightstand with a pen and my lucky dime on top of it. I'll leave it that way overnight, if that's okay with you. Tomorrow, I'll transcribe my notes from today into the book for you to proofread and edit."

Mrs. Schwartz smirked. "To this day, I still sprinkle salt over my left shoulder before eating. My husband checked dresser drawers every night to ensure he closed them. We all have our little quirks and idiosyncrasies. Who am I to criticize yours? That sounds like a perfect plan."

Mrs. Schwartz shared highlights from her life while Louise took copious notes. Mrs. Schwartz's face glowed during her reminiscence, which brought a feeling of genuine joy to Louise. Louise glanced at her watch and realized they had been speaking for almost two hours. For residents mobile enough to go to the dining room, dinner was typically served at 5:30 and it was already nearly 6:00.

"Mrs. Schwartz, I'm so sorry, it is almost six. You'll be late for dinner. Would you like me to go with you to the dining room? Better yet, I have an idea. Would you like to have dinner brought to the room, and I'll stay with you till we finish?"

"If you don't mind. I'd love that."

At 7:15, Louise said, "I think we should call it a night. I'll be back to see you tomorrow around 11:30, and afterwards I'll begin transcribing my notes into the book. Again, please excuse my little superstition, so I'd appreciate you leaving the book, pen and my lucky dime in place without disturbing it."

The following morning, Louise strolled in to Mrs. Schwartz's room with two paper cups and a white bag in tow. "Did you have a good night's sleep, Mrs. Schwartz? I hope you like cappuccino and cinnamon Danishes."

"Both sound great, thank you so much! Once I was able to fall asleep, I slept well. I haven't had something to keep me awake for a long time. I was so excited about our writing! I can't remember the last time I was so looking forward to doing something. I want to thank you very much for giving me something to keep me awake at night."

Louise felt her palms sweating. She had sort of resigned herself to the possibility that there might not be a biographical text of Mrs. Schwartz ready for review and editing. Louise was fully prepared to give it her best shot and serve as Mrs. Schwartz's biographer based on the notes she had taken if the composition book was empty. She dried her hands on her slacks as she first reached over to pick up the dime, which she carefully placed in a pocket of her slacks. She then retrieved the book and pen and sank back into the chair. Taking a deep breath, she opened the book, saw many filled pages, and smiled broadly.

"Mrs. Schwartz, are there any additional details you would like to add to our conversation from yesterday? I'm going to need to make my rounds shortly, and tonight I'm going to start putting my notes into writing for you to review and edit as you see fit."

"I believe I said enough yesterday. Thanks so much, Mrs. Graber. I have a feeling I won't be able to fall asleep too easily tonight either!"

Chapter 42

"This is wonderful," Mrs. Schwartz said as she dabbed at her tears with a tissue. "This is one of the most generous gifts anyone has ever given me. The writing is so beautiful, and you've done an amazing job capturing my love of teaching. You should have been a writer."

"I'm so glad you like it. You've truly had such a positive influence on so many young people, and it's important there is a keepsake, so people don't forget it. It's funny, I've always had a fear of writing, which I guess is one of the reasons I have these quirks when I prepare to write," Louise said as she looked down sheepishly while checking her fingernails.

"Louise, could I ask you for one more favor?"

Louise smiled. "Of course, Arlene."

"Would it be possible to make a copy or two of my biography?"

Louise followed the same procedure to create written biographical records for Mr. Morrison and Mrs. Rotkowski. Mr. Morrison choked up after reading his. He barely able to utter "Thanks." His biography brought tears to Louise's eyes so she only imagined the emotional impact it had on him. It was, she thought, a remarkable story of a gifted dancer and teacher, embedded within a decades-long love story. Sadly, a love story kept silent and invisible to the outside world.

Mrs. Rotkowski was similarly moved by reading a memorial tribute to her son Gary, who gave his life fighting bravely for the United States in the Battle of Hue in Vietnam. He died at 19 years old, having never attended college. Mrs. Rotkowski's guilt that she didn't encourage him to pursue an education still pained her daily. If only he had attended college, he might have avoided the draft, lived a full life, and perhaps had a family of his own. When Gary died, his death left a cavernous void and a heartache that forever defined her.

><

Louise sat in Mr. Young's office alongside Mrs. Crawford, who was sipping from a mug of tea with steam rising from it.

"Mrs. Graber, I've heard only wonderful things about you and the work you're doing with your assigned residents."

"Thank you, Mr. Young. I'm not sure I'm making much headway with Ms. Carmichael yet, but I'm still cautiously optimistic."

Mrs. Crawford grimaced slightly. "I'm not sure anyone can get that woman to become more pleasant and sociable, but your effort is appreciated."

"I must tell you," Mr. Young continued, "I've received calls from three of the residents, Mr. Morrison, Mrs. Rotkowski, and Mr. Morrison, expressing their gratitude for the time you've spent with them. Mr. Morrison, who is a man of some wealth, has pledged a very generous gift to the home in your honor. He does not want any type of recognition for his generosity, but I wanted to make you aware of it and thank you for what you've already done for us. I understand you have helped each of these residents create a sort of historical record of their lives."

Louise demurely looked down. "I'm really touched. I assure you, I've gotten as much from spending time with them as they have received from me. Perhaps more. Mr. Kramer, who is a bit challenging, as you indicated he would be, has also been fine. I'm going to suggest he and I work on a personal history of his own, if he is interested."

Mr. Young smiled and said, "That's wonderful to hear. When you feel you might have some more time, we would love for you to visit with some other residents. I believe we will soon have a waiting list of residents requesting to meet with you!"

Louise left Mr. Young and Diane, and figured she would visit Mr. Kramer to see if he would have an interest in creating a book of his own. But he was not in his room. She figured she would make another attempt with Miss Carmichael, so she headed to the second floor.

"Good afternoon, Miss Carmichael. How are you?"

Miss Carmichael looked up from the book she was reading, *The Exorcist* by William Peter Blatty. "Oh, fine."

Louise once again attempted to engage the reluctant woman. "Do you like reading horror stories?"

Miss Carmichael begrudgingly looked up. "I enjoy all genres, and I'm really enjoying this book, so if you don't mind..."

With a sigh, Louise left the room. She helped in the Activities Room for a while before deciding to check in on Mr. Kramer. As she turned down the corridor towards his room she heard yelling.

"Shut off that damn music before I come in there and throw your goddamn radio out the window!"

Louise quickened her pace and found Mr. Kramer outside his neighbor's room, menacingly waving a cane at a man in a wheelchair who could not have been any younger than 95. The recipient of Mr. Kramer's tirade was cupping his hand around his ear, yelling, "What did you say?"

Louise reached Mr. Kramer as he entered the other man's room. "Mr. Kramer, put down that cane right now," Louise implored. "What is the matter with you?"

Mr. Kramer belligerently began to answer before he saw the woman intervening was Louise. "This breathing corpse always plays his goddamn radio so fu—" His voice suddenly lowered. "Oh, hi, Mrs. Graber. I was trying to rest, but Mr. Roland always plays his radio loud enough to wake the dead."

"Mr. Kramer, I'm truly surprised that you would threaten a man who is in a wheelchair and at least twenty years older than you."

Mr. Kramer sheepishly looked at his feet. Addressing Mr. Roland, he said, "I'm sorry for yelling at you."

Mr. Roland again cupped his ear and barked, "What?"

Louise accompanied Mr. Kramer back to his room and sat down in a chair. There were two chairs in the room, and Mr. Kramer manipulated the other one across from Louise. "I'm really sorry about my outburst. That really isn't like me."

Louise suppressed her initial response and instead said, "Hopefully that is the case, and there aren't any future incidents like this. Mr. Kramer, what I came here to tell you is that I've worked with a couple of other residents here on a sort of biographical sketch of their lives. They were interested in recording some of their thoughts and life experiences in the form of a memoir. Would something like that be of interest to you?"

Mr. Kramer smirked. "First of all, I'd like you to call me Bob, and can I call you Louise?"

"Mr. Young prefers we use the more formal way of addressing the residents, and as he is the boss, we must really follow his guidelines."

"I don't really see the sense in that. After all, this isn't the army. I was in the army but got out before the big war. I wouldn't have minded killing some of those Nazi scum."

Louise felt herself thinking about the contrast between the man sitting in front of her and the much more pleasant and erudite Mr. Morrison. She quickly gathered herself and with a smile suggested, "That is why you should let me assist you with a writing of some of your thoughts and experiences. I'm sure you have so much to tell. I'll come back tomorrow and you can let me know if you're interested in such a project."

Chapter 43

Louise was pleasantly surprised by how at home she felt working at North Shore. She had always enjoyed interacting with people and now through these personal interactions, she regained a true sense of purpose. She believed she even had made a bit of headway with Ms. Carmichael. Louise had picked up a copy of Stephen King's new book, *Cujo*, and given it to Ms. Carmichael as a gift. Louise found Stephen King a bit too scary herself. She had barely made it through *The Shining*, and then had nightmares for a week, but many people loved his books. *Cujo* was not her cup of tea—it was about a demonic dog. But Ms. Carmichael seemed genuinely appreciative of the present. She had even said thank you in what was—for her—a pleasant voice.

In a way Louise almost preferred Ms. Carmichael to Mr. Kramer. He seemed too calculating, manipulative, false and mean-spirited. She had seen his true colors when he menaced that old man, and now seated across from him, she did her best to maintain a smile.

"All you need to do, Mr. Kramer, is to talk me through some of the memorable moments of your life, and I'll take notes. We can then review everything tomorrow, and I'll put together a few pages of your autobiography for you to review. What do you think of that idea?"

"Well, I got paid good money to talk and sell myself so that sounds right up my alley."

For the next forty-five minutes Mr. Kramer spoke tirelessly about himself. Unlike the other three autobiographical efforts Louise recently assisted with, this experience she found tedious and distasteful. Her mind wandered throughout, particularly as Mr. Kramer extolled his own self-importance. According to Mr. Kramer, he could have played major league baseball, was able to take apart and rebuild an automobile, and was the most accomplished hardware salesman in the entire Northeast. Louise's mind was elsewhere Mr. Kramer yelled, "Are you even paying attention to me? I'm asking you what type of car you drive?"

Louise quickly returned to the moment. "I'm so sorry. I was thinking about some of the fascinating things you have done and were telling me about."

Mr. Kramer asked impatiently, "So what kind of car do you drive?"

"Oh, it's a 1979 silver Honda Accord. As a matter of fact, we can probably see it from the window." Louise got up and walked over to the window and separated the curtain. "There it is."

Mr. Kramer got up and went to the window. "Hondas are good cars. Got to be honest, the Japs make better cars than we do in the good old USA. Everyone knows the Krauts make better cars than we do too. Hell, we kicked both of their asses in the big war, and now they make better cars than us. Who would have thought it?"

Louise sighed as she tried to recall the daydream she was enjoying before being interrupted by this bigoted blowhard. She realized she best try to get Mr. Kramer back on topic and finish his story. "So, what about your family? It would be interesting to incorporate some of your personal life into the account. Any relationships or family members you would like to include?"

Mr. Kramer's forehead creased, and his lips puckered. "I was married to a bitch of a woman for twenty-four miserable years. One day she decided to pick up and leave. She probably ran off with some loser after she spent all my money. Good riddance."

Not certain how best to respond, Louise cautiously offered,

"I'm sorry your marriage didn't last. Twenty-four years is a long time. May I ask if you were blessed with any children?"

"Blessed—no. Cursed is more like it. Two daughters, brainwashed by their mother to turn against me. Every criticism their mother made of me, my nasty daughters parroted."

Louise couldn't find anything to say.

Mr. Kramer continued, "I gave those ingrates everything, and they turned on me. I haven't heard from either of them in over two damn years. I wish I had sons instead. Fathers and sons are lifelong buddies, and sons are loyal to their father."

Desperately wanting to wrap up the session, Louise said, "I'm sorry I brought up unpleasant memories for you, Mr. Kramer, but you have certainly lived such a fascinating life with so many wonderful achievements. I have a procedure I follow when writing up these biographies, and a portion of it is—I guess you could say—superstitious. Tonight, I'm going to study all my notes from the information you have provided, and I'm going to leave a composition book that I will write your story in on your dresser. I know it sounds silly, but I'm going to place my lucky coin on the book along with a pen. I'm going to ask you to please not touch the book, pen or coin until I return to collect them tomorrow morning. This process is quite important to me, and if you disregard my request, I won't be able to write the story with you. All you need to do is continue thinking about your life story, and please feel free to tell me any more anecdotes you might have thought of when I return tomorrow. Is that a deal?"

"It's a deal," Mr. Kramer said while giving Louise a conspiratorial wink.

Louise left the room with less confidence than she had with the others that Mr. Kramer would honor her request.

When Louise returned to Mr. Kramer's room, she saw he was once again not in his room. Mr. Kramer was in his early seventies and much more mobile than most of the other residents, so he was frequently up and about. Louise crept into the room and spotted the book, pen, and most importantly, the dime, in the exact locations she had left them. She went back to the hallway and looked in both directions to see if Mr. Kramer was in the vicinity, but he was nowhere in sight. She hastily returned to the dresser, and with a pang of guilt picked up the coin and pen. She took a quick glance at the book, and sure enough, the coin had worked again. She put everything back in place and left the room with plans to come back in an hour.

Louise assisted Mrs. Colby in the Activities Room for a while, then returned to Mr. Kramer's room to find him in an armchair resting his eyes. She cheerily greeted him, "Good day, Mr. Kramer. How did you sleep?"

"Lousy," he responded. "Thinking about my miserable wife and daughters gave me damn nightmares."

Not sure how to answer, Louise offered, "I'm sorry to hear that. If you would prefer not to proceed with the writing, that's fine. It's supposed to be an exercise that you derive satisfaction from, so if it upsets you, we can put it aside."

"Nah, it's fine. It's a good idea talking about what I've done. I think I just want to leave out the bad parts, like my wife and daughters."

Louise could not imagine a more miserable sentiment. But she forced a smile and said, "I'll take my notebook, review everything tonight, and return tomorrow with a first draft for you to read and edit. Is that okay?"

From his chair, Mr. Kramer stared out the window with a vacant stare. "Sure."

Louise sat at her dining room table eating a tuna fish sandwich as a feeling of melancholy overcame her. She used to love to cook, and dinnertime had always been a special time. When the kids were still at home the dinner meal was a time for the four of them to recount their days and discuss problems and successes. It was the venue where Philip and Esther discussed their new school friends, test results, athletic accomplishments, and latest crushes. Once the kids were out of the house, Louise and David enjoyed extravagant dinners, just the two of them, almost every night. After all those years of marriage, they truly enjoyed each other's company and those quiet evenings together.

A sense of bitterness swelled inside her as she thought about Mr. Kramer's disdain for his family and how much she missed David. She would give anything to once again have him sitting by her side. She pushed aside the half- eaten sandwich, positioned the composition book in front of her and began to read the thoughts of an angry, egocentric man.

She read the words with limited interest or commitment until she gasped audibly as she read:

How much goddamn abuse can one man take? Everyone has a breaking point. She mouthed off to me one time too often. When she said I was a complete failure as a salesman, as a father, as a husband and in bed, I just snapped. I hit her harder than Muhammad Ali in his prime. It felt so good to unload all that anger, but I then realized when she fell, she had hit her head on the wood floor, hard. I heard the cracking sound of her skull and saw all the blood. It was strange the mixed emotions I felt. I realized she might be dead, and I was both happy that she would be out of my life forever but also scared that I could spend the rest of my life in jail.

She appeared to still be breathing a bit and I knew I had to put her out of her misery and mine. I took a pillow from our bedroom, placed it over her face and counted slowly to one hundred. Once I knew she was dead, I started to clean up the mess. Shit, it must have taken me two hours to make sure all the blood was gone. I then got the wheelbarrow from the garage along with a spade. It took me another two hours to dig a large hole next to the oak tree in our backyard so I could bury her. I figured this way if our daughters ever want to visit the house, they would be able to also visit their mother. Ha ha.

That night I slept as well as I had in a very long time. The six cans of Michelob certainly helped.

I called the girls the next day to say their mother left me and had they heard from her? Unbelievably they each said the same fucking thing to me: "It's about time."

I didn't hear from the girls for a couple of weeks and then out of the blue, they paid me a visit. I guess from all my years as a salesman I developed skills like an actor. I certainly was a good bullshit artist and put it to good use that afternoon.

I asked them what I owed the pleasure of their visit, and they told me they had not heard from their mother. I couldn't help myself so I said, "She probably didn't like the two of you either. It was about time she left you." Finally, Carol, the older of the two, asked me if I killed their mother. Can you imagine that? My own daughter asking me such a thing?

At that point I started to act as if I was worried about my late wife. I was so convincing that my daughters believed I had nothing to do with the bitch's disappearance. After that afternoon, I never heard from either one again. Good riddance.

Louise trembled as she rushed out of her chair to the bathroom, where she violently threw up. She cleaned up, and haltingly sat on the covered toilet seat. Was this possible? Had the coin truly transcribed the confession of Mr. Kramer killing his wife and burying her body in his backyard? What should she do? She thought of calling the police , but what would she say? That her magic coin had written a confession from a man who killed his wife? She knew she needed to do something—but what?

Louise recalled Rabbi Alder all those years ago telling her she needed to be very careful with the power of the coin. His prophecy seemed to have come to fruition.

She turned off the downstairs lights, held tightly onto the banister, and climbed up the stairs to her bedroom.

Louise tossed and turned in bed all night thinking about that vile man who had kept the most horrific of secrets. She finally determined the course of action she would take with Mr. Kramer. It would include a bit of manipulation of the truth—a little white lie. That went against her values, but one must fight fire with fire. Exhausted, she was able to sleep for three hours.

Chapter 44

With repulsion Louise looked at the disheveled looking man sitting on his bed. He was wearing a bathrobe and had a dark five o'clock shadow, which gave his face a menacing appearance. She again felt like vomiting but managed her disgust with great effort, saying, "Good morning, Mr. Kramer. I've started writing your biography, but there is something I need to tell you that is upsetting and frankly, badly scared me."

"You looked tired, Mrs. Graber. Didn't you sleep well?"

"I didn't, and when you hear what I have to say, you will understand why."

The lines in Mr. Kramer's forehead bunched together as he said, "All right, tell me what the problem is."

Louise took a deep breath as she actively tried to control her emotions. "The night before last I was here very late and I walked past your room. Perhaps you were sleeping and talking in your sleep, or maybe you were awake and talking to yourself, but I heard you saying things that were extremely disturbing."

As Louise was gathering her thoughts, Mr. Kramer asked, "What exactly did you hear me say?"

Louise could feel her heart beating as she sensed she was losing her battle with her nerves. Finally she blurted out, "You said you had killed your wife by punching her and then smothering her with a pillow, and that you then buried her in your backyard."

Mr. Kramer's face darkened.

"You said your daughters at one point accused you of killing your wife but you were able to convince them otherwise."

Mr. Kramer began to tremble, and Louise was uncertain if his trembling was due to fear or anger, or a combination of the two. Louise stood in the event she would have to run for assistance, but Mr. Kramer steadied himself and said, "I can't believe what you're saying. Obviously I was having a nightmare and was calling out in my sleep. My wife left me, and I've been upset ever since that horrible time. Isn't it logical to have bad dreams about such a thing and to remain troubled about it?"

Everything Mr. Kramer had said made perfect sense, but Louise knew for a fact this man had killed his wife. The problem was that Louise was unable to explain to Mr. Kramer, or anyone else for that matter, the true source of her information. Recognizing this reality, Louise sat again and took another measured breath. "Of course, that makes sense. I'm sorry I presented such a horrible thing. However, I hope you understand that I had to say something."

Mr. Kramer leaned back casually, wearing a smug grin. "Of course you did. I'm terribly upset you had to hear something so horrible, and I can only imagine what you must have thought of me, or anyone, who might do such a despicable thing. Let's just put this behind us, all right?"

Louise forced a smile. "For me personally, I'm going to put it behind me. However, as an employee of the North Shore Home, I will need to report the incident to Mr. Young, who is my supervisor. Of course, I will tell him that your explanation makes complete sense, and that the whole situation can be attributed to me hearing you talking in your sleep. Mr. Young is away until Tuesday so I will just mention it when I see him next. In the meantime, I'm going to spend a portion of my weekend working on your biography. Have a good weekend."

Louise could feel the heat of Mr. Kramer's glare as she turned and left his room.

Louise did not want to spend her weekend alone so she called Esther, and pretty much invited herself to spend the weekend at her daughter's house. Louise loved to spend time with both of her children and their families. Her most recent visit was with Philip so this time she reached out first to Esther. She was grateful Esther and Donald did not have any special plans for the weekend, and Esther sounded genuinely thrilled to have her as a houseguest. Esther and Donald would have a special "date night" Saturday and Louise could happily have her granddaughter to herself.

As Louise did not go to the North Shore Home on Fridays, she was able to leave for the hour and a half drive to Esther's house in Englewood in the early afternoon.

Louise timed her arrival for just after 3:30, as she knew that was when Esther got home from teaching school. When she pulled into the driveway at Esther's two-story red brick home, she saw Esther waiting for her with her beautiful granddaughter, holding her hand. Once Louise got out of the car, Esther put Molly down so she could toddle over to her.

"Gwamma, Gwamma."

Louise picked up her granddaughter and smothered her with kisses as Esther took her mother's suitcase into the house.

Molly's eyes widened, and her mouth opened as Louise scooped up another piece of egg smothered with grape jelly. Molly opened her mouth to receive the spoon-fed breakfast. Jelly omelets were Louise's favorite breakfast from childhood, and it seemed her granddaughter had inherited this culinary appreciation.

"You're spoiling her. Now she is going to expect me and Donald to feed her on our laps," Esther said with a smile.

"That's what grandmothers are supposed to do, spoil their grandkids. You and Donald are supposed to love her, set boundaries, and discipline her. My role is simply to love and spoil her."

While her daughter said, "more, more, more" in the background, Esther happily said to her mother, "That sounds about right."

"Esther, I really want to thank you and Donald so much for having me here this weekend. It's what I really needed. I'll call Donald later to thank him myself."

"He and a friend went hiking for the day and left at the crack of dawn. I was still sound asleep when he went out. We always love having you, and obviously Molly does too. My guess is there will be a few tears when you leave. Are you feeling a bit less anxious about dealing with that horrible sounding Mr. Kramer this week?"

"I know it's something I have to do. It's my responsibility to explain to Mr. Young what I overheard, and then it will be up to him if he wants to investigate further. If he doesn't, I've made my peace with just letting it go, as horrible as that might sound."

Esther reached over, held her mom's hand, and said, "You've always done the right thing, and you're handling this perfectly fine. Besides, chances are, what Mr. Kramer said is true—he was almost certainly talking out loud during a bad dream."

Louise looked away worriedly. "I'm sure you're right."

Chapter 45

Silver raindrops gathered on Louise's windshield and slid off, driven by the wind. A smattering of rain pelted the roof like drumming as Louise waited for the light to change. A man on the sidewalk smiled smugly under his tent-like umbrella, pleased with the forethought he'd exercised that morning.

Her grip on the steering wheel tensed as she guiltily thought of how she had shared Mr. Kramer's horrific crime with Esther and Donald but omitted the magic dime's role. She forced herself to sit up tall and cleared her throat. She turned off the radio and said, "Mr. Young, something happened with Mr. Kramer that I need to discuss with you." No, no, that's too demanding. She tried again, more gently, higher pitched. "Mr. Young, you were kind enough to suggest I could speak with you if the need arose. I'd appreciate a few minutes of your time to discuss a situation regarding Mr. Kramer."

Comfortable with the knowledge she was as prepared as she could be, Louise turned the radio back on and began to hum along. After tomorrow, this horrid situation with Mr. Kramer would be behind her.

As much as she didn't want to, she felt it was a good idea to keep up appearances and include Mr. Kramer in her daily visits. She stuck her head into his room and observed him sitting in his chair looking out of his window.

"Good morning, Mr. Kramer. Did you have a nice weekend?"

His faraway look changed into one of recognition, and he replied, "Oh, good morning, Mrs. Graber. It was just fine. By the way, do you still plan on talking with Mr. Young about what you overheard?"

"We went over this, Mr. Kramer. I'm obligated to report to my supervisor my weekly activities, and I will simply make a mention of it tomorrow morning. As I promised, I will explain to him that what I heard was the result of you talking in your sleep during a bad dream. I'm sure that will be the end of it. I have other things to discuss with him too. As special as you are, there are other residents I also need to discuss with him."

The bile rose in her throat, and Louise hastily retreated from the room. The feeling of disquietude decreased with every step she took away from room 315.

Her day improved after that: she always enjoyed the time she spent with Mrs. Schwartz, Mrs. Rotkowski and Mr. Morrison. She had even thawed Miss Carmichael's frosty demeanor. The two women had recently begun having lengthy conversations about books, movies and social issues, particularly Miss Carmichael's fervent belief in greater equality for women. She really was a fascinating person with diverse interests and strong opinions, although she remained curt and abrasive.

Louise genuinely appreciated these new relationships, which more than made up for the unpleasant time with Mr. Kramer. Blessedly, her involvement with that wretched man would be over soon.

Louise decided she would indulge herself and pick up a pastrami sandwich from her favorite deli for dinner. She was somewhat relieved that the rain had stopped, so the drive to the deli and then home would not be so laborious. She began to fit her key into the passenger door when she realized the door was already unlocked. Shaking her head at her stupidity for being in such a state in the morning that she forgot to lock the car door, she maneuvered her back into a comfortable position, attached the seatbelt, and inserted her key to start the ignition. Ready for the short trip to the deli, she released a sigh of relief, knowing that by this time tomorrow, the situation with Mr. Kramer would be behind her and her mind would once again be on pleasant thoughts.

The tension in her neck and shoulders relaxed as she listened to Barbara Streisand on the radio. She hummed along to "The Way We Were" as the roadway sign posted the familiar notice that it was two miles to the next exit, the one she needed to take. Louise had always been a very cautious driver, particularly when the roads were slick. She flipped on her right blinker and navigated to the right lane. As the brake lights on the car a few hundred feet in front of her appeared, she calmly pumped her foot on the brake as an inexplicable sense of unsettledness rushed through her. The brake lights in front of her were getting closer, and she realized the brakes on her own car were not working. Panicked, Louise yanked the steering wheel to her left seconds before she would have collided into the car in front of her.

The truck coming from the opposite direction never had a chance to avoid smashing head-on into Louise's Honda Accord. Seconds before the crash, Louise's screams completely drowned out Barbara Streisand singing, "So it's the laughter we will remember whenever we remember the way we were."

Chapter 46

The mortician was surprised to find a loose coin on the embalming table next to the recently deceased Louise Graber. It was only a dime, though it appeared to be an old one. He placed the dime in the jar on his assistant's desk, where she collected loose change for buying coffee.

Chapter 47

Once I stopped screaming "Holy shit! Holy shit!" I realized there was another sound in the room. I turned to my right and saw tears streaming down Julie's face.

In between deep, painful-sounding heaves, she rasped, "Oh no, I can't believe it. She's dead. I can't believe it. How's that possible?"

Trying my best to calm her, I replied, "If she was alive today she'd be like what, 95? She'd probably be dead anyway."

Unfortunately my attempt to console her was totally ineffectual. Julie ranted at me, "How could you be so insensitive? Louise was a kind and considerate woman who went through so much personal heartbreak. To die in such a manner was tragic."

To reverse the damage my prior words had done, I offered, "I'm sorry, I guess I was just so upset myself that I tried to rationalize the situation." I allowed a few moments to pass before I attempted further consoling, though I did affectionately pat Julie's knee several times. After what I felt a sufficient time had gone by, I said, "You obviously know that her death was no accident."

Julie had gotten some toilet paper from the bathroom, which she was now using to dry her eyes. She looked at me and sniffled. "What do you mean?"

"Mr. Kramer killed her. He said he was an expert at taking apart automobiles, and he knew which car was Louise's. Frequently when Louise went to visit Mr. Kramer's room, he was out and about, so we know he had the time and mobility. He must have tampered with her car, most likely the brakes, causing the accident. Louise said the car door was unlocked when she returned to it after work, so he must have been able to open the car, but didn't lock it."

Julie crossed to the room and back, clutching her head. "Of course. You're absolutely right. I can't believe that didn't dawn on me."

My astute insight had put me back into Julie's good graces. I held her hand and said, "You were in shock and were understandably overcome with emotion. Once the initial shock wore off, you would have come to the same conclusion."

We looked at each other and asked the same question simultaneously: "What do we do now?"

Requiring sustenance to do my best thinking, we decided to order in Chinese food. Over dumplings, Dan Dan noodles, chicken with diced peanuts, and beef with broccoli, we mapped out our game plan. Louise's demise impacted our appetites differently: Julie toyed with her food, eating about half a plateful, while I left no traces behind.

My whole life I've been obsessed with writing, particularly mysteries. This situation gave me the perfect opportunity to put my passions to practical use. Julie and I needed to prioritize what we wanted to accomplish, so together we created a list of questions:

+ What was reported about Louise's fatal accident?

+ Was there a criminal investigation into the accident, and if so, was Robert Kramer ever charged?

+ Was the disappearance of Robert Kramer's wife ever questioned?

+ How did Robert Kramer spend the rest of his life?

+ Where are Robert Kramer's daughters today?

+ Where are Esther and Philip now?

+ How do we bring closure for the families involved?

We would begin our search the next day.

I had read every volume of Sherlock Holmes that Arthur Conan Doyle had written. Now I was stepping into similar shoes more than a century later. I even had my very own Watson, though I was hesitant to tell Julie that was the role I envisioned her playing. And of even greater help, we had at our fingertips a resource Sherlock Holmes never had: the internet.

That Tuesday we each had two tutoring sessions scheduled, so we agreed to meet in my apartment at 3:15 to begin delving into what happened to Louise. Julie brought her laptop over, allowing us to work simultaneously.

We uncovered similar news reporting in both *The Long Island Press* and *New York Newsday* regarding Louise's death. We found this brief article from the Wednesday, December 16, 1981, edition of *Newsday*:

Louise Graber, 58, a longtime resident of Great Neck, died as a result of injuries suffered in a vehicular accident on Monday, November 14. Mrs. Graber was returning home from volunteering at The North Shore Nursing Home around 5:30 p.m. when she lost control of her car and swerved into an oncoming truck. Police have theorized that slick road conditions were a contributing factor in the accident.

Charles Cafiero, 44, the truck driver suffered minor injuries. Initial indications are that Mr. Cafiero is blameless, though the investigation is still underway.

Mrs. Graber was for many years an elementary school teacher in Great Neck. She had only recently begun volunteering at The North Shore Home, where in a very short time she formed many relationships with residents.

North Shore Home Director Ralph Young had this to say. "Mrs. Graber was only with us at North Shore briefly but had a profound impact on so many of our residents. She was a wonderful woman, and the entire North Shore Home community sends our deepest sympathy to the Graber family. She will be sorely missed."

North Shore resident Linda Carmichael, while fighting back tears, commented, "I was only beginning to know Mrs. Graber, but she was one of the kindest and most compassionate people I've ever met. Her passing is a tremendous loss to all who knew her. May she rest in peace."

Other than the obituary notices, neither Julie or I were able to uncover anything else discussing Louise or her accident. We found no criminal investigation, and assumed authorities considered it an accident—a driver simply losing control on a wet road.

We then scoured search engines to find out what had happened with Robert Kramer. Over the years, there were several obituaries published about men named Robert Kramer, but we couldn't confirm which was the correct one. Julie went through state death records and located listings for all men named Robert Kramer who had passed away in New York State in the eighties and nineties. We figured as a starting point we would only look at those two decades. But when the results remained unspecific, we called the North Shore Nursing Home to see if they could help.

Fortunately, the home was still in existence, though it was now called The North Shore Rehabilitation Center and Home. I called and pretended to be doing some family history research. I asked if they had records dating back to the early 1980s. I was put on hold, got disconnected, called back, and was placed on hold again. Then I finally spoke to someone in administration. Surprisingly, she eagerly offered to help and told me that North Shore now digitized all records, but only to the last 15 years. However, she said there were some paper files going back a few years longer in a large room on the fourth floor. They maintained files prior to 2000 in basement storage, but she couldn't say how far back they went.

"Do you think you could find out, and perhaps locate my great-uncle's file?" I asked.

The woman said she would have to call me back with those answers.

At 4:55 my phone rang. "Hi, Mr. Howard, this is Kim from North Shore. I followed up on your inquiry, and the good news is we do have resident files going back to the early days of the home. The bad news is the files are disorganized and rather cumbersome. As you can imagine, there are probably thousands of records—so many people have lived here. Finding one person in all those files would be a huge undertaking, and there is no way we wouldn't have the time to look. Also, you should be aware that none of the files we have in storage contain medical records, so if you are looking for those, I cannot help you, nor are we permitted to let you see them."

Hearing a small opening I asked, "Thanks very much. I don't need any medical information. Would it be possible for me and a friend to look through them? Any chance you happen to know if they categorized files by year?"

"I believe they are and let me check if you are permitted to come here. Please hold on."

I took the opportunity to update Julie that Kim was checking and received in response, "That's nice of her. Please let your *friend* know what she says."

Julie's response somewhat baffled me but at that point, Kim returned to the line and said, "I was told that would probably be fine, but you can't take or copy any of the files. When would you like to come in? Better yet, I have to leave now so let me give you my email address and email me the day and time you would like to come in. Any weekday should be okay."

After receiving Kim's email information, I thanked her, turned to Julie, and asked, "When would you like to go?"

Julie smiled. "I don't know, let me check my hair washing schedule."

I thought there was a message in there somewhere but I wasn't sure what it was so I figured I was best off not saying anything.

Thursday was going to be an appointment-free day for both Julie and me, so I emailed Kim requesting Thursday at 10:00 a.m. I heard back from her Wednesday morning confirming the appointment.

We pulled into the parking lot of the North Shore Rehabilitation Center at 9:55 in the morning. It was likely the same lot Louise had parked her Honda in forty years earlier. The first glance at the red-brick facade with institutional looking windows gave me the impression we were about to enter an office building. We walked from the asphalt parking lot up a very slight incline through automated doors and approached a security station where two men in brown uniforms sat. One of the guards approached me and asked who we were visiting. I told him we had an appointment with Kim, and he pointed us in the direction of an office a little ways down the lobby.

I knocked at the door of the Administration Office and entered. A dour-looking woman sitting at the front desk peered up at me. I thought to myself that this couldn't be the pleasant-sounding Kim, but I couldn't be sure.

"Hi, I'm Zach Howard and we have a ten o'clock appointment. Are you Kim?"

The woman's harsh voice matched her appearance, confirming she was certainly not Kim.

"Hold on. I'll check to see if she is available."

"Thanks very much."

A couple of minutes later a smiling Asian woman who appeared to be in her late twenties came out and said, "Mr. Howard? I'm Kim Lee, nice to meet you."

"Hi, Kim," Julie said, "I'm Zachary's *friend*, Julie."

"Oh, sorry," I said sheepishly as I realized I mishandled the social nicety of introductions. I did my best to rebound by saying, "We really appreciate you allowing us to search through the files."

"No problem at all, it's my pleasure. If you follow me, we can take the stairs down to the basement to the storage facility."

Julie gave me a nudge as I looked at her quizzically. She then stared at me and then down to the bag I was holding, which was a reminder I needed to hand the bag to Kim and say, "We picked up a couple of muffins to thank you for your help. We weren't certain what you like but one is blueberry, and the other is cinnamon apple. There's a great bakery in our neighborhood."

"Oh, that's so sweet of the two of you, and both sound delicious. Where do you two live?"

"Astoria," Julie answered."Are you familiar with it?"

"Of course. I grew up in Queens myself. Flushing."

We followed Kim down a staircase where we opened the door to the basement of the building. The temperature, once we entered the hallway, was considerably warmer than the lobby level as we passed a closed door with the words "Heating Plant" posted on it. At the end of the hall, we reached a locked storage room. Kim took out a keychain with several keys on it, and on her second attempt, opened the padlock. She pushed open the door and turned on a series of lights, which quickly illuminated the room. All around us were boxes and boxes of files. There must have been several hundred boxes stacked and surrounding us. Fortunately, most of the file cartons appeared to have years posted on them, and many included more identifying writing such as: Expenses, Payroll, Admissions.

The three of us looked at one another thinking the same thing: this might end up being a massive undertaking.

Kim left us and said she would be back in a couple of hours if we had not returned to her office before then. We thanked her again, and rolled up our sleeves to begin our tedious task.

For the next hour or so, we primarily excavated boxes we thought might have a chance of containing the information we were seeking. We focused exclusively on 1981 as we knew Mr. Kramer was in residence by then. Our efforts were delayed a bit due to Julie's shrieking fit upon discovering one of the glue traps contained a victim. She ordered me to take the trap and its inhabitant out of the room and locate a trash can. For the duration of our efforts, Julie kept one eye on the files and one on the floor for scurrying creatures. This exercise slowed her down a bit.

It would have been easier if North Shore had alphabetized the residents' files. If a box had been labeled "1981 J-M," we probably would have finished in time to for lunch.

But that didn't happen. Around noon I tried to declare a lunch break. But Julie said, "Can't you forget about food just once? We have to keep looking. Come on, Zach, let's focus. We're trying to solve a murder here. Does Sherlock Holmes break for lunch in the middle of an important case?"

"I think Watson usually brought him a sandwich."

"No, he didn't You're making that up."

When I said I was going to go to Kim's office to ask for the muffins back, Julie she snapped at me. She then didn't speak to me for an extended period when I told her that the next mouse I found I was going to eat. Finally she searched her bag and gave me a granola bar, which I gobbled up in two bites. Frankly, it only made me hungrier, but I decided not to share that information with Julie.

We didn't hit pay dirt until 3:30, when Julie uttered her first words to me in a couple of hours. "Zach, I found it! I've got his admission form!"

With great adeptness, I shimmied and twisted between the stacks of boxes, reaching Julie. I peeked over her shoulder at the document she was holding. We eased our way into sitting positions on top of stacked file boxes and quietly read the information. We learned that Robert Samuel Kramer was born on May 6, 1910. Prior to taking up residence in the North Shore Home, he lived in Uniondale, Long Island. When it said he was a retired salesman with marital status listed as divorced, we knew we had our man. His closest relatives were his daughters, Valerie and Rhonda. Valerie had an address in Suffolk County, Long Island, and Rhonda lived in Chicago. His health had been considered relatively good, though he had some arthritis, particularly in his right knee.

Slightly disregarding the instructions given to us, Julie and I surreptitiously took photos of the page, and then restored the room as best we could to its former condition, *sans* dead rodents. We informed Kim that our search was successful, thanked her, and left the home a little before 5. With the mission accomplished, I insisted we walk to a Burger King a block away.

Julie and I have a lot in common, but our dietary habits still are stratospheres apart. Who knew that Burger King served salads? More surprisingly, why would anyone ever order a salad from Burger King? While I warily eyed Julie's Chicken Garden Salad, Julie seemed equally uncomfortable with my two Whoppers, fries, chocolate shake and ten-piece spicy chicken nuggets. I offered Julie some nuggets, but she shook her head so vigorously from side to side, I thought she would injure her neck.

I sat back and patted my full stomach with contentment. I've always loved the feeling of knowing my belly was full. Feeling fueled and calm, I knew I could accomplish anything—at least until hunger returned. "That hit the spot," I said with a smile. "How about we get back in the car and see if we can find the house Louise lived in?"

We parked in front of a ranch style white house with green trim. A smokestack protruded from dark roofing and there were several large trees on the property, which if I was to hazard a guess, were red maple. The property was probably about a third of an acre or so. There was a

Lexus parked in the driveway; someone was likely home.

"It's kind of strange, isn't it?" I said, turning to Julie. "There's probably a new family living there now—people who know nothing of Louise or her family. Fifty years ago, Louise, David, Philip and Esther were living here, and they were one big, happy family. Ten years later, both David and Louise were dead, due to car accidents. A home is kind of like the magic dime in a way. How many lives and stories intertwine with a coin, and how many lives intertwine with a house?"

Julie continued to regard the house. "You're right. I never thought about it like that."

After another few minutes of quiet contemplation, I knew it was time to leave. We went to Julie's apartment to formulate our next steps. She expressed surprise that I said I was still hungry, but she made me a couple of tuna fish sandwiches, and we resumed our work.

With the specifics we uncovered regarding Robert Kramer, we were then able to learn that he had died on April 9, 1992, in a nursing home in Riverhead, New York. It was probably impossible to unearth the reasons for his move to a new nursing home, but it wouldn't be a stretch to assume his cantankerous personality played some part in his being asked to leave the North Shore Home.

Search engines helped us to find his two daughters. Rhonda Sykes (formerly Kramer) was born in 1937 but passed away in 2018 in Chicago, Illinois. Valerie Miller (Kramer) was born in 1939, with her current address listed in Jamesport, New York. Jamesport was only a few miles from Riverhead so perhaps Robert Kramer had moved to be closer to his daughter? Had they reconciled?

We next turned our attention to Louise and her family.

Unfortunately, additional efforts turned up no indication that Louise's death was anything but an accident.

Dr. Philip Graber, 80, was living on Park Avenue and 83rd Street in

Manhattan. He and his wife, Cindy, also owned a home in Boca Raton, Florida. Cindy, 72 was his second wife. There was no mention of his first wife, Donna, who, as we recalled, was the mother of his children, Sam, 43, and Rachel, 41. Our further investigation turned up that Philip now had six grandchildren of his own. Those grandkids were Louise's great-grandchildren.

Rachel and her husband, Donald, also lived in Manhattan, on the Upper West Side. They had a second residence in East Hampton. In addition to Molly, 40, they had a second daughter, Samantha, 37. We determined that it was very possible that Esther had been pregnant when Louise last saw her.

Esther had three grandchildren. Louise and David Graber had grandchildren who would never know their grandparents.

We had the familial information we needed. The next step was to determine if and how to share what we knew about the murder of Robert Kramer's wife and our theory about the death of Louise Graber.

Julie and I stayed up well past midnight discussing the ins and outs of this conundrum. We knew the easiest way to validate our claims about what Robert Kramer had done was to show Philip and Esther the coin's capabilities. We could share with them an experiment, much like the one Louise performed with her mother and Sarah. Another option was to share the coin's magic with the police and conduct a similar presentation. The concern of course was being labeled lunatics.

Frankly, I was not anxious to divulge the coin's existence with anyone at this stage of the investigation; I preferred to never share it. I wasn't certain what my long-term plans were for the coin, but I knew I wanted to keep it as Julie's and my secret until I could figure things out. After all, there were a multitude of ways I would be able to use the coin's unique ability to my professional benefit. I did not want to relinquish such a gift unless forced.

We decided the best course of action was to meet with

representatives of the Great Neck police department in person. I offered to go by myself but Julie thought it might make a better impression if we went together. At first, I was a bit offended that Julie doubted my ability to make a convincing case on my own, but I quickly realized that she just wanted to be by my side for every facet of the investigation. We decided we would drive to the Great Neck police precinct Monday afternoon to make our presentation.

That Monday Julie made me change my shirt twice. My initial attempt was a T-shirt, which I had forgotten was in my dresser, that said, "Honk if you like gaming." My second attempt, a green t-shirt that said, "That's dope," with a decorative plant in the middle of the O had Julie howling. She had tears in her eyes by the time she stopped laughing. I wasn't sure why she found it so hysterical, but I took her reaction to mean that this shirt wasn't acceptable either, requiring me to try again. My third attempt was a simple hoodie, met by an eyeroll and head shaking. Julie walked me back to my apartment, where she scrutinized my closet and dresser in which she discovered a blue button-down shirt that was apparently to her liking. As a practice I like to be amenable, but I drew the line when she pointed at my feet, recommending I replace my sneakers with loafers.

Once I was dressed to her satisfaction, Julie said, "When this is all over, I think you and I should go on a clothes shopping excursion." Now it was my eyeroll turn.

Driving to the precinct, we discussed our strategy as to how we were going to explain things to the police. Midway through what I thought was a very cogent strategic approach, Julie put her hand on my arm and said, "Please don't take this the wrong way, but sometimes I'm a little bit better at reading people than you are. If you wouldn't mind, I may interrupt you when we are speaking with the police if I feel the police officer is, let's say, resistant to what you are saying. Is that okay with you?"

I must admit I was fuming inside a bit at that point. I liked Julie an awful lot and really enjoyed her in my life, but I didn't appreciate her bullying behavior. I've heard many situations where once a woman gets involved in a relationship, she tries to change and manipulate the guy. Well, I wasn't going to stand for it. No one was going to manipulate me. I didn't respond for a while. Finally, Julie said in a conciliatory voice, "I'm sorry. If I hurt your feelings, I certainly didn't mean to. It's just that you've done everything. You've led this whole process from the beginning, and you've had all the insight. Frankly, I'm feeling like I'm not contributing anything substantive to this project. I just thought that maybe, if I took the lead a bit with the police, I'd feel a little bit better about myself."

What Julie said made complete sense, but I did my best not to smile. "Of course you can take the lead in the discussions," I said, "and if you feel it's appropriate to interrupt me at any point during the meeting, please do so."

I relaxed a bit with what must have been a grin of self- satisfaction. It was funny—Julie and I were becoming so much alike. When I looked over at her she appeared to also have a look of accomplishment.

It was the first time either of us had ever been inside of a police station. I envisioned a tough cop bellowing "Out of my way!" as he hauled a handcuffed thug to a dank cell. Instead, the well-lit surroundings showed off an elongated gray desk serving as the focal point with several small desks throughout the remainder of the space. Women and men, some in uniform and some not, sat behind the smaller desks talking on phones and studying computer screens. By all appearances we could have walked into an insurance or financial office.

There was a man in uniform sitting behind the main desk with a paper-filled tray in front of him and a phone in his ear. We walked towards him, and once he completed his call he asked, "Can I help you?"

I quickly answered, "I'd like to report two mur—" at which point,

Julie interrupted.

"If possible, we would like to speak with someone regarding two old crimes."

The officer looked at both of us quizzically. "Let me see who is available. Why don't the two of you sit over there and wait?" He pointed us in the direction of a waiting area furnished with six chairs, two already occupied.

I thought about the plot of *Murder Most Mundane* for as long as I could. In fact, I thought about changing it significantly. But I didn't have my laptop to record my ideas, and when my mind, grew restless, I told Julie I was going to ask how much longer we would have to wait. She patted my hand, stood up and said, "I'll ask."

Julie came back a minute later with an update. "A detective is finishing up with something else and should be out in a few minutes."

About fifteen minutes later, an African American man about my age, in slacks and a sports shirt, with a well-groomed mustache, approached us and said, "Hi, I'm Detective Royster. I understand you have some information about two crimes? I'm sorry, I didn't get your names."

Figuring I could handle this one, I replied, "I'm Zachary Howard, and this is Julie Fields."

Detective Royster instructed us to follow him to a small conference room, where he asked us to sit down.

Once seated he asked, "So, what would you like to tell me?"

Respecting Julie's wish, I waited for her to start. She nodded at me and said, "Thank you, Detective Royster. I'm sure you receive a lot of wild claims and reports, and this one may sound way off-the-wall, but I promise you it is completely legitimate. Zach and I have come across some information regarding a man who lived on Long Island over thirty years ago who was certainly responsible for one murder, and very likely two. The first one, the man's wife, was attributed to the victim running away on her own, and the second one, an acquaintance of his, in a car accident. The problem Zach and I have is how to prove to you both were cases of murder. You see, we are unable to disclose our source at this time."

Detective Royster squinted pensively and reclined in his chair. "I'm sure your intentions are good, but as you can no doubt understand, there are serious complications with the claims you are presenting."

I tried to clarify things but the detective quickly cut me off. "Let me finish. There are a lot of TV crime dramas out there focusing on cold cases, but the reality is, to simply start investigating two murders that occurred over thirty years ago is not something we just pick up and jump into. Secondly, you haven't told me where these murders allegedly took place, so I don't even know who would have jurisdiction. Lastly, as you told me you can't divulge the source of your information. Am I supposed to simply start an investigation based on unsupported allegations?"

Detective Royster saw the looks on our faces and softened his tone a bit. "Look, I know you're trying to help and do what you feel is your civic duty, but you get my dilemma, right?"

"Detective Royster," I said, "the last thing we would want to do is waste the department's time or yours. I've heard of detectives relying on psychics to help solve a crime, and I'm certainly not saying we are psychics, or had a vision or anything outlandish like that. But we have information from what would best be called a non-mainstream source. We have knowledge that makes us one hundred percent certain that a man named Robert Kramer killed his wife, most likely in 1980. We also are ninety-five percent certain that this man, while a resident of the North Shore Home, a nursing home here in Great Neck, tampered with the brakes of a car owned by a Great Neck resident named Louise Graber, resulting in a fatal accident. Louise Graber was a volunteer at the nursing home. The reason Mr. Kramer tampered with the brakes of her car was because she told him she had found out he had killed his wife and that she was going to report it. Mr. Kramer had car mechanic skills and was capable of rendering her car brakes ineffective."

At this point Detective Royster wanted to interrupt me but I continued. "Please, let me finish. We know one of Mr. Kramer's daughters is still alive, and at one time she and her now deceased sister believed their father had killed their mother. Mrs. Graber's two children are still alive. Aren't they entitled to learn the truth about their mother's death?"

With that, I sat back, noticing a combination of surprise and delight on Julie's face.

"Mr. Howard, that was quite a compelling argument. However, there is still a great deal involved here. Do you live in the area?"

"No, we live in Astoria, Queens."

"Would it be possible for the two of you to come back later this week when my supervising officer is here so we can both sit down with you? Of course, it would be helpful if you were to bring with you all evidence or supporting documentation you can."

Julie and I looked at each other. Julie responded, "It would be our pleasure to return."

We set an appointment to go to the precinct on Wednesday afternoon, and we promised Detective Royster we would bring as much information as we could.

Chapter 48

"I'd like to thank both of you for coming in again. Detective Royster explained to me that your allegations are based on some unverifiable methods, but he seems to feel that there is enough you presented to at least warrant a follow-up discussion. I'd like you to walk us through everything you know with as much detail as possible."

Julie and I sat in the same conference room where we had met with Detective Royster two days earlier. Detective Royster was sitting across from me and had a pad and pen in front of him. The man to his left had introduced himself as Captain Bill Sheridan. Captain Sheridan appeared to be in his early fifties and frankly looked more like a bank executive than a police captain. He had dark well-groomed hair, which was graying at the sideburns, and his blue eyes looked out at us from behind horn-rimmed glasses. To be honest, neither Captain Sheridan nor Detective Royster fit my image of what a law enforcement agent would be like. They were both extremely articulate and professional, which also did not fit into my preconceived notion of a policeman.

For the better part of the next hour Julie and I reviewed with them everything we believed we knew about the two murders and answered their follow-up questions to the best of our ability. The only thing we were unable to divulge was how we came upon this information, which understandably was a large point of frustration for them. We did come to an understanding that if they launched an investigation, and they found sufficient justification to pursue either or both matters, we would revisit divulging how we gathered our information.

Captain Sheridan excused himself and a couple of minutes later concluded the meeting by saying, "Based on what we have, or actually don't have, I hope you understand we are unable to begin a full investigation. However, what you have explained has piqued our interest, and what I'll do is try to get into contact with Valerie Kramer. If anything comes out of my discussion with her, I will let you know."

Our drive back to Queens was a blast. We sang along with songs from Kings of Leon and Fallout Boy. Julie does not have a great voice but it's a helluva lot better than mine. We had to be back by 5 as Julie had a tutoring session scheduled. We decided to go out for at a local Chinese place later to celebrate. I was on cloud nine until I was parking the car and Julie said, "My parents would like to meet you and take us out to dinner."

My mood deflated noticeably to the point that Julie asked, "What's the matter? Don't you think it's time you met my parents?"

I sighed and said, "It's not that I don't want to meet them. Of course I do. It's just that everything is going so well. For some reason my friends' parents have not always taken a liking to me. What happens if I say stupid things and they don't like me, or even worse, if they try to persuade you that I'm not right for you?"

At that point we had gotten out of the car. Julie came around and took my hand. "The Zach Howard who met with Detective Royster the other day, and with Detective Royster and Captain Sheridan today, would impress any parent. Besides, I'm a grown woman, and I can formulate my own opinions without influence from my parents. Would it be okay if I told them this Saturday night?"

I ignored the butterflies in my stomach and any misgivings I had and responded, "Of course."

><

I didn't even bother attempting to dress myself Saturday evening. The only clothing item I selected on my own that night was my boxers. The rest of my attire, from my socks to my tie—yes, I wore a tie—was picked out by Julie. I should mention that my boxers were green with pink little piglets on it. I could tell Julie wanted to say something about that choice, but she refrained from doing so; clearly, she recognized my need for some independence. The blue pin-striped shirt and gray Brooks Brothers slacks I wore were recent presents from Julie. By recent, I mean she handed them to me when she arrived at my apartment to assist with the dressing process along with a yellow tie that had small sailboats on it. I barely had time to unwrap my presents and thank her before she instructed me to put them on. She diffused my concern that I had never gone sailing in my life and was somewhat prone to seasickness with a finger to her lips and a "Shhh."

Julie looked great, wearing a light blue blazer over a white silk blouse and black pants. I told her so and headed over to the fridge.

"Zach, what are you doing?"

"I figured to calm my nerves I'd get a little snack."

"We're going to have a great dinner, and you have nothing to be nervous about. Besides, it would be a shame if you got a stain on your new clothes. Sit next to me on the couch," she said, patting the cushion by her side.

We were meeting Julie's parents at one of the top Italian restaurants in Astoria. I was a bit surprised that her parents had been able to secure a reservation there for a Saturday night on such short notice, so I asked Julie about it.

"Do your parents go to La Roma often?"

"No, I don't think they've ever been there."

"Gee, I'm surprised they were able to get a reservation for 8:00 o'clock dinner on a Saturday night with only two to three days' notice. I figured a place like that would be booked weeks in advance."

Julie bit her lip and said, "Well, to tell you the truth, my mother made the reservation about a month ago. I kind of had a feeling you might be a bit nervous about meeting them, so I didn't want to ask you too far in advance."

I thought about what Julie just told me and my response was

apparently perfect. "I think that was a great idea."

Julie blurted out something no woman besides my mother has ever said to me: "I love you, Zach." She looked somewhat embarrassed and rose from the couch.

Admittedly stunned, I nonetheless instinctively placed my hand on Julie's shoulder and gently coaxed her back down. "I love you too," I whispered.

We arrived at dinner at precisely the same time as Julie's parents, so we walked in together. Her parents, a nice-looking couple, appeared somewhat tense. Mrs. Fields was a small woman with short blonde hair and bangs. Mr. Fields was a gangly six feet tall. Both were extremely cordial. My nerves started melting.

Once seated, Mr. Fields immediately invited me to call them Richard and Carol. The tension I still felt lifted when Richard added, "You know, you didn't have to wear a tie."

I winked at Julie. "Oh, yes I did."

For the next ten minutes Richard and Carol provided a summation of Julie's lifelong commitment to proper etiquette. I was really enjoying the conversation, and Julie was a great sport. The conversation slowly segued in my direction, primarily orchestrated by Richard. "So, Zach, I understand you're a writer. I'm a huge reader myself, mostly nonfiction. What do you write?"

Julie noticeably squirmed a bit but I confidently smiled at her, then answered her father, "I write exclusively fiction. Mysteries, detectives, that sort of thing. I've always been a fan of Sherlock Holmes, Hercule Poirot—truly cerebral detectives."

"That's fascinating, Zach. Of course I've read a great deal of Sherlock Holmes. I would love to read some of your books. If you give me a couple of titles of your books you most recommend, I'll order them first thing in the morning. Of course, if the author wants to send me a couple of signed copies himself, I wouldn't say no," he said with a wink.

I opened my mouth, but Julie jumped in. "Dad, it is extremely difficult to get a book published, particularly for a first-time writer. Zach is working on something now that I'm confident a publisher will pick up. But it's not out yet."

Eyebrows arched, Richard looked at his daughter, then at me. "So you don't have anything published?"

I felt my confidence, and appetite, dissipating rapidly and hesitantly responded, "Not yet, but I've written a lot, and as Julie said, my current story is showing promise."

Conversation went quiet as everyone gathered their thoughts. Carol gave me a small encouraging smile. I hoped the newly arrived appetizers would prompt new topics as the clams oreganata looked delicious. Unfortunately, Richard continued.

"What I don't understand is, if you're a writer but you haven't written anything that actually sells, how do you pay your bills? Can you be a professional writer if you don't earn a living? You see, guitar is one of my hobbies. I like playing the guitar—sometimes for myself, sometimes for Carol, who enjoys my playing. But she doesn't pay me to play for her, and as a matter of fact, no one pays me to play the guitar for them. So, playing the guitar is my hobby, not my job. For my job, I guide people towards the best investment approaches for their future. People pay me for that service. Therefore, that's my job, and it is how I pay my bills. How do you pay your bills, Zach?"

"Richard," Carol said, "that's enough. You're being unpleasant."

I looked over at Julie, white as a ghost and trembling. My knees shook under the table, which I tried to relax while wiping my clammy hands on my pants. To calm my nerves, I speared two clams and put them in my mouth. (They were delicious.) Swallowing, then summoning up courage, I said, "Mr. Fields, do you know that Toni Morrison, Mark Twain and J.R.R. Tolkien all had their first books published after they turned 40? Raymond Chandler didn't publish until he was past 50. I think I'm a good writer, and as I don't have the responsibility of a family yet,"—and with that I looked over at Julie—"I still have time to pursue my writing dream. If the time comes when I can no longer pursue that dream, and I need to get a nine-to-five job, that's what I'll do."

We were at the restaurant for close to three hours but after that uncomfortable exchange, the evening went by quickly. We drank two bottles of wine, and if nothing else, at least my appetite impressed Richard. He insisted I order whatever I wanted. I didn't want to insult him, so I followed the clams oreganata with burrata and roasted peppers, and then a veal chop parmigiana. All the food was delicious. I also shared the Caesar salad, made for the whole table. I was full by the time the main courses arrived, but the waiter asked if we wanted dessert, at which point I noticed a barely perceptible side-to-side shaking of the head from Julie. Richard, however, insisted I have dessert, so feeling stuck between Julie's head shaking and Richard's insistence, I asked for the smallest piece of ricotta cheesecake the waiter could slice.

Richard and Carol gave us a lift home and we promised we would go to their house in Connecticut for a weekend very soon.

Julie was beaming when we walked into her apartment. When we got back to my apartment, Julie literally jumped on top of me. She ripped the clothes off me in a frenzy, completely disregarding that they were brand new. Afterwards, lying in bed, she said, "Zach, you were phenomenal tonight."

"Oh, thanks," I said with a broad smile. "You were great too. After all, you were the one who initiated everything and was so anxious to get started."

Julie giggled and said, "You were phenomenal here too, but I meant dealing with my father at dinner. I've never seen him be quite that rude. He had no right to be so rude to you. I guess that was him being overprotective of his only child. But you handled him exceptionally well."

"Do you think he likes me now?"

"Knowing him, I'm sure he would prefer you to have a more lucrative profession, but he'll come around."

I rolled over and considered getting up for a snack. But I rolled back over. "Julie," I said, "something has been bothering me for a while. There are so many reasons for me to like you, but um, why do you like me?"

Julie gathered her hair into a pony tail, as if gathering her thoughts. "Remember when I first met you, in your injured state? You seemed so fragile and vulnerable, but there was a goodness to you that came through even while in pain. Then I ran into your brother outside your apartment, and he was so obnoxious. I could not imagine what it must have been like growing up with such a conceited oaf. He told a story about how your mother referred to you as a delicate butterfly. As kids, our teachers taught us how a plain, nondescript caterpillars eventually turn into beautiful butterflies, and it made me realize that to survive in a household with someone like Roger, you needed to stay in your cocoon for a very long time. However, when I first met you, I got the feeling there was so much beauty and quality inside of you waiting to blossom, and I wanted to be a part of it."

We made love again.

><

Sunday afternoon we were sitting in Julie's apartment when my phone pinged with a text from Roger.

Julie asked, "What's wrong?"

"Nothing really. Roger is taking Roger Jr. to a birthday party in the city tomorrow and asked if they could swing by afterwards."

"Zach, they're your brother and nephew. It would be nice to see them, and besides, babies are so cute."

"I guess you're right. I'll text him to say I'm looking forward to it." Before I could hit send, my phone rang and I answered it, something I usually don't do. As soon as I hit the green phone icon I heard, "Mr.

Howard, this is Detective Royster. How are you?"

"Good afternoon, Detective. What's up?"

My stomach clenched a bit in anticipation as I waved frantically to get Julie's attention. As Julie hurried over, I put the phone on speaker.

"I just left Valerie Miller's house. She has not seen or heard from her mother for over 40 years and is certain that she is dead and likely murdered. She said that under no circumstance would her mother have walked out of the lives of her daughters. She was a loving mother, married to an abusive man, whom she desperately wanted to leave, but would never have left her girls. Valerie was always convinced that her father had killed her mother. She and her sister reported their concerns when their mother disappeared, and apparently there was a brief investigation, but nothing came of it. She claims her father was, as she put it, "silver tongued." He was quite a con man, and not only did he convince the police his wife had left him, but even put doubt in Valerie's and her sister's mind that he was responsible. I told Mrs. Miller that something came across my desk regarding a potential lead concerning her mother's disappearance but certainly nothing close to concrete."

"Zach, Julie, I'm sure you understand that no judge in his right mind would approve an order to dig up someone's backyard in search of a body without evidence justifying it."

"Detective Royster, this is Julie. I'm here with Zach. Would it be possible for Zach and me to meet with or speak to Valerie Miller? I know it might be a longshot, but if we were able to convince her our evidence is valid, perhaps she would be able to work something out with the current owner of her former home to allow for an excavation?"

"Look, there is nothing preventing you from being in touch with her. Let me think about it some more, and I may speak with her again. I'll call you back in a day or two."

"Thank you," Julie and I said in unison.

Two days later, Detective Royster told me he had spoken with

Mrs. Miller and she had agreed to meet with Julie and me. Royster had given her my number. After a Tuesday morning SAT tutorial, I saw I had a missed call from a 631 area code and listened to the voicemail message. It was from Valerie Miller.

Julie was working at the dining table as I handed my phone to her and replayed the message. I pulled a chair next to Julie and asked, "Ready?" She nodded, and I hit the missed call number and turned on speaker mode. There were three rings, and then the voice of an older woman answered, "Hello."

"Hi, Mrs. Miller, my name is Julie Fields and my boyfriend Zach is also on the phone with us. Detective Royster was kind enough to arrange for us to speak with you."

Recognizing my cue, I immediately said, "Hi, Mrs. Miller."

"Yes, my dears, Detective Royster is a very nice man and I told him I was most interested in what you had to say."

"Thanks so much," Julie added sweetly. "We would love the opportunity to meet with you and discuss in person the information we have to share, which we believe will be of interest to you."

"That would be lovely. However, you would need to come visit me. My husband Larry is not doing so well, and I really can't leave him for too long. Have you ever been to the North Fork of Long Island?"

"I have not but I've heard about it. Zach, have you been?"

I shook my head before realizing that my answer needed to be verbal. "No, I haven't but I've heard it's very nice."

"Oh, it's beautiful. Larry and I have been here for a long time. His family had property here when he was growing up, mostly farmland, and then we built a house here in the late eighties. The North Fork has flown under the radar seemingly forever, but now it's been discovered, and everyone comes here. We have beaches, vineyards, wineries, farm stands, though the farm stands don't reopen until the spring. It's really a little slice of heaven."

"That sounds amazing. We would love to come out to visit you, and perhaps Zach and I could explore the area afterwards."

We made plans to visit Mrs. Miller on Friday at 11 a.m. for tea.

Chapter 49

Forcing myself to smile, I watched Roger Jr. toddle around the apartment babbling incessantly and picking up everything his stubby, sticky fingers could find. The funny thing is, I've always liked babies, and Roger Jr. was certainly cute enough, but Roger's play-by- play of the baby's "amazing achievements" ruined the experience.

As my brother blabbed about how his offspring was superior to the other 15 diaper-wearing attendees at the birthday party he had just come from (held in a 4,000-square-foot apartment on 88th Street and Park Avenue) I wondered why Junior wasn't smart enough to know that he shouldn't shove a laptop off a table.

"Zach, when you have a toddler visiting, you really need to baby-proof the place. At this age, they pick up everything, particularly those as intelligent and inquisitive as Junior here. Much of it ends up in their mouths."

Junior picked up anything and everything that didn't weigh more than he did. What he couldn't fit into his mouth he handed to his father.

Mercifully, after thirty minutes, my brother said, "I hate to cut this visit short, but I've got to get my little dynamo to take a nap. As soon as I get him into the car, he'll be sound asleep. Hell, the ride in the Bentley is so smooth, half the time *I* feel like taking a nap."

Friday morning Julie and I got into the car at nine o'clock sharp. Google Maps said it would take an hour and 45 minutes to get to Mrs. Miller's home in Jamesport. Julie had picked up a bouquet of flowers as a gift, and we brought with us printouts of some of the texts of the coin, particularly those pertaining to Robert Kramer. Our hope was that we would not need to tell her how we had garnered our information, but we knew we had to be prepared to be asked.

At the end of the Long Island Expressway is the town of Riverhead. At Riverhead you can either go southeast towards the well-known region of the Hamptons, or northeast toward the North Fork, which includes the towns of Greenport, Southold, Mattituck, and Jamesport, where Mrs. Miller lived. We headed north and arrived in front of Mrs. Miller's house, which was located one turn off the main road, by 11:50. We parked next to a white picket fence in front of the house and waited in the car for a few minutes, as we did not want to be too early. The house itself was a white one-story with a gray roof. The well-maintained grounds included a flower bed just waiting in anticipation for the warm weather to arrive.

Julie said, "This certainly is quaint."

"It is," I said. "I've got to be honest, I'm a bit nervous. If we can't convince Mrs. Miller of our information's legitimacy, the investigation will have to come to an end, and it would be the end of Louise's story."

"Yeah, I'm a bit nervous too. It's 11:58, I guess we should go up to the house."

We exited the car and I used the door knocker to announce our arrival. A sprightly woman with reddish brown hair and a big smile opened the door. "You must be Julie and Zach. Please come in. Did you have trouble finding the house? Was there much traffic?"

I answered, "There was not as much traffic as I would have thought. Our GPS led us straight to your door."

"Oh, we've never used those things. I guess we do it the old- fashion way and rely on maps when we need directions. Please come in."

Julie handed Mrs. Miller the bouquet of flowers and said, "These are for you. We really appreciate you seeing us."

"Oh, that is so sweet and totally unnecessary, but thank you. They're lovely."

Mrs. Miller led us into a cozy living room, where a frail, aging man with a few remaining strands of gray hair over his ears sat in a large leather reclining chair. He appeared in his late eighties, with crusty, rheumy eyes.

"Larry, this is the nice young couple I told you about, Julie and Zach."

I approached the man extending my hand, and said, "It's nice to meet you, Mr. Miller."

Mr. Miller returned my handshake without much force, while nodding absentmindedly.

Mrs. Miller said on her husband's behalf, "Larry doesn't speak much anymore. He's content sitting here in the living room and watching the fire."

Julie and I took notice of the old-fashioned stone fireplace, which had several lit logs giving off a soothing warmth as well as a pleasant smell. Mrs. Miller picked up a log tong, which she used to rearrange some of the flaming wood. Then she gestured to the couch, saying, "Both of you please sit down. Would you like some tea? I have Earl Grey or chamomile."

Julie responded, "Earl Grey please," and I quickly agreed.

With the tea, Mrs. Miller brought out warm, just-baked chocolate chip cookies. I took one, and Julie handed me a napkin.

We had agreed that Julie would start the presentation as a woman-to-woman approach might be most effective.

"Mrs. Miller, I know this is a very difficult and awkward situation, and Zach and I are only motivated to do what we believe is right. I apologize if anything I say is painful and upsetting for you. We inadvertently came across information that led us to believe that your father had, um, killed your mother."

Mrs. Miller's facial expression remained the same as she responded, "The detective told me you had found something out concerning my mother, and my father's role in her disappearance. He also said you were not comfortable divulging how you learned the information. I'm curious as to why that is. I'd also like to know if you have any idea how he killed her, and hopefully where my mother's remains might be."

I could see Julie trying to compose her thoughts. "I'm sorry to say this, but it seems your father punched your mother very hard in a fit of anger. She hit her head and he then smothered her with a pillow. Then he buried her in the backyard of the house next to an oak tree."

We were silent as we observed the impact of Julie's words on Mrs. Miller. She looked anguished at first, but acceptance gradually sank in. Finally, Mrs. Miller said in a restrained voice, "I know that oak tree well. At one time, Valerie—my sister—strung a hammock there. We had it up for a few years. My father had a terrible temper. My mother, sister and I lived in constant fear of him. He never actually hit me or Valerie, that I was aware of, but he would scream at us with such ferocity that we felt trapped. I know my mother used to have deep bruises on her sometimes. Never on her face but frequently on her arms and legs."

Neither Julie nor I felt comfortable enough to speak, so the three of us sat in silence for a few minutes. Finally, Mrs. Miller asked, "Zach, did you finish all the cookies?"

Julie looked embarrassed as I sheepishly answered, "I'm sorry. I did. They were delicious."

Mrs. Miller smiled and said, "Larry used to eat like that. He used to love my cookies. I've always prided myself on my baking, and it does my heart good to see you enjoy them like that. Before you go, I will pack up some for you to take home."

I felt like sticking my tongue out at Julie but instead I said, "I'd love that. Thank you so much."

Mrs. Miller looked at us warmly."You two are so cute together. Larry and I were like that at one time. Now we are nothing but old relics."

Before either one of us could refute what she said, she continued, "I'd really like to have my mother's remains back to give her a proper burial. I owe her that, she deserves it. My mom was a warm, wonderful woman, and a great mother. She made us feel safe and loved, even while we lived with that horrible man. I only wish divorce had been as common then as it is today."

I figured it was time I offered something besides my hearty appetite to the discussion. "Mrs. Miller, you asked us how we learned the circumstances of your mother's death, and this is where it gets complicated. The information came to us in an unconventional manner. We strongly prefer not to divulge the discovery details unless it becomes necessary. Even if it does become unavoidable, we're afraid that a judge would question our evidence. So, a court order to exhume your mother's remains seems extremely unlikely. We must think of another way, and Julie and I believe the best solution is to ask the current owner directly seeking approval to dig up around the oak tree."

Mrs. Miller closed her eyes, took a deep breath, and settled back into her chair. Emotions, both fragile and palpable seeped into all of us. Suddenly she sat up and said, "My mother used to tell my sister and me that you trust people until they do something to lose your trust. I might be a naive old woman but I trust that you both are telling me the truth. It's inconceivable that two seemingly nice people would concoct this story to con someone old enough to be their grandmother. We're not wealthy people, but comfortable. If I have to spend a few thousand dollars excavating the garden to bring peace to my mother, it's money well spent. The only problem is, I don't know the current owner or if they will grant us permission."

Julie chimed in, "We hope Detective Royster might help with that."

We got up to leave, saying our goodbyes. I made Julie a bit anxious as I dawdled a minute or so by the front door, trying to look bereft and empty-handed. A moment later Valerie returned, handed me a small brown paper bag and said, "Sorry Zach. I almost forgot your cookies."

Mrs. Miller asked us to promise we would return to see her and the beautiful North Fork in spring, when everything was green and in full bloom. We promised to do so, providing she bake more cookies, provoking a huge grin. We got back to Astoria at 4:30, and I immediately called Detective Royster on his cell. He answered with a harried voice, "Detective Royster."

"Hi, Detective Royster, this is Zachary Howard. Sorry to bother you, but we just got back from seeing Mrs. Miller, and I just wanted to update you."

"Thanks, Zach. Valerie Miller beat you to the punch. It sounds like things went well. I'm going to contact the current Uniondale house owner, and request permission to dig in their backyard as part of an old case we are investigating. If we don't receive their voluntary cooperation, Mrs. Miller said she would try as well. And if that doesn't work, the only other option is disclosing the evidence you have to a judge and seeking permission for a court order to excavate. I've got to go now. I'll be in touch."

That night Julie and I decided to order pizza in and enjoy a quiet evening, joyously basking in the progress we made. Julie, lying on the couch, nestled in my arm, suggested, "You might want to clean up a bit. I've never seen your place such a mess."

"Sorry. Roger Jr. made a mess when he was here, picking up everything and throwing things about. I've been meaning to straighten up, but haven't had the chance."

The following Tuesday, I finally heard back from Detective Royster in a voicemail message, which said, "We've received permission from the owner to excavate a portion of the yard. I made the necessary arrangements based on your information provided, and we scheduled the work for next week. It's important you understand that I've taken a risk here, and in the event our efforts don't determine a crime was committed, we'll need to discuss consequences. If you have questions, call me."

I took a deep breath. It had never occurred to me that the information the coin had been producing might have been inaccurate, but I guess that was certainly a possibility. I had done checks on other information we received based on writings the coin generated, all verified. I guess it was also possible that what the coin reported as accurate at a time had later changed. What if Robert Kramer did bury his wife's body in the backyard initially but moved it later?

That whole week I was a nervous wreck. I had difficulty sleeping, couldn't concentrate on my work, and deep circles developed under my eyes. Astoundingly, I completely lost my appetite. Julie was handling the stress much better. She kept suggesting we go for long walks, but as I wasn't really sleeping, I didn't have the energy to even make it around the block. Finally, a week after Detective Royster's message, I received a follow-up from him confirming excavation first thing Wednesday morning. He promised to call me upon completion.

Julie and I spent all Wednesday together. We even held our tutoring sessions that morning simultaneously in my apartment— headphone on, voices low. Concentration was near impossible. Zoning out, my student's "Earth to Zach, earth to Zach," jolted me back to reality.

My appetite still nonexistent, Julie insisted that I eat something, so I nibbled on two peanut butter and jelly sandwiches.

The phone rang at 5:14, with Detective Royster's name popping up. Paralyzed, I handed Julie the phone, watching intently as she and the detective spoke. "Yes, Detective. Thank you for calling. Yes, I understand. Of course. She had to know. Certainly, I know it takes time. I will tell him. Yes, I believe that is all right. The afternoon is better for us. OK, see you then."

I felt my throat tightening up. "So what did he say?"

Julie calmly replied, "If you really wanted to know, you would have answered your own phone." Julie then laughed and gave me a big hug. "They found human bones buried near the oak tree! They're human!"

"Oh my god!" Waves of tension washed away from every pore of my body and my breathing normalized. I asked, "I heard you say the afternoon is better for us. What was that about?"

"He wanted to know if we could return to the station tomorrow. The captain would like to thank us and discuss further the information about the likelihood of a second murder."

With that Julie took a step back and said, "We did a great thing. I love you, Zach."

Beaming, I replied, "I'm starving. Do you think we could go out for gyros?"

><

Walking home from the restaurant, Julie took my hand as she told me, "What you did was remarkable."

I honestly felt humbled but responded the best I could. "What *we* did was remarkable. I certainly couldn't have done it without you. I needed your support and partnership on this journey. We approached everything methodically and responsibly. The coin was a gift, a gift that we had use properly. Someone else might have only focused on how to use the coin selfishly for monetary gain, without considering the benefit it might have to others. I really couldn't have done it without you. We're a team, kind of like"—here I thought carefully and swallowed hard—"Sherlock Holmes and a young Jane Marple."

Julie giggled, bit her lip, and said, "All of that is true, but when I said you're amazing, I meant I didn't think it was possible for a person to eat a plate full of grape leaves, a bowl of baba ghanoush with pita, a gyro platter with rice, a souvlaki sandwich and an order of French fries. Not to mention half of my tilapia."

I think I blushed a bit.

Chapter 50

We were back in the conference room with Captain Sheridan and Detective Royster. To our pleasant surprise, we saw Valerie Miller already there. Detective Royster had sent a car to pick her up; Mrs. Miller's daughter was home with Larry. On the table sat an overflowing cookie tray. Mrs. Miller winked at me and said, "This time I added walnuts—I hope you like them."

Reaching for two, I said, "I love walnuts."

Captain Sheridan turned to us and said, "The three of us really want to thank you both. I have no idea how you got your information, and I'd love to know your source. I understand your continued reluctance, but I'm hopeful that at some point you'll tell us...Any chance that time is now?"

I looked at Julie before replying, "Honestly Captain, we prefer not to do so."

Captain Sheridan grinned and said, "I figured you'd say that. We brought Mrs. Miller in to tell her that we confirmed the bones found were those belonging to a woman approximately 50-60 sixty years old. We're not yet able to positively identify, but it seems possible the remains are Mrs. Miller's mother. As you were both instrumental in finding her, Mrs. Miller asked us to invite you here today. Mrs. Miller, our goal is to confirm the remains' identity within a few weeks. Of course, we'll keep you informed, in real time."

For the first time, Mrs. Miller struggled with her emotions. As her breath deepened and eyes teared, Julie reached out grabbing Valerie's hand. In a halting voice, Valerie added, "I don't know how to thank the four of you enough. I've had a tremendous void in my life these past forty years. My sister died without ever knowing what happened to our mother, and I'm sure that loss took years off her life. Knowing my family will now properly bury and memorialize my mom is a blessing. Thank you, thank you."

Detective Royster stood up and placed a Kleenex box in front of Valerie. "Mrs. Miller, if you'd like, I'll have an officer drive you home now."

Julie stood up, hugged Mrs. Miller and said, "We plan on visiting you on the North Fork in the spring if that's okay with you."

"I insist, and I'll have a dozen cookies waiting for Zach."

Julie and I got up to leave but Captain Sheridan asked, "Would you both mind staying a few minutes longer?"

Detective Royster escorted Mrs. Miller out, and upon returning, Captain Sheridan spoke. "Last time we met, you said you had evidence that Robert Kramer may have killed someone else." He looked down at his notes. "The alleged victim, a Mrs. Graber. I hope you will tell us why you believe Mr. Kramer murdered her."

I looked over at Julie, who nodded, and I began. "Mrs. Graber worked with Mr. Kramer while she volunteered at the North Shore Home. During her interactions with him, she discovered that Kramer killed his wife, burying the body in his backyard. She confronted him with this information, telling him she found out by overhearing Mr. Kramer talking in his sleep. Kramer became agitated and denied everything. He was having a nightmare, he said. To placate him and buy herself some time, Louise—that's Mrs. Graber—told him that she believed his explanation but that she was obligated to report the incident."

"Before you ask how she was so certain Kramer had killed his wife, and it wasn't actually a delirious nightmare—Louise learned this information through the same source that Julie and I learned he had killed his wife. And I'm sorry, but we still can't divulge the source."

"Louise's work supervisor left town for a few days. So, she told Kramer that when the supervisor returned, she would report the incident to the administration. The day before her boss returned, she stopped by to see Mr. Kramer. At first it seemed he had calmed down, but when he asked if she was still going to mention the alleged confession to her supervisor and she said yes, he became grim and dark again. She quickly left his room with the hope that she wouldn't need to interact with him again. She figured that all she had to do was speak with the higher-ups, and they would determine the appropriate course of action, such as contacting the police."

"So how do you know Kramer killed her?" Detective Royster asked.

Julie answered, "We really don't know for certain. We are speculating. However, there is a good deal of circumstantial evidence to support the theory." Julie stopped and smiled guardedly at the troubled looks on the faces of Captain Sheridan and Detective Royster.

"I know, I stream too many police dramas. We do know that Mr. Kramer was an expert mechanic, and unlike many of the other residents, he was mobile. He was frequently walking around the building and the grounds of the home. He also knew which car belonged to Louise, and where she typically parked it. To further quote the shows I stream, he had the means, motive, and opportunity to commit the crime." With that Julie sat back and smiled while everyone else laughed.

I took the opportunity to add, "We have the contact information for Louise Graber's two children. Wouldn't it be a good idea to reach out to them to tell them there may be new information on their mother's death? That in fact, it might have been murder, and not death by accident?"

At that moment, I felt the atmosphere in the room change. I looked over at Julie, and she had a look on her face I couldn't describe. I wasn't certain what I said wrong, or perhaps even right for that matter, but something I said had made some sort of impact that I was unable to read.

Captain Sheridan cleared his throat authoritatively. "Detective Royster and I take our responsibilities very seriously. Based on the information the two of you provided, I would say there is certainly a likelihood that Robert Kramer tampered with Louise Graber's car, causing her accident and death. My initial thought was, What's the benefit of reopening an investigation now? The victim, dead for 40 years, the likely murderer also dead for decades. The victim, buried by her family shortly after the accident, allowing her children to say their goodbyes. Louise's family had closure all those years ago. To reopen those wounds now—I'm not sure anyone would benefit."

"The daughter of the murder suspect in the case has just learned what happened to her mother and will soon be receiving her mother's remains for a proper burial. As horrible as the realization must be for her that her father murdered her mother, she has accepted this grim reality as a horrific moment of uncontrollable rage. To additionally learn that perhaps he was also responsible for another woman's death might be too much to bear."

"To find evidence that someone had tampered with a car that was junked 40 years ago is close to impossible. I'm sorry, I honestly don't see anything good coming from pursuing this matter."

I started to respond. I was going to say that it's important that the truth comes out, allowing Louise's children to know what really happened, but Julie spoke up first.

"Captain Sheridan, I agree with you. I can't imagine the additional pain it would cause both Mrs. Miller and Louise's family."

I opted to stay silent.

Captain Sheridan and Detective Royster stood up, which was our cue that the meeting was over.

Detective Royster said, "I'd like to again thank you both. What the two of you did was amazing and you gave a true gift to a very deserving woman. I haven't been doing this as long as Captain Sheridan, but I'd venture a guess that this may end up being the most unique case I'll ever see in my career."

Captain Sheridan added, "I guarantee it. If either of you ever have information to share with us regarding a crime in the future, please do not hesitate to reach out. And, if you ever want to disclose your source of information to us, dinner and drinks will be on me."

As I turned onto the Grand Central Parkway, Julie said, "Zach, that was the right thing to do. I know you wanted to take this further, but Captain Sheridan was right, there was nothing else to achieve by reopening painful wounds."

"I guess you're right," I said with a sigh. I contemplated taking the L.I.E. home but figured at 4:00 p.m. on a weekday the traffic would be worse. As we inched along at ten miles an hour, I was not too confident I made the right choice.

"I'm just sad it's over—the investigating, the discoveries, and, um, working with you. I'm going to miss it now that it's over."

"Zach, it's not over. We can figure out other adventures the dime can take us on. Not only that, but even without the dime we can make new adventures."

A horn blasted, and I advanced a total of 20 feet to the apparent satisfaction of the asshole behind me.

"Look, I'm certainly hoping that's the case, but my novel's going nowhere, I haven't figured out how I can write about the dime, and it's fairly clear I'm not exactly your father's top choice for his daughter. Making matters worse, Roger told my parents that he thinks I have a girlfriend, and tonight I've got a Howard family conference call scheduled at 7:00."

A cacophony of car horns drowned Julie out. "What did you say?"

"I said I'm not certain what the problem is with you letting your family know you have a girlfriend. Are you ashamed of me?"

"Of course not. It's just that once they find out, they're going to want to meet you."

"And what's wrong with that?"

The parking lot in front of me began to move forward at a brisker pace, and I did too. "If you think your father gave me a hard time about not being good enough for you, that will be nothing compared to the abuse my family, particularly my mother, will dish out."

"Zach, I don't get it. I may not be a supermodel or working on a solution to achieve world peace, but I think I'm a pretty nice person. And I'm good for you."

"No, no, it's not you they will criticize. They won't understand what you're doing with me and will likely try to talk you out of it. Hell, I wouldn't be surprised if my mother tried to fix you up with a son of one of her friends."

"Zach, you are too funny."

"I wish I was joking."

Chapter 51

Julie helped me straighten out my apartment, even lending me her vacuum cleaner. We sat on my couch, me sipping on a Coors Lite and Julie drinking Fiji water she brought from her apartment. Apparently, she preferred drinking water from a plastic bottle rather than from my garage sale beer steins.

"Zach, you've got to admit your place looks a lot better."

"Absolutely. Thanks for helping. I really should buy a vacuum. How about we set up the laptop for one more try? We really don't know what happened to the dime once Louise passed."

"I don't know, Zach. Do we really want to completely close Louise's chapter? It almost feels as if we are in a mourning period and out of respect, we should savor her life before moving on."

"You know what, you're one hundred percent right. There is no reason to start anything new. I'm not ready to say goodbye to Louise yet."

Julie smiled. "What's the matter, Zach? You look confused."

"Mmm, I'm not sure where the dime is. Do you see it anywhere?"

We both got up and looked around, cautiously at first, and then picking up and moving things around with greater urgency. A queasy feeling overtook me as I considered the possibility that the coin was nowhere in the apartment. My efforts to find it became more harried as the apartment soon began to look as messy as it had before. Suddenly the reality struck me like a dagger in the pit of my stomach.

"Roger Jr.! Julie, Roger's kid either flung the coin underneath something or put it in his mouth and swallowed it. If he did swallow it, I'm going to have his stomach pumped. Hey, if he swallowed it, do you think it, you know, eventually comes out? How many days ago was that? Shit, it probably was in a goddamn diaper that Roger threw out days ago."

"OK, Zach, calm down."

Only then did I realize I was close to hyperventilating. Julie put her hand on my arm and said, "Listen to me, the first thing we should do is get on our hands and knees and search every inch of the apartment. If we don't find it, you should call Roger and calmly explain the situation."

We spent the next thirty minutes searching every inch of the apartment. I frequently thought I'd like a much larger apartment, but this was one time I was thrilled to live in a space no more than 350 square feet in size.

Our intensive search turned up three pennies, all 1988 and later, two paper clips, a half dozen rubber bands, a beer cap, and multiple dust balls, but no dime. I had to reach out to my brother.

I figured the situation warranted a phone conversation rather than an exchange of texts, so I called. Of course he didn't pick up, and in response to my call I received a text back advising "I am on the other line and will get back to you when I can." I then texted him to say I needed to speak with him as soon as possible. As soon as possible turned out to be four hours later.

"Hey, what's the emergency, big brother?"

Julie gave me excellent advice: don't lose my temper and absolutely do not make any disparaging remarks about my nephew. I took a deep breath. "Remember me telling you I found an old dime that was very important to me? I must have left it out when you and Roger Jr. visited, and now it's missing. I remember how inquisitive Junior was, picking up everything in sight, and I was wondering if you might know what happened to it? I'm also very concerned that he may even have put it into his mouth and accidentally swallowed it. I wouldn't want him to get sick." I braced myself for Roger's response.

"No way could he have swallowed a coin. He's much too smart to do that. I don't remember seeing it—gotta run!" And with that, my brother hung up.

While I was contemplating the mantra, "I hate my brother" for the five-hundredth time, my phone rang. To my surprise, it was Roger.

"Sorry, I was in the middle of ten things earlier. But I remembered that Junior was handing me different things from your apartment, and I believe he handed me a coin."

"What did you do with it? What did you do with it?"

"Chill, bro, I was just about to tell you. You really need to calm down."

I remembered what Julie had told me and took another deep breath. "I'm sorry, Roger. Do you happen to recall what you did with the coin?"

"I guess I just put it in my pocket without really thinking. To me, it was just a dime, and I figured I'd just keep it out of harm's way."

While I was fantasizing about various ways of placing Roger in harm's way, I took another few deep breaths and asked, "So, do you think it's still in the pocket of the pants you wore that day?"

"No, that's the funny thing. I usually don't carry any change with me but when we left your apartment to walk to the garage, we passed some bum sitting on a corner with a cardboard sign saying he was a homeless vet. I was only carrying big bills, and remembered the dime I had in my pocket, so I flipped that into the guy's can. What made me remember it is that I must have been a good ten or fifteen feet from the can, and my aim was spot on."

I didn't think that breathing exercises similar to the type women utilize during labor would get me through this but gritting my teeth I replied, "Roger, that coin meant a lot to me. What did the guy look like? Where was he sitting?"

"Are you serious? What did the guy look like? He looked like a bum. He had stringy gray hair that looked like he hadn't washed in weeks. Oh, and he had a dog with him—some kind of mutt, kind of cute, though, for a mutt. He was on the block with the garage. What are you going to do, go up to a homeless guy and ask him for your dime back? Listen, it's my fault. I'll send you a hundred bucks. What's your Venmo?"

Breathing exercises be damned. "Roger, it's not about money!

That dime was special to me and irreplaceable. I'll try to find that poor unfortunate man and see if I can get it back. You truly don't care about anyone else, do you?" I hung up this time.

At 7:00 p.m. I joined the conference call only to hear my mother's joyous words. "Zach, why are you always the last one to join? Roger and Suzy have been on the call forever, and they are very busy professionals."

"Mom, the call was set for 7, the time on my phone says 7:01, which means that taking into account the time spent on your warm greeting, I arrived on the call at 7:00, which was the scheduled time."

"Never mind, I don't want to argue with you," she said, which of course is precisely what she wanted to do. The volume of her voice escalated. "Now tell us about this girl Roger says you've been seeing."

It felt like only ten seconds passed, yet my mother cried, "Zach, Suzy, Roger, your dad and I are patiently waiting."

Patience and my mother have never belonged in the same sentence.

"Hi, Dad, Suzy. Hello again, Roger. Yeah, I've been seeing this woman for a couple of months now—she's my neighbor and really great. We spend a lot of time together."

Suzy asked, "Is it getting serious?"

"I think it might be."

My dad chimed in, "That's really great, Zach. We're happy for you. You deserve to be with someone nice."

I silently counted to myself, hoping I would get through the conversation unscathed. But Roger said, "I've met her. She isn't half bad. Zach's doing okay for himself."

Gee, that wasn't too bad, I thought, as I prepared to say goodbye and hang up.

And then my darling mother asked, "So, what's wrong with her?"

"There is absolutely nothing wrong with her, Mom. She is a wonderful person and genuinely likes me and—"

Before I could finish, I heard my mother scream.

My father yelled, "Beth, are you okay?"

In unison, Suzy, Roger and I asked, "What's happened?"

My dad hurriedly said, "She fell and hit her head. I think she's unconscious. I'll call you back."

"I'm sure she'll be fine," Julie said while rubbing the back of my neck. I had gone straight to her apartment once the conference call abruptly ended at 7:10.

"I imagined a lot of responses from my mother about my having a nice girlfriend, threatening to faint being one of them. However, actually fainting was unexpected."

"Zach, I've never seen you so upset. I'm sure she'll be fine. Your dad will call you soon. Would you like something to eat while we wait?"

"I'm not hungry, and it's not my mom that's got me so upset, it's the coin. Hmmmm, what food do you have? Maybe eating a little something would calm my nerves."

"I've got some Annie's macaroni and cheese. Would you like me to make some?"

"That would be great. Would you make two boxes?"

The phone's ping interrupted the meal planning. The text from Roger read, "Hey Bro. You really should be more careful before unloading some shocking news. LOL. I just spoke to Dad. Mom's going to be okay. She hit her head and will need a few stitches but will go home tonight. They'll check if she was concussed but she's coherent. Dad said she tripped on a rolled-up portion of a rug, but we all know the real reason. Ha."

Julie was looking at the text with me and said, "What an ass."

"That he is, but I guess everything is fine with my mom, and I'll call my dad in a little while. But first let me tell you how big an ass my brother truly is."

><

Come Saturday I tried my best not to think about the lost dime, and instead focused on the dreaded evening, only a few hours away. I usually enjoy Saturday nights, but anticipating this one gave me a severe case of indigestion. In less than six hours, Julie and I were going to Fort Lee, New Jersey, to have dinner with my parents, Roger, and his wife, Priscilla. My mother had fully recovered from her fall and insisted we bring Julie over to meet them. Naturally Suzy wasn't coming, as she was keynote speaker at a Stanford human genomics conference. Suzy promised to get together with Julie and me very soon, as she is "so looking forward to meeting Julie and catching up." Yeah, sure. That will happen.

It was to be a grown-up only evening, so the second coming, Roger Jr., a.k.a. Sticky Fingers, wouldn't be there. I was sure in his absence we would hear all about how he's on pace to win the decathlon in the 2036 summer Olympics, assuming he can break away from discovering a new, clean fuel source and saving the planet.

"Zach, please stop pacing."

"I'm sorry, but I'm too upset to sit down, and I figure if I walk a few miles in your living room, I might work up an appetite to eat my mother's meatloaf tonight."

"How do you know she will be serving meatloaf?"

"She always serves meatloaf. She can only make about two or three things, and her meatloaf is the only one I'd categorize as edible. She serves them with these tiny potatoes she roasts, overcooked asparagus, and then for dessert, store-bought frozen apple pie, which she tries to pass off as homemade."

"It all sounds good."

"She puts ketchup and breadcrumbs in the meatloaf, and my guess is it's one part meat to five parts breadcrumbs with half a gallon of ketchup. Her meatloaf tastes like a ketchup sandwich."

"I'm sure it's not that bad. Besides, tonight is not about the food but about the company."

I grimaced. "The food will be far and away the best part."

"Are you sweating?"

"Yes, I'm sweating," I said, wiping my forehead with a sleeve. "I'm a nervous wreck."

"Why are *you* nervous? *I'm* the one meeting your parents for the first time."

We had just gotten out of the elevator, and my feet felt like lead as I looked down the long corridor towards my parent's high-rise apartment. Fort Lee has more residential apartment buildings than most of New Jersey, which typically has private homes.

They've lived there for over 20 years.

"I'm nervous because I know how the evening will turn out. If you open a door to rabid, unleashed dogs behind it, you'd be nervous too."

Julie took my hand and led me down the hall. My dad opened the door, warmly shook my hand, and gave me a half hug.

"You must be Julie. It's so nice to meet you. Beth is in the kitchen. Let me tell her you guys are here."

Julie smiled knowingly at me while I mouthed, "Wait."

A moment later, my 5-foot 2-inch mother stormed into the living room, somehow soaking up all the oxygen. "Zach, so who is this?"

"Mom, you know very well, this is Julie."

"Well, let me see you." She spun Julie in a pirouette. "So, you're the woman who has stolen my Zach's heart. I can certainly understand what he sees in you, but whatever do you see in him?" My mother chortled. "Zach is a good boy, just taking his time finding himself. He's a late bloomer—very late. Ha ha, but Edgar and I always knew he had a lot of goodness in him. Didn't we, Edgar?"

"Beth, that's enough. No reason to embarrass Zach. Nothing's wrong with him."

"Of course not. It's just, he hasn't completely found himself yet. Not like his sister and younger brother. Now, they're both extremely accomplished. You'll be meeting Roger and our amazing daughter-in-law soon. Priscilla is undoubtedly going to be the managing partner in a few years of the most prestigious law firm in the country. And to look at her, you'd think she was a Hollywood star. She's that beautiful and glamorous. They'll be here soon. They are both so busy with their successful careers, we can't expect them to get here on time. Their son, my grandson, is the most beautiful baby you'll ever see. With those genes, I wouldn't be surprised if he becomes president one day."

Julie saw an opening and took it. "Mrs. Howard, Zach and I bought you some assorted Greek dips as appetizers from our neighborhood."

Julie wanted to bring a floral arrangement but I insisted we bring food so I could have something edible to eat. Naturally my mother said, "That's nice of you, but I've made a delicious dinner already. Flowers might have been a bit more practical."

Fortunately, my father saved the day by saying, "I love Greek food. Why don't we put them out as appetizers?"

Just then, the doorbell rang, and my mother hurried to the door, calling, "That must be Roger and Priscilla!"

I sat down on the couch and glanced at the framed photographs throughout the living room. On the console table there was a photo of Suzy in a crimson cap and gown, receiving her doctoral degree. Next to that photo was one of Roger in a cap and gown receiving his MBA. Bordering those two were family shots of Suzy, her husband and their three children, and one of Roger, Priscilla and the baby messiah.

Julie was I looking at a prominent photo of my dad with his arm around Roger holding a large golf trophy, captioned "A Flight Men's Champion Acorn Country Club - 2014." Adjacent to that photo, in a sterling silver frame, was Suzy standing at a podium, authoritatively lecturing a huge audience. A small table just below the oversized television mounted on a wall contained two more framed photos: my parents holding hands on a beach while sipping fluorescent pink cocktails; and a photo of the four grandkids, with our future president on the lap of Suzy's eldest child. Try as I might, I couldn't find any visual proof of my existence.

"Edgar? Edgar! Roger and Priscilla are here, and they've brought the most beautiful floral arrangement. It's gorgeous. So thoughtful of them and appropriate too." Roger slapped me on the back and greeted me with, "Hey, bro."

I took Julie's hand and walked her over to my brother and his wife and said, "Roger, I believe you've already met Julie, and Julie, this is Priscilla."

Priscilla can be a bit intimidating. She's about 5 foot 10 with cascading blond hair and eyes that alternate between green and turquoise. She has a pert nose and full lips, and a body that epitomized "hot." Her black blouse and pleated slacks probably cost more than I make in a month. If you added the shoes, it would be more than three months of SAT tutoring. Beautiful, brilliant and accomplished, her existence was downright unjust. Thankfully, like Roger—she's awful.

Julie grasped Priscilla's extended hand and timidly said, "It's very nice to meet you."

Roger covered the two womens' hands, gave Julie a kiss on her cheek, and smiled radiantly. "It's great to see you again. Last time I saw you, poor old Zach was laid out moaning incessantly. It appears you've done a great job nursing him back to health."

At that moment my dad brought out the pita bread and dips and put them out in bowls on the glass table between the couch and chairs and asked, "What is everyone having to drink?"

I immediately reached over and placed a heaping serving of

hummus on a piece of pita, which motivated my mother to say, "Try not to eat too much of those hors d'oeuvres. I've made my specialty for dinner, so don't get too filled up."

My wonderful brother, acting as if he was so genuinely excited, said, "Mom, don't tell me, did you make your delicious meatloaf?"

At that moment, a pita triangle became lodged in my esophagus, causing my mother to hold her words. But then Roger overzealously pounded me on the back with what felt like a two-by-four.

"And I've made the most scrumptious tiny potatoes to go with it," my mother said. "I'm also serving asparagus."

"That sounds wonderful, Mom. Doesn't it, Zach? After all, you're the big eater in the family."

I was beginning to lament that I hadn't choked to death on the pita. My father continued to be my salvation, playing the good host. "We have wine, beer, or I could make mixed drinks. What would everyone like?"

I had a beer, as did my father, while Julie and my mother had white wine. Roger asked for a scotch and then announced, "But Priscilla will not be drinking, at least not for the next few months."

My mother seemed to levitate out of her chair and fly in Priscilla's direction. "Are you—are you pregnant?"

Priscilla gave her signature radiant smile, her glistening, perfectly white teeth coming together all at once. "I am. I'm due in June, and this time we're going to have a girl."

I forced myself to smile and join in the chorus of boisterous congratulations.

Roger went to his wife's side, put his arm around her and said, "It's just what we wanted, a boy and a girl. We've decided two is the perfect number. That way we can spread our love and attention equally, and each will be special."

A beaming Priscilla chimed in, "Of course, if we were having another boy, we'd be thrilled too, but having one of each has always been my dream. A boy to follow in Roger's footsteps, and a daughter to follow in mine."

"That's wonderful," my father said.

"Congratulations to both of you," Julie said. "That's so exciting."

Not wanting to feel left out, I offered, "In this modern day, wouldn't it be okay if a boy followed in his mother's footsteps and a girl in the footsteps of her father?"

My mother glared at me and in her ever-diplomatic way added, "Don't be obtuse, Zach. Priscilla, you are absolutely right, two is the perfect number of children to have."

Julie and I shared a grimace as I once again couldn't hold my tongue. "Mom, you do realize that Suzy has three kids right? By the way, you and Dad also have three kids, though you tend to forget that fact. Of course, if you had decided to only have two kids, Roger here would never have been born, so maybe two is the right number."

"Don't be so argumentative, Zach. You should be thrilled for Roger and Priscilla. Let's sit down and eat."

My mother and father sat at opposite ends of the dining room table, while I sat next to Julie across from Priscilla. My mother continued to serve as the enthusiastic emcee of The Roger and Priscilla Show, and plated everyone's meals. During the first course, my mother's version of a salad—lettuce with mayonnaise—we learned that they were naming the baby Abigail in honor of Priscilla's grandmother. Accompanied by stale rolls we discussed riveting details about Priscilla's groundbreaking merger and acquisition negotiation and Roger's new client with a $3 billion portfolio.

At last, my father turned his attention to Julie. "So, Julie, tell us a bit about yourself."

Julie blushed and wiped her mouth. "Well, I grew up in Connecticut, went to Trinity College and majored in math. I've always been a bit of a math geek and loved working with numbers. Now, I'm primarily a math tutor at the same company Zach works for. Of course, Zach is only doing it part-time while he writes his book, which is great and will undoubtedly be a bestseller. Zach and I discussed starting our own tutoring business once he finishes the novel. With my expertise in math and Zach's in English and writing, we don't really need to work for someone else, do we, Zach?"

I just shook my head. I was stunned, as Julie and I had never discussed starting our own company. But it certainly sounded good. Hell, my book, which currently was going nowhere fast, turning into a bestseller was a startling revelation as well, but Julie was on a roll and I wasn't about to stop her.

"Of course, my family's primary focus is philanthropy. It's not well-known, and my parents are very private people, but my mother's grandfather had a series of patents that made him extremely wealthy. The money has passed down from generation to generation so realistically my great-grandchildren should never actually need to work. Of course, my parents don't advertise, or even discuss, their immense wealth. They feel it's important to have a strong work ethic, and being the proverbial trust fund baby would limit one's initiative. Fortunately, Zach and I are completely in agreement with this philosophy, so if we do decide one day to make a lifetime commitment to one another, it would still be our intention to work as if we didn't have an enormous safety net."

Everyone's mouths were now chewing less vigorously, if at all, and the clicking of dinnerware on china ceased entirely. All eyes were on Julie.

"I share a lot of the same interests as Zach, which is fortunate. We both love nature, hiking, and cooking, particularly healthy food."

At this point, an ashen Roger, looking in need of mouth-to-mouth resuscitation, stammered, "Zach likes healthy food? He likes hiking?"

I just shrugged.

Julie continued. "Roger, I'm not sure how much time you've spent with Zach recently, but over the past year, he engaged in introspection and soul searching. Many a time he has told me he wants to be a true difference-maker. Sure, material things are important to him, and to both of us, but at what expense? He wants to help people, rather than live an empty superficial life. Buying fancy cars and expensive things—that screams insecurity and unfulfillment. Don't you agree?"

"Well, geez, I, uh..." Roger said. He looked confused as to whether he should take offense.

"For the past month, Zach has led me on the most fascinating expedition. Through some research he was doing for his new book, he discovered evidence about a crime committed forty years ago. He uncovered things that the police were unable to uncover—facts leading to the exhumation of the remains of a long-lost woman. Zach found the project so fascinating and fulfilling that he generously allowed me to join him in his work. Together, we not only identified a two-time murderer, we also brought closure to two grieving families. Zach plans on using this experience as material for his next book."

"Surely, Mr. and Mrs. Howard, you both know how truly gifted Zach is?"

My mother's jaw was somewhere between her shoulders and her belly. My father answered, "We always knew Zach had a great deal of potential, and he's always been kind and considerate."

The rest of the dinner, blissfully silent, improved the meatloaf's taste.

><

I opened the car door for Julie and rushed around to the driver's side. Once seated I blurted out, "You were un-fucking-believable! You shut my mother and Roger up, and made the dinner not only survivable, but almost enjoyable. You were kidding about your great-grandfather and that whole inheritance thing, right?"

"My great-grandfather was actually a bartender who died of alcoholism at the age of forty-five."

In a firm and confident voice, I said, "You're amazing. I love you."

Basking in the triumph of the evening lasted several minutes before a pang of disquietude settled in the pit of my stomach. I exhaled heavily. "Do you think it's gone forever?"

"Listen, Zach, the odds of finding the homeless man and somehow getting it back seem very long, but why don't we at least try? Tomorrow, we can spend the day searching."

Chapter 52

Julie and I were on a mission. We split up and walked in opposite directions, searching for a homeless man with a dog on the streets of Astoria, Queens, stopping at local businesses and asking if anyone knew the guy. We checked each other's progress, or lack thereof, with regular texts. I started off speaking with the on-duty garage attendant where Roger parked his Bentley. Unfortunately, the guy didn't speak a great deal of English and didn't seem to understand who I was looking to find. Julie found a couple of people who thought they had seen our guy around—they remembered the dog more than the man. At 1:00 p.m. we met up for lunch at a pizza place I like on 31st Avenue to compare notes.

"Zach, if he's in the area, we will find him. If we aren't successful today, we can check at the closest homeless shelter tomorrow."

"Yeah, good idea. But even if we find him, what are the chances he still has the dime or even lets us look through his change?"

Julie grabbed my hand and said, "It's possible, or likely, you'll never get the dime back, but you need to recognize all the positive things the dime helped you experience. It took you on an unbelievable adventure and helped to bring closure to a lovely woman."

I could tell Julie had more to say, but I inserted, "It helped bring us close together. As the commercial says, that was priceless."

Julie's smile made bearable the realization that I may never hold the dime again.

After lunch, Julie took me to a Greek bakery nearby and bought me a box full of pastries: *baklava*, *katafi*, walnut cake, and my favorite, *galaktoboureko*. The last one I have difficulty pronouncing but no difficulty eating. I was about to cross the street, pastries in hand, when Julie asked, "Zach, do you see what I see?"

"Sure, a Häagen-Dazs store. But I'm looking forward to these pastries later and don't want to ruin my appetite with ice cream now."

"No, Zach, look! By the tree on the corner!"

I carefully followed Julie's gaze. There was a dog on a leash tied to a tree and a man sitting in the shade. My pulse quickened, and I grabbed Julie's hand, pulling her towards them. I guess we approached too hastily because the dog, small- to mid-sized with the snout of a poodle and the body of a Golden Retriever, started barking at us.

"Hi, I'm Julie and this is Zach. Who is this adorable fellow?"

The man looked up and in a halting voice said, "This is Garcia, as in Jerry. What a great tragedy when we lost that genius."

Julie magically pulled a baggy out of her pocket, and the man's eyes lit up. They darkened, though, as Julie said, "I've got a chunk of cheddar cheese here. Do you think Garcia would like a piece?"

Garcia wagged his tail. "He'd love it, and Herman—that's me—wouldn't mind a slice too, if you can spare it."

"My pleasure." My very prepared girlfriend produced a plastic knife and cut two chunks of cheese, one small, and one considerably larger. She handed the small one to me and as I was about to put it in my mouth, her eyes widened, directing me to the anxiously waiting dog.

"I was just kidding," I sheepishly offered while I hesitantly extended the piece to the dog. Garcia took it from my fingers in a second, even licking them in the process.

Julie handed the remaining cheese to Herman. "Zach recently lost something very special to him, and we think there is a possibility someone may have given it to you."

Herman seemed to digest this information as he began to nibble at the cheese. "What is it that you think I may have? I guess you can tell that other than Garcia, I don't have too much."

Finally, I thought, it was my turn to speak. "My baby nephew accidentally took a coin from my apartment and gave it to my brother. I believe my brother, not even looking at the coin or knowing its value to me, might have given it to you."

"Are you talking about that old dime?"

Julie and I were a bit taken back by the immediate recognition of my lost treasure. Feeling a rush of adrenaline I responded, "Herman, that's amazing! That's exactly what I'm talking about. It's a 1921 Mercury dime, and I'd be pleased to buy it back from you. I'll give you fifty dollars for it."

A shadow crossed over Herman's face as he muttered, "Shit, shit, shit."

Julie asked, "What's the matter?"

Herman scratched his beard. "I think it was Monday night. At the end of each day, I count how much I've collected. Most people are generous, and they give me bills, usually a dollar. A lot of people come over and play with Garcia and sometimes give me a five or a ten."

At the sound of his name, Garcia's tail started wagging, and he approached Julie in search of more cheese. Julie looked over at Herman, who nodded approvingly, and she cut off another slice to feed the dog. Another Herman nod led Julie to offer Herman another slice, immediately devoured in one bite. "This one smug-looking guy tossed a dime in my direction. It hit me in the chest and landed in my can. This ass yelled out a whoop and made a fist pump as if he just hit a game-winning shot. What an asshole."

"That's my brother Roger."

"You have my sympathy. Anyway, that night, I went through my change, though there wasn't much. As I said, I usually get bills. But lo and behold, here was this dime, nearly a hundred years old! I don't know much about coin collecting but I know a coin that old—as you said, 1921—has some value. I took it to a collectibles place a few blocks from here. The guy gave me fifteen bucks for it. He said it wasn't that valuable because it wasn't in good condition. I figured he was getting over on me, but what was I going to do? Fifteen dollars is fifteen dollars."

I knew exactly who he had sold it to and where we were heading next. I gave Herman a twenty, and Julie gave him the remaining cheese.

Julie and I stood in front of Carl Caruso's Classic Collectibles. I told Julie the proprietor was not exactly a charmer, and I wasn't looking forward to dealing with him again.

"Well, it seems likely you won't have to deal with him again—after this. Besides, a lot has happened since you dealt with him last. You're a different person now, with a fresh perspective."

"You're right. Let's go inside."

A bell above the door announced our arrival, and Carl turned his attention from his ever-present *Racing Form* toward us. He picked up an unlit cigar stump from the counter and called out, "Looking for anything in particular?"

I marched right up to him. "Actually yes. I understand that you recently purchased a 1921 silver Mercury dime that was formerly mine and through a series of unfortunate events came to you. Do you have it?"

Carl smiled his tobacco-stained smile and said, "I can't be certain it's the same coin as the one that was yours, but I just so happen to have that type of coin in the same year over here." He walked to a locked case with several coins of varying sizes and styles. He pointed a grubby finger toward the piece of silver, which I easily recognized.

Next to the coin was a price tag that read "$95.95." I blurted out, "That price is outrageous."

From across the shop, Julie asked, "How much is he asking, Zach?"

"$95.95!"

"That's ridiculous!"

"I know."

Julie pulled me away from the case, and from Carl, who was looking bemused.

"Listen, Zach. Forget the money, I'll split it with you. This coin means so much to you—to both of us. Just pay this crook his money and let's walk out of here with the coin."

I grimaced with determination. "Let me handle it," I said, and I walked back over to Carl, who was still in the vicinity of the case. "Carl, do you remember me?"

"You look vaguely familiar."

"Well, I was in here a few weeks ago and I was contemplating selling this same dime. Do you know what you offered me for it as your best offer?"

"I get a lot of customers..." He shrugged.

"Twenty-five dollars. Do you think that was fair?"

"Hey, I'm a businessman and I strike the best deal I can."

"So, the next time you see this dime, you buy it from someone clearly down on his luck, and what did you pay him for it? Fifteen dollars!"

"What do you know about it?! As I said, I'm a businessman. If you don't like the way I conduct my business, there's the door." He peered over his spectacles and down his long, pointing arm.

"Carl, do you know what I do for a living? I'm a writer. I've had several pieces published in *The New York Times*. Perhaps in a week or two you'll put down the *Racing Form* for a few minutes and read about yourself in the *Times* and how you swindle people in general and particularly, the homeless. When you're not reading the *Times* or the *Form*, you might want to go online to read follow-up comments to my blog posts about shady business practices at Carl Caruso's Classic Collectibles in Astoria, Queens. The part that might really get your attention—and the local police precinct's—is how you purchase stolen goods, no questions asked. The homeless man you bought the coin from didn't steal the coin, but I'd venture a guess some of your stuff, might be, let's say, questionable. Shit, I forgot to mention, my brother is a NYC Police Department captain."

Carl folded his *Form*, shifted in his seat, and sputtered a few shocked sounds.

I continued, "As you said, you're a businessman, and I appreciate the fact you need to make a profit. However, I caution you to be much more careful in the future. I'll give you thirty for the coin, twice as much as you paid for it, and we will put this whole mess behind us."

Scowling but silent, Carl walked to his desk and retrieved a key ring. At the cabinet, he manipulated the keys and opened the case. He picked up my magical coin and barked, "Give me my thirty bucks."

I decided not to ask for a receipt.

On the pavement outside the store, Julie said, "Wow, Zach, you continue to shock me."

"I've got to be honest—I kinda shocked myself too."

Chapter 53

The last few weeks have been a whirlwind.

It was strange—once we concluded the work on the investigations and Julie had straightened out my family for me, my imagination and writing flowed like they never had before. In the past, I'd struggled to write more than a page at a time. Since Julie's jolt started my system, my computer screen has been a canvas and my keyboard a paintbrush. I've been continuously cranking out my masterpiece.

I changed my protagonist from a stodgy, middle-aged male detective to a female detective in her thirties named Lois Wine. Get it? Lois Wine, inspired by Louise Weinstein.

Lois has insights into personalities and situations that dwarf those of her peers, in no small part due to the lucky coin she always carries around with her. This coin, unlike any other, picks up on clues and information others can't see or may miss. At the end of a work day, Lois places the old dime on a piece of paper, and by the morning the coin fills the page with clues and their significance.

As I'm writing this, I have meetings scheduled with two different publishers interested in speaking with me about possible book deals. Hell, I've never received a follow-up letter from a publisher, and now there may be two interested in publishing my Lois Wine detective stories. Both publishers really like the mystery book with a magical realism slant. They even like the title, *Wine and Coin*.

So, everything is great. Well, almost everything. Julie hasn't exactly put me on a diet, but she has taken some steps to adjust my food preferences. Through some mildly heated negotiations we agreed to limit my meat intake to six days a week, and my consumption of red meat to no more than two times a week. She's reduced fast food, fried food and bacon only to months with thirty days, and no more than twice in those months. Baked goods or ice cream are permitted every other night. The changes and sacrifices one must make in the name of love!

Julie and I agreed to pool our resources, and rather than paying for two apartments fifty yards apart, give up one and live together in hers. Julie's apartment is a one-bedroom, so it is the logical choice. Julie insisted that my kitchenware does not join in the move. I suggested we give it to charity but as she put it, "We want to help people in need, not offend them."

Next weekend we have a romantic weekend planned to return to the North Fork, staying over at a bed and breakfast in Southold Saturday night. We figured we would go to a few wineries, explore Greenport, and lunch at Valerie Miller's. Jule reluctantly agreed that if Valerie bakes me a dozen cookies, it would be wasteful not to eat them at once.

Saturday, April 13, 2019

As we ate tuna fish sandwiches made with the perfect amount of mayonnaise and diced sweet pickles mixed in, Valerie told us about her mother's memorial service.

"She's buried close to Rhonda, and I just know they are together again, and somehow aware they've been reunited."

I looked over at Larry, who was staring out the window at the budding trees.

"How's Mr. Miller doing?"

"He has his good days and bad ones. I wish I knew what he was thinking. I'm just grateful that he's comfortable and not in pain. I enjoy him being here. I just don't want him to be suffering."

Julie said, "If there's anything we can do to help you, please let us know. We're going out to East Marion this afternoon to this winery that we heard has the most beautiful view of the Sound. Would you like to join us?"

"That's very sweet of you, but I really can't leave Larry alone. Besides, you two should enjoy it. You don't want an old lady like me intruding on your romantic afternoon."

I noticed a subtle wink from Valerie directed towards Julie. "I know a lot of people have their bachelor and bachelorette parties at the wineries. Of course, these wineries are also beautiful sites for weddings. Just something to keep in mind."

"Now, it's a bit early in the season, but I want to show you my garden in the back. I don't have a lot in yet but some lettuce is ready, and I also have some delicious arugula. I'd love to send you home with some."

I could barely contain my excitement as I exclaimed, "I love rugelach. It's probably my favorite dessert. Did you make the chocolate ones or cinnamon? I love them both."

Both women laugh uproariously, and I could have sworn there was even a smile on Larry's face. I just sat there a bit confused. Finally, Julie said, "Zach, arugula is a type of lettuce. You're confusing it with rugelach."

I felt kind of silly but mostly I felt disappointed. Fortunately, Valerie broke my melancholy by saying, "Sorry I don't have any rugelach, but in addition to taking back some arugula, would you take a dozen of the white chocolate macadamia nut cookies I just baked?"

Valerie was right, the North Fork was beautiful in the spring. It was a cool and cloudy day, but we were able to see the emerging lush green farmland all around us as we headed further east.

The North Fork, known as "Long Island wine country," was immediately apparent as we passed several wineries on both sides of the highway. Wine tastings and tours were prominently advertised, and tour buses and limousines filled parking lots.

We also passed several farm stands, but unfortunately most were not yet open for the season. Valerie told us many would be open in a week or two, and all would be open by Memorial Day. We were able to see glimpses of the Long Island Sound to the north of us, and decided we would go for a walk on the beach on our way home. After a few more picturesque miles, we saw a sign for the Nicholas Winery on our left and pulled into their parking lot.

We drove slowly down the winding, gravelly road for about half a mile. Although it was a bit nippy out, we rolled down the windows, luxuriating in crisp, moist air from the Sound and earthy aromas from the seemingly endless rows of grape vines. The car parked, Julie and I entered the large wooden structure which was both inviting and intimidating. Once inside, expecting a dark barn-like interior, 360 degrees of sunlight blinded us as the rays baked their way through the floor-to-ceiling windows. Endless meticulous rows of perfectly spaced vines dominated our view to the left, while to our right a welcoming park-like area seemed to go on indefinitely. The cavernous tasting room with two long wooden tables, each hosting fifteen to twenty wooden chairs, consumed much of the space, and the eighty-foot-high ceiling, so far above our heads, made us feel as though we were among the vines outside. In front of us, but still a good distance away, two bartenders, a woman and a man, graciously served flights of wine to a handful of people hanging on to every precious bit of wine knowledge they parceled out.

We walked to the bar, and not knowing what to do, I pretended to study the menu intently, hoping to project a modicum of wine sophistication. Not knowing much beyond the most limited of basics, I summoned my deeply embedded masculine, authoritative voice and asked the bartender for a "reserve" flight of whites. Not sure it was worth the extra $5 per person, but I was trying my best to impress both Julie and the unnamed bartender who had yet to make eye contact with me.

We watched as she poured five very chintzy glasses of wine, as she droned on about each one. Julie listened intently to the descriptions of "wafts of blackberry and apricot with notes of mossy straw," while my mind wandered to the Greek restaurant we had passed on the way here. I was hoping we might have time to try it.

Julie put down a couple of dollars as a tip for the waitress, and I picked up the tray of wine. We walked through the doors to go outside. It was too bad the temperature was not warmer, and the sun wasn't out, but nevertheless, the view was amazing. The landscape was massive with a half a mile walk to the vineyard's edge, a cliff overlooking Long Island Sound.

There were several tables immediately outside the door of the main house, and I initially placed the tray on one of the tables so we could sit. Julie placed her hand on my forearm and said, "Let's walk further. There are other places to sit closer to the water."

We walked a couple of hundred yards past several other picnic tables and I periodically gestured to a table, while shook her head. Julie led me to bluffs overlooking the beach.

We sat down at a table no more than fifteen yards from the edge.

A neighboring table was a few feet away with a solitary woman with long brown hair underneath a straw hat, writing busily in a ledger book. From our spot all we could see by looking down was a portion of a rocky beach leading out to the ripple of waves cascading onto the shore. I was about to speak but Julie closed her eyes and put her finger in front of her lips. The only sounds we could hear were the waves and an occasional seagull. Looking outward, I was able to see water for miles and the outline of what must have been Connecticut. I had to admit, nothing could have been more serene.

The moment was gently interrupted by a woman's voice asking, "It's beautiful, isn't it? I've been here for twenty years, and I don't think I'll ever get enough of it. My parents took me and my sister out here when we were very young, in the eighties. Where are the two of you from?"

Julie answered for us, "We live in Queens."

"So, it's probably about a two-hour trip for you, of course depending on the traffic. Two months from now, coming out here on a Friday afternoon, it would probably take you closer to four hours. I grew up in New Jersey, but I guess a part of me always remembered the North Fork. Perhaps it was fate that I ended up here."

Julie asked, "So you live here now?"

"Yup. I married a man from out here, and this has been home since. It's really a great place to bring up a family. We have two kids, and I feel it's such a healthy and well-balanced life out here. I'm sorry—my name is LuLu."

"Oh, I'm Julie, and this is my boyfriend, Zach. We're only here for the weekend. We've heard such great things about the North Fork. We have a friend who lives in Jamesport. She insisted we come out here in the spring, and I'm glad we did, but we certainly will come again this summer. I could sit here all day drinking wine and taking in this view. I can only imagine this must be the most perfect place to have a wedding."

As I pondered how all this recent wedding talk had come about, LuLu said, "It certainly is. But then again, I'm somewhat biased. My husband and I own this winery, and we've hosted many breathtaking weddings."

Feeling a bit left out, I figured I'd join the conversation. "How's the food at the Greek restaurant we passed on our way here?"

"It's very good. There are a couple of wonderful upscale restaurants in Greenport that are a bit on the pricey side, but definitely worth it. In the summer, you need to make reservations three to four weeks in advance for those. However, my favorite place is another restaurant in Greenport that serves the absolute best thin crust pizza and phenomenal cocktails."

"That sounds perfect."

"I'm so sorry, I have to run inside to help out. We have a bachelorette party here this evening. Please, if you have any questions about restaurants or things to do out here, don't hesitate to get in touch." LuLu glanced at me, then back towards Julie, and back again towards me. A small smirk developed as she winked at both of us.

Stifling a giggle, LuLu added, "Or of course, if you personally know of anyone looking for a beautiful wedding venue..." She winked again, just as Mrs. Miller had winked at Julie earlier. Perhaps the pollen count was high that day.

LuLu reached into her pocket and said, "Here's my card."

Julie took a card, handed one to me and said, "Thank you, LuLu." I looked down at the card Julie just handed me and read:

Louise "LuLu" Graber Hanes
Co-Proprietor
Nicholas Winery
Lulu@Nicholaswinery.com
631-477-0067

Lulu walked away.

As what I was seeing began to sink in, Julie tried speaking, but before her words came out, I screamed "PLEASE STOP!" I guess I was speaking to time itself—and it seemed to listen. Everything was silent around me except the waves slapping against rocks. I was transported to a different existence, savoring every moment in slow motion.

I sensed Julie's presence, but at the same time bombarded with my own isolated thoughts in a liminal space like I'd never visited in my life. I'm not certain if seconds or minutes passed but eventually, I spoke. "I'm sorry, I didn't mean to shush you. I just had a feeling that overwhelmed me, one I've never experienced before."

As Julie stared at the card, she replied, "No need to apologize. This entire experience is way beyond my comprehension as well."

As we walked back towards the parking lot, hand in hand, I led us on a detour, toward the main house. "I need to do something. Something I know in my heart is the right thing to do. I hope you will support my decision."

I could tell Julie wanted to ask me something but instead simply said, "Of course I will."

I opened the glass door leading into the house and took a quick glance around. As I didn't see Lulu, I asked the male bartender if he knew where she was. Holding a tray full of glasses, he motioned with his head over his shoulder. "She just went into her office. I know she's really busy."

"I promise I'll only bother her for a minute. I need to give her something."

As the waiter walked off with a shrug, I approached a half-opened door with an "Office" sign on it. With Julie following close behind me, I knocked on the door twice and saw Lulu looking down at a stack of papers.

"Lulu, I'm very sorry to disturb you, but it occurred to me I have something to give to you. Actually, it's something that belonged to your grandmother."

"My grandmother? My grandmother's been dead for almost ten years."

I was confused by her response.

"Lulu," Julie said. "We're talking about your *other* grandmother."

"My other grandmother? She died before I was born. I'm named after her. I'm sorry, I don't understand what the two of you are going on about, and I'm really busy."

The last thing I wanted to do was upset Lulu, which was all I seemed to be accomplishing. Reaching into my pocket I took out my wallet and from a side compartment extracted a clear plastic coin sleeve. Inside it was the 1921 Silver Mercury dime. Handing it to her, I said, "This belonged to your grandmother Louise Graber, and I want you to have it."

Lulu's eyebrows raised and her posture straightened with uncertain appreciation.

"I realize you have many questions," I continued, "including those about my sanity, but I—we—promise you that this dime belonged to your grandmother."

Lulu looked at me with an intensity that made me uncomfortable. "I'm not sure what this is about, but this clearly requires a longer conversation."

I smiled. "That is an understatement. It is an amazing story and one we would love to share with you. " On a blank piece of paper, I wrote down our contact information and handed it to LuLu. "Your grandmother was an extraordinary woman with a rich history. She'd want you to have this. If, and when you are ready, please reach out. Louise's story awaits you."

Acknowledgements

Trying to achieve a goal is rarely an easy task, particularly something as daunting as writing a first-time full-length novel. Fortunately, I have received a great deal of much-needed support.

Flying on the Wings of Mercury would never have gotten off the ground without the guidance and expertise of Benjamin Obler. Claudia Eff, Jesse Blumberg, Ed Irwin, Jon Schaffzin, Kaitlyn Butterfield, Sara Rothman and Scott Raulsome kindly provided me with their time, insight, and invaluable suggestions.

Thank you to Mark and Muriel Graber, my initial readers, who graciously let me know that the story was promising but still required much editing.

Special thanks to Dr. Marion Nestle who generously offered not only insight and commentary, but also inspiration.

And thank you to my son William, who has promised me he will do something he rarely does and read a novel from cover to cover. Lastly, without the countless hours of review and editing spent by the two most important women in my life, Jennifer Berg and Elizabeth Berg, the book would not be worthy of publication.